Celtic Fairy Tales

SAY THIS

Three times, with your eyes shut

Moṫuiġim bolaḋ an Éireannaiġ ḃinn ḃreuġaiġ

faoi m'ḟóidín dúṫaiġ

And you will see

What you will see

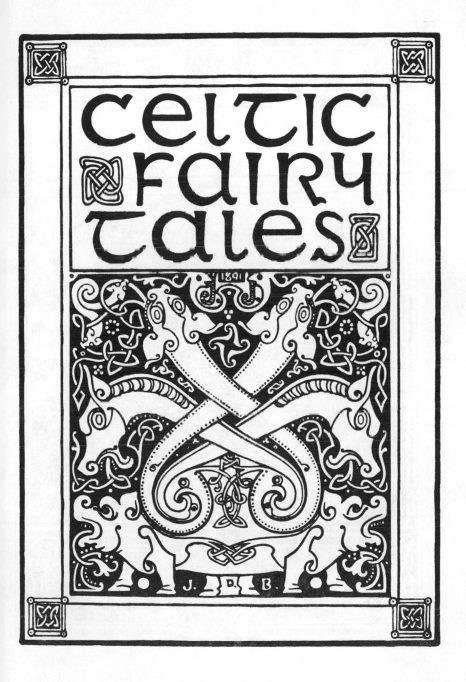

Celtic Fairy Tales

Collected by
JOSEPH JACOBS

Illustrated by
JOHN D. BATTEN

Dover Publications, Inc.
New York

Published in Canada by General Publishing Company, Ltd., 30 Lesmill Road, Don Mills, Toronto, Ontario.
Published in the United Kingdom by Constable and Company, Ltd., 10 Orange Street, London WC 2.

This Dover edition, first published in 1968, is an unabridged republication of the work originally published in a limited edition by David Nutt in 1892.

International Standard Book Number: 0-486-21826-0
Library of Congress Catalog Card Number: 67-24223

Manufactured in the United States of America
Dover Publications, Inc.
180 Varick Street
New York, N. Y. 10014

TO

ALFRED NUTT

Preface

AST year, in giving the young ones a volume of English Fairy Tales, my difficulty was one of collection. This time, in offering them specimens of the rich folk-fancy of the Celts of these islands, my trouble has rather been one of selection. Ireland began to collect her folk-tales almost as early as any country in Europe, and Croker has found a whole school of successors in Carleton, Griffin, Kennedy, Curtin, and Douglas Hyde. Scotland had the great name of Campbell, and has still efficient followers in MacDougall, MacInnes, Carmichael, Macleod, and Campbell of Tiree. Gallant little Wales has no name to rank alongside these ; in this department the Cymru have shown less vigour than the Gaedhel. Perhaps the Eisteddfod, by offering prizes for the collection of Welsh folk-tales, may remove this inferiority. Meanwhile Wales must be content to be somewhat scantily represented among the Fairy Tales of the Celts, while the extinct Cornish tongue has only contributed one tale.

In making my selection I have chiefly tried to make the stories characteristic. It would have been easy, especially from Kennedy, to have made up a volume entirely filled with " Grimm's Goblins " *à la Celtique*. But one can have too much even of that very good thing, and I have therefore avoided as far as possible the more familiar " formulæ " of folk-tale literature. To do this I had to withdraw from the English-speaking Pale both in Scotland and Ireland, and I laid down the rule to include only tales that have been taken down from Celtic peasants ignorant of English.

Having laid down the rule, I immediately proceeded to break it. The success of a fairy book, I am convinced, depends on the due admixture of the comic and the romantic : Grimm and Asbjörnsen knew this secret, and they alone. But the Celtic peasant who speaks Gaelic takes the pleasure of telling tales somewhat sadly : so far as he has been printed and translated, I found him, to my surprise, conspicuously lacking in humour. For the comic relief of this volume I have therefore had to turn mainly to the Irish peasant of the Pale ; and what richer source could I draw from ?

For the more romantic tales I have depended on the Gaelic, and, as I know about as much of Gaelic as an Irish Nationalist M.P., I have had to depend on translators. But I have felt myself more at liberty than the translators themselves, who have generally been over-literal, in changing, excising, or modifying the original. I have even gone further. In order that the tales should be characteristically

Celtic, I have paid more particular attention to tales that are to be found on both sides of the North Channel. In re-telling them I have had no scruple in interpolating now and then a Scotch incident into an Irish variant of the same story, or *vice versâ*. Where the translators appealed to English folk-lorists and scholars, I am trying to attract English children. They translated ; I endeavoured to transfer. In short, I have tried to put myself into the position of an *ollamh* or *sheenachie* familiar with both forms of Gaelic, and anxious to put his stories in the best way to attract English children. I trust I shall be forgiven by Celtic scholars for the changes I have had to make to effect this end.

The stories collected in this volume are longer and more detailed than the English ones I brought together last Christmas. The romantic ones are certainly more romantic, and the comic ones perhaps more comic, though there may be room for a difference of opinion on this latter point. This superiority of the Celtic folk-tales is due as much to the conditions under which they have been collected, as to any innate superiority of the folk-imagination. The folk-tale in England is in the last stages of exhaustion. The Celtic folk-tales have been collected while the practice of story-telling is still in full vigour, though there are every signs that its term of life is already numbered. The more the reason why they should be collected and put on record while there is yet time. On the whole, the industry of the collectors of Celtic folk-lore is to be commended, as may be seen from the survey of it I have prefixed to the Notes and References at the end of the volume. Among these, I would call attention to the study of the legend of Beth Gellert, the origin of which, I believe, I have settled.

While I have endeavoured to render the language of the tales simple and free from bookish artifice, I have not felt at liberty to retell the tales in the English way. I have not scrupled to retain a Celtic turn of speech, and here and there a Celtic word, which I have *not* explained within brackets—a practice to be abhorred of all good men. A few words unknown to the reader only add effectiveness and local colour to a narrative, as Mr. Kipling well knows.

One characteristic of the Celtic folk-lore I have endeavoured to represent in my selection, because it is nearly unique at the present day in Europe. Nowhere else is there so large and consistent a body of oral tradition about the national and mythical heroes as amongst the Gaels. Only the *byline*, or hero-songs of Russia, equal in extent the amount of knowledge about the heroes of the past that still exists among the Gaelic-speaking peasantry of Scotland and Ireland. And the Irish tales and ballads have this peculiarity, that some of them have been extant, and can be traced for well nigh a thousand years. I have selected as a specimen of this class the Story of Deirdre, collected among the Scotch peasantry a few years ago, into which I have been able to insert a passage taken from an

Irish vellum of the twelfth century. I could have more than filled this volume with similar oral traditions about Finn (the Fingal of Macpherson's " Ossian "). But the story of Finn, as told by the Gaelic peasantry of to-day, deserves a volume by itself, while the adventures of the Ultonian hero, Cuchulain, could easily fill another.

I have endeavoured to include in this volume the best and most typical stories told by the chief masters of the Celtic folk-tale, Campbell, Kennedy, Hyde, and Curtin, and to these I have added the best tales scattered elsewhere. By this means I hope I have put together a volume, containing both the best, and the best known folk-tales of the Celts. I have only been enabled to do this by the courtesy of those who owned the copyright of these stories. Lady Wilde has kindly granted me the use of her effective version of " The Horned Women ;" and I have specially to thank Messrs. Macmillan for right to use Kennedy's " Legendary Fictions," and Messrs. Sampson Low & Co., for the use of Mr. Curtin's Tales.

In making my selection, and in all doubtful points of treatment, I have had resource to the wide knowledge of my friend Mr. Alfred Nutt in all branches of Celtic folk-lore. If this volume does anything to represent to English children the vision and colour, the magic and charm, of the Celtic folk-imagination, this is due in large measure to the care with which Mr. Nutt has watched its inception and progress. With him by my side I could venture into regions where the non-Celt wanders at his own risk.

Lastly, I have again to rejoice in the co-operation of my friend, Mr. J. D. Batten, in giving form to the creations of the folk-fancy. He has endeavoured in his illustrations to retain as much as possible of Celtic ornamentation ; for all details of Celtic archæology he has authority. Yet both he and I have striven to give Celtic things as they appear to, and attract, the English mind, rather than attempt the hopeless task of representing them as they are to Celts. The fate of the Celt in the British Empire bids fair to resemble that of the Greeks among the Romans. "They went forth to battle, but they always fell," yet the captive Celt has enslaved his captor in the realm of imagination. The present volume attempts to begin the pleasant captivity from the earliest years. If it could succeed in giving a common fund of imaginative wealth to the Celtic and the Saxon children of these isles, it might do more for a true union of hearts than all your politics.

JOSEPH JACOBS.

Contents

Full-page Illustrations

Connla and the Fairy Maiden

ONNLA of the Fiery Hair was son of Conn of the Hundred Fights. One day as he stood by the side of his father on the height of Usna, he saw a maiden clad in strange attire coming towards him.

"Whence comest thou, maiden?" said Connla.

"I come from the Plains of the Ever Living," she said, "there where there is neither death nor sin. There we keep holiday alway, nor need we help from any in our joy. And in all our pleasure we have no strife. And because we have our homes in the round green hills, men call us the Hill Folk."

The king and all with him wondered much to hear a voice when they saw no one. For save Connla alone, none saw the Fairy Maiden.

"To whom art thou talking, my son?" said Conn the king.

Then the maiden answered, "Connla speaks to a young, fair maid, whom neither death nor old age awaits. I love Connla, and now I call him away to the Plain of Pleasure,

Moy Mell, where Boadag is king for aye, nor has there been complaint or sorrow in that land since he has held the kingship. Oh, come with me, Connla of the Fiery Hair, ruddy as the dawn with thy tawny skin. A fairy crown awaits thee to grace thy comely face and royal form. Come, and never shall thy comeliness fade, nor thy youth, till the last awful day of judgment."

The king in fear at what the maiden said, which he heard though he could not see her, called aloud to his Druid, Coran by name.

"Oh, Coran of the many spells," he said, "and of the cunning magic, I call upon thy aid. A task is upon me too great for all my skill and wit, greater than any laid upon me since I seized the kingship. A maiden unseen has met us, and by her power would take from me my dear, my comely son. If thou help not, he will be taken from thy king by woman's wiles and witchery."

Then Coran the Druid stood forth and chanted his spells towards the spot where the maiden's voice had been heard. And none heard her voice again, nor could Connla see her longer. Only as she vanished before the Druid's mighty spell, she threw an apple to Connla. (the forbidden fruit)

For a whole month from that day Connla would take nothing, either to eat or to drink, save only from that apple. But as he ate it grew again and always kept whole. And all the while there grew within him a mighty yearning and longing after the maiden he had seen.

But when the last day of the month of waiting came, Connla stood by the side of the king his father on the Plain of Arcomin, and again he saw the maiden come towards him, and again she spoke to him.

CONNLA AND THE FAIRY MAIDEN

" 'Tis a glorious place, forsooth, that Connla holds among shortlived mortals awaiting the day of death. But now the folk of life, the ever-living ones, beg and bid thee come to Moy Mell, the Plain of Pleasure, for they have learnt to know thee, seeing thee in thy home among thy dear ones."

When Conn the king heard the maiden's voice he called to his men aloud and said :

" Summon swift my Druid Coran, for I see she has again this day the power of speech."

Then the maiden said : " Oh, mighty Conn, fighter of a hundred fights, the Druid's power is little loved ; it has little honour in the mighty land, peopled with so many of the upright. When the Law will come, it will do away with the Druid's magic spells that come from the lips of the false black demon."

Then Conn the king observed that since the maiden came Connla his son spoke to none that spake to him. So Conn of the hundred fights said to him, " Is it to thy mind what the woman says, my son ? "

" 'Tis hard upon me," then said Connla; " I love my own folk above all things ; but yet, but yet a longing seizes me for the maiden."

When the maiden heard this, she answered and said : " The ocean is not so strong as the waves of thy longing. Come with me in my curragh, the gleaming, straight-gliding crystal canoe. Soon we can reach Boadag's realm. I see the bright sun sink, yet far as it is, we can reach it before dark. There is, too, another land worthy of thy journey, a land joyous to all that seek it. Only wives and maidens dwell there. If thou wilt, we can seek it and live there alone together in joy."

When the maiden ceased to speak, Connla of the Fiery Hair rushed away from them and sprang into the curragh, the gleaming, straight-gliding crystal canoe. And then they all, king and court, saw it glide away over the bright sea towards the setting sun. Away and away, till eye could see it no longer, and Connla and the Fairy Maiden went their way on the sea, and were no more seen, nor did any know where they came.

Guleesh

HERE was once a boy in the County Mayo; Guleesh was his name. There was the finest rath a little way off from the gable of the house, and he was often in the habit of seating himself on the fine grass bank that was running round it. One night he stood, half leaning against the gable of the house, and looking up into the sky, and watching the beautiful white moon over his head. After he had been standing that way for a couple of hours, he said to himself : " My bitter grief that I am not gone away out of this place altogether. I'd sooner be any place in the world than here. Och, it's well for you, white moon," says he, "that's turning round, turning round, as you please yourself, and no man can put you back. I wish I was the same as you."

Hardly was the word out of his mouth when he heard a great noise coming like the sound of many people running together, and talking, and laughing, and making sport, and the sound went by him like a whirl of wind, and he was listening to it going into the rath. " Musha, by my soul," says he, " but ye're merry enough, and I'll follow ye."

What was in it but the fairy host, though he did not know at first that it was they who were in it, but he followed them into the rath. It's there he heard the *fulparnee*, and the *folpornee*, the *rap-lay-hoota*, and the *roolya-boolya*, that they had there, and every man of them crying out as loud as he could : " My horse, and bridle, and saddle ! My horse, and bridle, and saddle ! "

" By my hand," said Guleesh, " my boy, that's not bad. I'll imitate ye," and he cried out as well as they : " My horse, and bridle, and saddle ! My horse, and bridle, and saddle ! " And on the moment there was a fine horse with a bridle of gold, and a saddle of silver, standing before him. He leaped up on it, and the moment he was on its back he saw clearly that the rath was full of horses, and of little people going riding on them.

Said a man of them to him : " Are you coming with us to-night, Guleesh ? "

" I am surely," said Guleesh.

" If you are, come along," said the little man, and out they went all together, riding like the wind, faster than the fastest horse ever you saw a-hunting, and faster than the fox and the hounds at his tail.

The cold winter's wind that was before them, they overtook her, and the cold winter's wind that was behind them, she did not overtake them. And stop nor stay of that full race, did they make none, until they came to the brink of the sea.

Then every one of them said : " Hie over cap ! Hie over cap ! " and that moment they were up in the air, and before Guleesh had time to remember where he was, they were down on dry land again, and were going like the wind.

At last they stood still, and a man of them said to Guleesh:
" Guleesh, do you know where you are now ? "

" Not a know," says Guleesh.

" You're in France, Guleesh," said he. " The daughter
of the king of France is to be married to-night, the handsomest woman that the sun ever saw, and we must do our
best to bring her with us, if we're only able to carry her
off; and you must come with us that we may be able to
put the young girl up behind you on the horse, when we'll
be bringing her away, for it's not lawful for us to put her
sitting behind ourselves. But you're flesh and blood, and
she can take a good grip of you, so that she won't fall off
the horse. Are you satisfied, Guleesh, and will you do
what we're telling you ? "

" Why shouldn't I be satisfied ? " said Guleesh. " I'm
satisfied, surely, and anything that ye will tell me to do I'll
do it without doubt."

They got off their horses there, and a man of them said
a word that Guleesh did not understand, and on the
moment they were lifted up, and Guleesh found himself and
his companions in the palace. There was a great feast
going on there, and there was not a nobleman or a gentleman in the kingdom but was gathered there, dressed in silk
and satin, and gold and silver, and the night was as bright
as the day with all the lamps and candles that were lit, and
Guleesh had to shut his two eyes at the brightness. When
he opened them again and looked from him, he thought he
never saw anything as fine as all he saw there. There
were a hundred tables spread out, and their full of meat and
drink on each table of them, flesh-meat, and cakes and
sweetmeats, and wine and ale, and every drink that ever a

man saw.   The musicians were at the two ends of the hall,
and they were playing the sweetest music that ever a man's
ear heard, and there were young women and fine youths in
the middle of the hall, dancing and turning, and going round
so quickly and so lightly, that it put a *soorawn* in Guleesh's
head to be looking at them.   There were more there
playing tricks, and more making fun and laughing, for such
a feast as there was that day had not been in France for
twenty years, because the old king had no children alive
but only the one daughter, and she was to be married to
the son of another king that night.   Three days the feast
was going on, and the third night she was to be married,
and that was the night that Guleesh and the sheehogues
came, hoping, if they could, to carry off with them the king's
young daughter.

Guleesh and his companions were standing together at
the head of the hall, where there was a fine altar dressed up,
and two bishops behind it waiting to marry the girl, as soon as
the right time should come.   Now nobody could see the
sheehogues, for they said a word as they came in, that made
them all invisible, as if they had not been in it at all.

" Tell me which of them is the king's daughter," said
Guleesh, when he was becoming a little used to the noise
and the light.

" Don't you see her there away from you?" said the little
man that he was talking to.

Guleesh looked where the little man was pointing with
his finger, and there he saw the loveliest woman that was,
he thought, upon the ridge of the world.   The rose and the
lily were fighting together in her face, and one could not tell
which of them got the victory.   Her arms and hands were

like the lime, her mouth as red as a strawberry when it is ripe, her foot was as small and as light as another one's hand, her form was smooth and slender, and her hair was falling down from her head in buckles of gold. Her garments and dress were woven with gold and silver, and the bright stone that was in the ring on her hand was as shining as the sun.

Guleesh was nearly blinded with all the loveliness and beauty that was in her ; but when he looked again, he saw that she was crying, and that there was the trace of tears in her eyes. " It can't be," said Guleesh, " that there's grief on her, when everybody round her is so full of sport and merriment."

" Musha, then, she is grieved," said the little man ; " for it's against her own will she's marrying, and she has no love for the husband she is to marry. The king was going to give her to him three years ago, when she was only fifteen, but she said she was too young, and requested him to leave her as she was yet. The king gave her a year's grace, and when that year was up he gave her another year's grace, and then another ; but a week or a day he would not give her longer, and she is eighteen years old to-night, and it's time for her to marry ; but, indeed," says he, and he crooked his mouth in an ugly way—" indeed, it's no king's son she'll marry, if I can help it."

Guleesh pitied the handsome young lady greatly when he heard that, and he was heart-broken to think that it would be necessary for her to marry a man she did not like, or, what was worse, to take a nasty sheehogue for a husband. However, he did not say a word, though he could not help giving many a curse to the ill-luck that was laid out for himself, to be helping the people that were to snatch her away from her home and from her father.

He began thinking, then, what it was he ought to do to save her, but he could think of nothing. "Oh! if I could only give her some help and relief," said he, "I wouldn't care whether I were alive or dead; but I see nothing that I can do for her."

He was looking on when the king's son came up to her and asked her for a kiss, but she turned her head away from him. Guleesh had double pity for her then, when he saw the lad taking her by the soft white hand, and drawing her out to dance. They went round in the dance near where Guleesh was, and he could plainly see that there were tears in her eyes.

When the dancing was over, the old king, her father, and her mother the queen, came up and said that this was the right time to marry her, that the bishop was ready, and it was time to put the wedding-ring on her and give her to her husband.

The king took the youth by the hand, and the queen took her daughter, and they went up together to the altar, with the lords and great people following them.

When they came near the altar, and were no more than about four yards from it, the little sheehogue stretched out his foot before the girl, and she fell. Before she was able to rise again he threw something that was in his hand upon her, said a couple of words, and upon the moment the maiden was gone from amongst them. Nobody could see her, for that word made her invisible. The little maneen seized her and raised her up behind Guleesh, and the king

nor no one else saw them, but out with them through the
hall till they came to the door.

Oro! dear Mary! it's there the pity was, and the
trouble, and the crying, and the wonder, and the searching,
and the *rookawn*, when that lady disappeared from their
eyes, and without their seeing what did it.   Out of the

door of the palace they went, without being stopped or
hindered, for nobody saw them, and, "My horse, my
bridle, and saddle!" says every man of them. "My horse,
my bridle, and saddle!" says Guleesh; and on the moment
the horse was standing ready caparisoned before him.
"Now, jump up, Guleesh," said the little man, "and put
the lady behind you, and we will be going; the morning is
not far off from us now."

Guleesh raised her up on the horse's back, and leaped up

himself before her, and, " Rise, horse," said he ; and his horse, and the other horses with him, went in a full race until they came to the sea.

" Hie over cap!" said every man of them.

" Hie over cap!" said Guleesh ; and on the moment the horse rose under him, and cut a leap in the clouds, and came down in Erin.

They did not stop there, but went of a race to the place where was Guleesh's house and the rath.   And when they came as far as that, Guleesh turned and caught the young girl in his two arms, and leaped off the horse.

" I call and cross you to myself, in the name of God !" said he ; and on the spot, before the word was out of his mouth, the horse fell down, and what was in it but the beam of a plough, of which they had made a horse ; and every other horse they had, it was that way they made it.   Some of them were riding on an old besom, and some on a broken stick, and more on a bohalawn or a hemlock-stalk.

The good people called out together when they heard what Guleesh said :

" Oh ! Guleesh, you clown, you thief, that no good may happen you, why did you play that trick on us ? "

But they had no power at all to carry off the girl, after Guleesh had consecrated her to himself.

" Oh ! Guleesh, isn't that a nice turn you did us, and we so kind to you ?   What good have we now out of our journey to France.   Never mind yet, you clown, but you'll pay us another time for this.   Believe us, you'll repent it."

" He'll have no good to get out of the young girl," said the little man that was talking to him in the palace before that, and as he said the word he moved over to her and struck her a slap on the side of the head. "Now," says he, "she'll be without talk any more ; now, Guleesh, what good will she be to you when she'll be dumb ? It's time for us to go—but you'll remember us, Guleesh ! "

When he said that he stretched out his two hands, and before Guleesh was able to give an answer, he and the rest of them were gone into the rath out of his sight, and he saw them no more.

He turned to the young woman and said to her : " Thanks be to God, they're gone. Would you not sooner stay with me than with them ?" She gave him no answer. " There's trouble and grief on her yet," said Guleesh in his own mind, and he spoke to her again : " I am afraid that you must spend this night in my father's house, lady, and if there is anything that I can do for you, tell me, and I'll be your servant."

The beautiful girl remained silent, but there were tears in her eyes, and her face was white and red after each other.

" Lady," said Guleesh, " tell me what you would like me to do now. I never belonged at all to that lot of shee-hogues who carried you away with them. I am the son of an honest farmer, and I went with them without knowing it. If I'll be able to send you back to your father I'll do it, and I pray you make any use of me now that you may wish."

He looked into her face, and he saw the mouth moving as if she was going to speak, but there came no word from it.

" It cannot be," said Guleesh, " that you are dumb.

Did I not hear you speaking to the king's son in the palace to-night ?   Or has that devil made you really dumb, when he struck his nasty hand on your jaw ? "

The girl raised her white smooth hand, and laid her finger on her tongue, to show him that she had lost her voice and power of speech, and the tears ran out of her two eyes like streams, and Guleesh's own eyes were not dry, for as rough as he was on the outside he had a soft heart, and could not stand the sight of the young girl, and she in that unhappy plight.

He began thinking with himself what he ought to do, and he did not like to bring her home with himself to his father's house, for he knew well that they would not believe him, that he had been in France and brought back with him the king of France's daughter, and he was afraid they might make a mock of the young lady or insult her.

As he was doubting what he ought to do, and hesitating, he chanced to remember the priest. " Glory be to God," said he, " I know now what I'll do ; I'll bring her to the priest's house, and he won't refuse me to keep the lady and care her." He turned to the lady again and told her that he was loth to take her to his father's house, but that there was an excellent priest very friendly to himself, who would take good care of her, if she wished to remain in his house ; but that if there was any other place she would rather go, he said he would bring her to it.

She bent her head, to show him she was obliged, and gave him to understand that she was ready to follow him any place he was going. " We will go to the priest's house, then," said he ; " he is under an obligation to me, and will do anything I ask him."

They went together accordingly to the priest's house, and the sun was just rising when they came to the door. Guleesh beat it hard, and as early as it was the priest was up, and opened the door himself. He wondered when he saw Guleesh and the girl, for he was certain that it was coming wanting to be married they were.

" Guleesh, Guleesh, isn't it the nice boy you are that you can't wait till ten o'clock or till twelve, but that you must be coming to me at this hour, looking for marriage, you and your sweetheart ? You ought to know that I can't marry you at such a time, or, at all events, can't marry you lawfully. But ubbubboo!" said he, suddenly, as he looked again at the young girl, " in the name of God, who have you here ? Who is she, or how did you get her ? "

" Father," said Guleesh, "you can marry me, or anybody else, if you wish ; but it's not looking for marriage I came to you now, but to ask you, if you please, to give a lodging in your house to this young lady."

The priest looked at him as though he had ten heads on him ; but without putting any other question to him, he desired him to come in, himself and the maiden, and when they came in, he shut the door, brought them into the parlour, and put them sitting.

" Now, Guleesh," said he, "tell me truly who is this young lady, and whether you're out of your senses really, or are only making a joke of me."

" I'm not telling a word of lie, nor making a joke of you," said Guleesh ; "but it was from the palace of the king of France I carried off this lady, and she is the daughter of the king of France."

He began his story then, and told the whole to the priest, and the priest was so much surprised that he could not help calling out at times, or clapping his hands together.

When Guleesh said from what he saw he thought the girl was not satisfied with the marriage that was going to take place in the palace before he and the sheehogues broke it up, there came a red blush into the girl's cheek, and he was more certain than ever that she had sooner be as she was—badly as she was—than be the married wife of the man she hated. When Guleesh said that he would be very thankful to the priest if he would keep her in his own house, the kind man said he would do that as long as Guleesh pleased, but that he did not know what they ought to do with her, because they had no means of sending her back to her father again.

Guleesh answered that he was uneasy about the same thing, and that he saw nothing to do but to keep quiet until they should find some opportunity of doing something better. They made it up then between themselves that the priest should let on that it was his brother's daughter he had, who was come on a visit to him from another county, and that he should tell everybody that she was dumb, and do his best to keep every one away from her. They told the young girl what it was they intended to do, and she showed by her eyes that she was obliged to them.

Guleesh went home then, and when his people asked him where he had been, he said that he had been asleep at the foot of the ditch, and had passed the night there.

There was great wonderment on the pricst's neighbours at the girl who came so suddenly to his house without any one knowing where she was from, or what business she had there. Some of the people said that everything was not as it ought to be, and others, that Guleesh was not like the same man that was in it before, and that it was a great story, how he was drawing every day to the priest's house, and that the priest had a wish and a respect for him, a thing they could not clear up at all.

That was true for them, indeed, for it was seldom the day went by but Guleesh would go to the priest's house, and have a talk with him, and as often as he would come he used to hope to find the young lady well again, and with leave to speak ; but, alas ! she remained dumb and silent, without relief or cure. Since she had no other means of talking, she carried on a sort of conversation between herself and himself, by moving her hand and fingers, winking her eyes, opening and shutting her mouth, laughing or smiling, and a thousand other signs, so that it was not long until they understood each other very well. Guleesh was always thinking how he should send her back to her father ; but there was no one to go with her, and he himself did not know what road to go, for he had never been out of his own country before the night he brought her away with him. Nor had the priest any better knowledge than he ; but when Guleesh asked him, he wrote three or four letters to the king of France, and gave them to buyers and sellers of wares, who used to be going from place to place across the sea ; but they all went astray, and never a one came to the king's hand.

This was the way they were for many months, and Guleesh was falling deeper and deeper in love with her every day, and it was plain to himself and the priest that she liked him. The boy feared greatly at last, lest the king should really hear where his daughter was, and take her back from himself, and he besought the priest to write no more, but to leave the matter to God.

So they passed the time for a year, until there came a day when Guleesh was lying by himself on the grass, on the last day of the last month in autumn, and he was thinking over again in his own mind of everything that happened to him from the day that he went with the sheehogues across the sea. He remembered then, suddenly, that it was one November night that he was standing at the gable of the house, when the whirlwind came, and the sheehogues in it, and he said to himself : " We have November night again to-day, and I'll stand in the same place I was last year, until I see if the good people come again. Perhaps I might see or hear something that would be useful to me, and might bring back her talk again to Mary "—that was the name himself and the priest called the king's daughter, for neither of them knew her right name. He told his intention to the priest, and the priest gave him his blessing.

Guleesh accordingly went to the old rath when the night was darkening, and he stood with his bent elbow leaning on a grey old flag, waiting till the middle of the night should come. The moon rose slowly, and it was like a knob of fire behind him ; and there was a white fog which was raised up over the fields of grass and all damp places, through the coolness of the night after a great heat in the day. The night was calm as is a lake when there is not a breath of wind to move a wave on it, and there was no sound to be heard but the *cronawn* of the insects that would go by from time to time, or the hoarse sudden scream of the wild-geese, as they passed from lake to lake, half a mile up in the air over his head ; or the sharp whistle of the golden and green plover, rising and lying, lying and rising, as they do on a calm night. There were a thousand thousand bright stars shining over his head, and there was a little frost out, which left the grass under his foot white and crisp.

He stood there for an hour, for two hours, for three hours, and the frost increased greatly, so that he heard the breaking of the *traneens* under his foot as often as he moved. He was thinking, in his own mind, at last, that the sheehogues would not come that night, and that it was as good for him to return back again, when he heard a sound far away from him, coming towards him, and he recognised what it was at the first moment. The sound increased, and at first it was like the beating of waves on a stony shore, and then it was like the falling of a great waterfall, and at last it was like a loud storm in the tops of the trees, and then the whirlwind burst into the rath of one rout, and the sheehogues were in it.

It all went by him so suddenly that he lost his breath with it, but he came to himself on the spot, and put an ear on himself, listening to what they would say.

Scarcely had they gathered into the rath till they all began shouting, and screaming, and talking amongst them-selves ; and then each one of them cried out : " My horse, and bridle, and saddle ! My horse, and bridle, and saddle ! " and Guleesh took courage, and called out as loudly as any of them : " My horse, and bridle, and saddle ! My horse, and bridle, and saddle ! " But before the word was well out of his mouth, another man cried out : " Ora ! Guleesh, my boy, are you here with us again ?   How are you getting on with your woman ?   There's no use in your calling for your horse to-night. I'll go bail you won't play such a trick on us again.   It was a good trick you played on us last year ? "

" It was," said another man ; " he won't do it again."

" Isn't he a prime lad, the same lad ! to take a woman with him that never said as much to him as, ' How do you do ? ' since this time last year ! " says the third man.

" Perhaps he likes to be looking at her," said another voice.

" And if the *omadawn* only knew that there's an herb growing up by his own door, and if he were to boil it and give it to her, she'd be well," said another voice.

" That's true for you."

" He is an omadawn."

" Don't bother your head with him ; we'll be going."

" We'll leave the *bodach* as he is."

And with that they rose up into the air, and out with them with one *roolya-boolya* the way they came ; and they left poor Guleesh standing where they found him, and the two eyes going out of his head, looking after them and wondering.

He did not stand long till he returned back, and he thinking in his own mind on all he saw and heard, and wondering whether there was really an herb at his own door that would bring back the talk to the king's daugh-ter.   " It can't be," says he to himself, " that they would tell it to me, if there was any virtue in it ; but perhaps the sheehogue didn't observe himself when he let the word slip out of his mouth. I'll search well as soon as the sun rises, whether there's any plant growing beside the house except thistles and dockings."

He went home, and as tired as he was he did not sleep a wink until the sun rose on the morrow. He got up then, and it was the first thing he did to go out and search

well through the grass round about the house, trying could he get any herb that he did not recognise. And, indeed, he was not long searching till he observed a large strange herb that was growing up just by the gable of the house.

He went over to it, and observed it closely, and saw

that there were seven little branches coming out of the stalk, and seven leaves growing on every branch*een* of them ; and that there was a white sap in the leaves. " It's very wonderful," said he to himself, " that I never noticed this herb before. If there's any virtue in an herb at all, it ought to be in such a strange one as this."

He drew out his knife, cut the plant, and carried it into his own house ; stripped the leaves off it and cut up the stalk ; and there came a thick, white juice out of it, as there comes out of the sow-thistle when it is bruised, except that the juice was more like oil.

He put it in a little pot and a little water in it, and laid it on the fire until the water was boiling, and then he took a cup, filled it half up with the juice, and put it to his own mouth. It came into his head then that perhaps it was poison that was in it, and that the good people were only tempting him that he might kill himself with that trick, or put the girl to death without meaning it. He put down the cup again, raised a couple of drops on the top of his finger, and put it to his mouth. It was not bitter, and, indeed, had a sweet, agreeable taste. He grew bolder then, and drank the full of a thimble of it, and then as much again, and he never stopped till he had half the cup drunk. He fell asleep after that, and did not wake till it was night, and there was great hunger and great thirst on him.

He had to wait, then, till the day rose ; but he determined, as soon as he should wake in the morning, that he would go to the king's daughter and give her a drink of the juice of the herb.

As soon as he got up in the morning, he went over to the priest's house with the drink in his hand, and he never

felt himself so bold and valiant, and spirited and light, as he
was that day, and he was quite certain that it was the
drink he drank which made him so hearty.

When he came to the house, he found the priest and the
young lady within, and they were wondering greatly why
he had not visited them for two days.

He told them all his news, and said that he was certain
that there was great power in that herb, and that it would
do the lady no hurt, for he tried it himself and got good
from it, and then he made her taste it, for he vowed and
swore that there was no harm in it.

Guleesh handed her the cup, and she drank half of it,
and then fell back on her bed and a heavy sleep came on

her, and she never woke out of that sleep till the day on the morrow.

Guleesh and the priest sat up the entire night with her, waiting till she should awake, and they between hope and unhope, between expectation of saving her and fear of hurting her.

She awoke at last when the sun had gone half its way through the heavens. She rubbed her eyes and looked like a person who did not know where she was. She was like one astonished when she saw Guleesh and the priest in the same room with her, and she sat up doing her best to collect her thoughts.

The two men were in great anxiety waiting to see would she speak, or would she not speak, and when they remained silent for a couple of minutes, the priest said to her : " Did you sleep well, Mary ? "

And she answered him : " I slept, thank you."

No sooner did Guleesh hear her talking than he put a shout of joy out of him, and ran over to her and fell on his two knees, and said: " A thousand thanks to God, who has given you back the talk ; lady of my heart, speak again to me."

The lady answered him that she understood it was he who boiled that drink for her, and gave it to her ; that she was obliged to him from her heart for all the kindness he showed her since the day she first came to Ireland, and that he might be certain that she never would forget it.

Guleesh was ready to die with satisfaction and delight. Then they brought her food, and she ate with a good appetite, and was merry and joyous, and never left off talking with the priest while she was eating.

After that Guleesh went home to his house, and stretched

himself on the bed and fell asleep again, for the force of the
herb was not all spent, and he passed another day and a
night sleeping. When he woke up he went back to the
priest's house, and found that the young lady was in the
same state, and that she was asleep almost since the time
that he left the house.

He went into her chamber with the priest, and they
remained watching beside her till she awoke the second
time, and she had her talk as well as ever, and Guleesh
was greatly rejoiced. The priest put food on the table
again, and they ate together, and Guleesh used after that
to come to the house from day to day, and the friendship
that was between him and the king's daughter increased,
because she had no one to speak to except Guleesh and the
priest, and she liked Guleesh best.

So they married one another, and that was the fine
wedding they had, and if I were to be there then, I would
not be here now ; but I heard it from a birdeen that there
was neither cark nor care, sickness nor sorrow, mishap nor
misfortune on them till the hour of their death, and may
the same be with me, and with us all !

The Field of Boliauns

NE fine day in harvest—it was indeed Lady-
day in harvest, that everybody knows to be
one of the greatest holidays in the year—
Tom Fitzpatrick was taking a ramble through
the ground, and went along the sunny side
of a hedge ; when all of a sudden he heard a clacking sort
of noise a little before him in the hedge. " Dear me," said
Tom, "but isn't it surprising to hear the stonechatters
singing so late in the season ? " So Tom stole on, going on
the tops of his toes to try if he could get a sight of what
was making the noise, to see if he was right in his guess.
The noise stopped ; but as Tom looked sharply through the
bushes, what should he see in a nook of the hedge but a
brown pitcher, that might hold about a gallon and a half of
liquor ; and by-and-by a little wee teeny tiny bit of an old
man, with a little *motty* of a cocked hat stuck upon the top

of his head, a deeshy daushy leather apron hanging before him, pulled out a little wooden stool, and stood up upon it, and dipped a little piggin into the pitcher, and took out the full of it, and put it beside the stool, and then sat down under the pitcher, and began to work at putting a heel-piece on a bit of a brogue just fit for himself. " Well, by the powers," said Tom to himself, " I often heard tell of the Lepracauns, and, to tell God's truth, I never rightly believed in them—but here's one of them in real earnest. If I go knowingly to work, I'm a made man. They say a body must never take their eyes off them, or they'll escape "

Tom now stole on a little further, with his eye fixed on the little man just as a cat does with a mouse. So when he got up quite close to him, " God bless your work, neighbour," said Tom.

The little man raised up his head, and " Thank you kindly," said he.

" I wonder you'd be working on the holiday ! " said Tom.

" That's my own business, not yours," was the reply.

" Well, may be you'd be civil enough to tell *us* what you've got in the pitcher there ? " said Tom.

" That I will, with pleasure," said he ; " it's good beer."

" Beer ! " said Tom. " Thunder and fire ! where did you get it ? "

" Where did I get it, is it ? Why, I made it. And what do you think I made it of ? "

" Devil a one of me knows," said Tom ; " but of malt, I suppose, what else ? "

" There you're out. I made it of heath."

" Of heath ! " said Tom, bursting out laughing ; " sure you don't think me to be such a fool as to believe that ? "

"Do as you please," said he, "but what I tell you is the truth.   Did you never hear tell of the Danes."

"Well, what about *them*?" said Tom.

"Why, all the about them there is, is that when they were here they taught us to make beer out of the heath, and the secret's in my family ever since."

"Will you give a body a taste of your beer?" said Tom.

"I'll tell you what it is, young man, it would be fitter for you to be looking after your father's property than to be bothering decent quiet people with your foolish questions. There now, while you're idling away your time here, there's the cows have broke into the oats, and are knocking the corn all about."

Tom was taken so by surprise with this that he was just on the very point of turning round when he recollected himself; so, afraid that the like might happen again, he made a grab at the Lepracaun, and caught him up in his hand; but in his hurry he overset the pitcher, and spilt all the beer, so that he could not get a taste of it to tell what sort it was.   He then swore that he would kill him if he did not show him where his money was.   Tom looked so wicked and so bloody-minded that the little man was quite frightened; so says he, "Come along with me a couple of fields off, and I'll show you a crock of gold."

So they went, and Tom held the Lepracaun fast in his hand, and never took his eyes from off him, though they had to cross hedges and ditches, and a crooked bit of bog, till at last they came to a great field all full of boliauns, and the Lepracaun pointed to a big boliaun, and says he, "Dig under that boliaun, and you'll get the great crock all full of guineas."

Tom in his hurry had never thought of bringing a spade with him, so he made up his mind to run home and fetch one ; and that he might know the place again he took off one of his red garters, and tied it round the boliaun.

Then he said to the Lepracaun, " Swear ye'll not take that garter away from that boliaun." And the Lepracaun swore right away not to touch it.

" I suppose," said the Lepracaun, very civilly, " you have no further occasion for me ? "

" No," says Tom ; " you may go away now, if you please, and God speed you, and may good luck attend you wherever you go."

" Well, good-bye to you, Tom Fitzpatrick," said the Lepracaun ; " and much good may it do you when you get it."

So Tom ran for dear life, till he came home and got a spade, and then away with him, as hard as he could go, back to the field of boliauns ; but when he got there, lo and behold ! not a boliaun in the field but had a red garter, the very model of his own, tied about it ; and as to digging up the whole field, that was all nonsense, for there were more than forty good Irish acres in it. So Tom came home again with his spade on his shoulder, a little cooler than he went, and many's the hearty curse he gave the Lepracaun every time he thought of the neat turn he had served him.

The Horned Women

 RICH woman sat up late one night carding and preparing wool, while all the family and servants were asleep. Suddenly a knock was given at the door, and a voice called, " Open ! open !"

" Who is there ?" said the woman of the house.

" I am the Witch of one Horn," was answered.

The mistress, supposing that one of her neighbours had called and required assistance, opened the door, and a woman entered, having in her hand a pair of wool-carders, and bearing a horn on her forehead, as if growing there. She sat down by the fire in silence, and began to card the wool with violent haste. Suddenly she paused, and said aloud : " Where are the women ? they delay too long."

Then a second knock came to the door, and a voice called as before, " Open ! open !"

The mistress felt herself obliged to rise and open to the call, and immediately a second witch entered, having two horns on her forehead, and in her hand a wheel for spinning wool.

" Give me place," she said ; " I am the Witch of the two Horns," and she began to spin as quick as lightning.

And so the knocks went on, and the call was heard, and the witches entered, until at last twelve women sat round the fire—the first with one horn, the last with twelve horns.

And they carded the thread, and turned their spinning-wheels, and wound and wove, all singing together an ancient rhyme, but no word did they speak to the mistress of the house. Strange to hear, and frightful to look upon, were these twelve women, with their horns and their wheels ; and the mistress felt near to death, and she tried to rise that she might call for help, but she could not move, nor could she utter a word or a cry, for the spell of the witches was upon her.

Then one of them called to her in Irish, and said, " Rise, woman, and make us a cake."

Then the mistress searched for a vessel to bring water from the well that she might mix the meal and make the cake, but she could find none.

And they said to her, " Take a sieve and bring water in it."

And she took the sieve and went to the well; but the water poured from it, and she could fetch none for the cake, and she sat down by the well and wept.

Then a voice came by her and said, " Take yellow clay and moss, and bind them together, and plaster the sieve so that it will hold."

This she did, and the sieve held the water for the cake ; and the voice said again :

" Return, and when thou comest to the north angle of the house, cry aloud three times and say, ' The mountain of the Fenian women and the sky over it is all on fire.' "

And she did so.

When the witches inside heard the call, a great and terrible cry broke from their lips, and they rushed forth with wild lamentations and shrieks, and fled away to Slievenamon, where was their chief abode. But the Spirit of the Well bade the mistress of the house to enter and prepare her home against the enchantments of the witches if they returned again.

And first, to break their spells, she sprinkled the water in which she had washed her child's feet, the feet-water, outside the door on the threshold ; secondly, she took the cake which in her absence the witches had made of meal mixed with the blood drawn from the sleeping family, and she broke the cake in bits, and placed a bit in the mouth of each sleeper, and they were restored ; and she took the cloth they had woven, and placed it half in and half out of the chest with the padlock ; and lastly, she secured the door with a great crossbeam fastened in the jambs, so that the witches could not enter, and having done these things she waited.

Not long were the witches in coming back, and they raged and called for vengeance.

" Open ! open !" they screamed ; " open, feet-water !"

" I cannot," said the feet-water ; " I am scattered on the ground, and my path is down to the Lough."

" Open, open, wood and trees and beam !" they cried to the door.

" I cannot," said the door, " for the beam is fixed in the jambs and I have no power to move."

" Open, open, cake that we have made and mingled with blood !" they cried again.

" I cannot," said the cake, " for I am broken and bruised, and my blood is on the lips of the sleeping children."

Then the witches rushed through the air with great cries, and fled back to Slievenamon, uttering strange curses on the Spirit of the Well, who had wished their ruin ; but the woman and the house were left in peace, and a mantle dropped by one of the witches in her flight was kept hung up by the mistress in memory of that night ; and this mantle was kept by the same family from generation to generation for five hundred years after.

Conall Yellowclaw

ONALL YELLOWCLAW was a sturdy tenant in Erin : he had three sons. There was at that time a king over every fifth of Erin. It fell out for the children of the king that was near Conall, that they themselves and the children of Conall came to blows. The children of Conall got the upper hand, and they killed the king's big son. The king sent a message for Conall, and he said to him—" Oh, Conall ! what made your sons go to spring on my sons till my big son was killed by your children? but I see that though I follow you revengefully, I shall not be much better for it, and I will now set a thing before you, and if you will do it, I will not follow you with revenge. If you and your sons will get me the brown horse of the king of Lochlann, you shall get the souls of your sons."

" Why," said Conall, " should not I do the pleasure of the king, though there should be no souls of my sons in dread at all. Hard is the matter you require of me, but I will lose my own life, and the life of my sons, or else I will do the pleasure of the king."

After these words Conall left the king, and he went home : when he got home he was under much trouble and perplexity. When he went to lie down he told his wife the thing the king had set before him. His wife took much sorrow that he was obliged to part from herself, while she knew not if she should see him more.

"Oh, Conall," said she, "why didst not thou let the king do his own pleasure to thy sons, rather than be going now, while I know not if ever I shall see thee more ? "

When he rose on the morrow, he set himself and his three sons in order, and they took their journey towards Lochlann, and they made no stop but tore through ocean till they reached it. When they reached Lochlann they did not know what they should do. Said the old man to his sons, "Stop ye, and we will seek out the house of the king's miller."

When they went into the house of the king's miller, the man asked them to stop there for the night. Conall told the miller that his own children and the children of his king had fallen out, and that his children had killed the king's son, and there was nothing that would please the king but that he should get the brown horse of the king of Lochlann.

" If you will do me a kindness, and will put me in a way to get him, for certain I will pay ye for it."

" The thing is silly that you are come to seek," said the miller ; " for the king has laid his mind on him so greatly that you will not get him in any way unless you steal him ; but if you can make out a way, I will keep it secret."

" This is what I am thinking," said Conall, " since you

are working every day for the king, you and your gillies could put myself and my sons into five sacks of bran."

"The plan that has come into your head is not bad," said the miller.

The miller spoke to his gillies, and he said to them to do this, and they put them in five sacks. The king's gillies came to seek the bran, and they took the five sacks with them, and they emptied them before the horses. The servants locked the door, and they went away.

When they rose to lay hand on the brown horse, said Conall, "You shall not do that. It is hard to get out of this ; let us make for ourselves five hiding holes, so that if they hear us we may go and hide." They made the holes, then they laid hands on the horse. The horse was pretty well unbroken, and he set to making a terrible noise through the stable. The king heard the noise. "It must be my brown horse," said he to his gillies ; "find out what is wrong with him."

The servants went out, and when Conall and his sons saw them coming they went into the hiding holes. The servants looked amongst the horses, and they did not find anything wrong ; and they returned and they told this to the king, and the king said to them that if nothing was wrong they should go to their places of rest. When the gillies had time to be gone, Conall and his sons laid their hands again on the horse. If the noise was great that he made before, the noise he made now was seven times greater. The king sent a message for his gillies again, and said for certain there was something troubling the brown horse. "Go and look well about him." The servants went out, and they went to their hiding holes. The servants rum-

maged well, and did not find a thing. They returned and
they told this.

" That is marvellous for me," said the king : " go you to
lie down again, and if I notice it again I will go out myself."

When Conall and his sons perceived that the gillies were
gone, they laid hands again on the horse, and one of them
caught him, and if the noise that the horse made on the
two former times was great, he made more this time.

" Be this from me," said the king ; " it must be that
some one is troubling my brown horse." He sounded the
bell hastily, and when his waiting-man came to him, he
said to him to let the stable gillies know that something
was wrong with the horse. The gillies came, and the king
went with them. When Conall and his sons perceived the
company coming they went to the hiding holes.

The king was a wary man, and he saw where the horses
were making a noise.

" Be wary," said the king, " there are men within the
stable, let us get at them somehow."

The king followed the tracks of the men, and he found
them. Every one knew Conall, for he was a valued tenant
of the king of Erin, and when the king brought them up out
of the holes he said, " Oh, Conall, is it you that are here ? "

" I am, O king, without question, and necessity made me
come. I am under thy pardon, and under thine honour,
and under thy grace." He told how it happened to him,
and that he had to get the brown horse for the king of
Erin, or that his sons were to be put to death. " I knew
that I should not get him by asking, and I was going to
steal him."

"Yes, Conall, it is well enough, but come in," said the king. He desired his look-out men to set a watch on the sons of Conall, and to give them meat. And a double watch was set that night on the sons of Conall.

"Now, O Conall," said the king, "were you ever in a harder place than to be seeing your lot of sons hanged to-morrow? But you set it to my goodness and to my grace, and say that it was necessity brought it on you, so I must not hang you. Tell me any case in which you were as hard as this, and if you tell that, you shall get the soul of your youngest son."

"I will tell a case as hard in which I was," said Conall. "I was once a young lad, and my father had much land, and he had parks of year-old cows, and one of them had just calved, and my father told me to bring her home. I found the cow, and took her with us. There fell a shower of snow. We went into the herd's bothy, and we took the cow and the calf in with us, and we were letting the shower pass from us. Who should come in but one cat and ten, and one great one-eyed fox-coloured cat as head bard over them. When they came in, in very deed I my-self had no liking for their company. 'Strike up with you,' said the head bard, 'why should we be still? and sing a cronan to Conall Yellowclaw.' I was amazed that my name was known to the cats themselves. When they had sung the cronan, said the head bard, 'Now, O Conall, pay the reward of the cronan that the cats have sung to thee.' 'Well then,' said I myself, 'I have no reward whatsoever for you, unless you should go down and take that calf.' No sooner said I the word than the two cats and ten went down to attack the calf, and in very deed, he did not last them long. 'Play up with you, why should you be silent ? Make a cronan to Conall Yellow,' said the head bard. Certainly I had no liking at all for the cronan, but up came the one cat and ten, and if they did not sing me a cronan then and there! 'Pay them now their reward,' said the great fox-coloured cat. 'I am tired myself of yourselves and your rewards,' said I. 'I have no reward for you unless you take that cow down there." They betook themselves to the cow, and indeed she did not last them long.

"'Why will you be silent ? Go up and sing a cronan to Conall Yellowclaw,' said the head bard. And surely, oh, king, I had no care for them or for their cronan, for I began to see that they were not good comrades. When they had sung me the cronan they betook themselves down where the head bard was. 'Pay now their reward, said the head bard ; and for sure, oh king, I had no reward for them ; and I said to them, 'I have no reward for you.' And surely, oh king, there was catterwauling between them. So I leapt out at a turf window that was at the back of the house. I took myself off as hard as I might into the wood. I was swift enough and strong at that time ; and when I felt the rustling toirm of the cats after me I climbed into as high a tree as I saw in the place, and one that was close in the top ; and I hid myself as well as I might. The cats began to search for me through the wood, and they could not find me ; and when they were tired, each one said to the other that they would turn back. 'But,' said the one-eyed fox-coloured cat that was commander-in-chief over them, 'you saw him not with your two eyes, and though I have but one eye, there's the rascal up in the tree.' When he had said that, one of them went up in the tree, and as

he was coming where I was, I drew a weapon that I had
and I killed him.   'Be this from me!' said the one-eyed

one—'I must not be losing my
company thus; gather round the
root of the tree and dig about it,
and let down that villain to earth.'
On this they gathered about the
tree, and they dug about the root,
and the first branching root that
they cut, she gave a shiver to fall,
and I myself gave a shout, and
it was not to be wondered at.
There was in the neighbourhood
of the wood a priest, and he had ten men with him delving,
and he said, 'There is a shout of a man in extremity and I
must not be without replying to it.'   And the wisest of the
men said, 'Let it alone till we hear it again.'   The cats
began again digging wildly, and they broke the next root;
and I myself gave the next shout, and in very deed it was
not a weak one.   'Certainly,' said the priest, 'it is a man
in extremity—let us move.'   They set themselves in order
for moving.   And the cats arose on the tree, and they
broke the third root, and the tree fell on her elbow.   Then I
gave the third shout.   The stalwart men hastened, and when
they saw how the cats served the tree, they began at them
with the spades; and they themselves and the cats began
at each other, till the cats ran away.   And surely, oh king,
I did not move till I saw the last one of them off.   And then
I came home.   And there's the hardest case in which I
ever was; and it seems to me that tearing by the cats were
harder than hanging to-morrow by the king of Lochlann."

" Och ! Conall," said the king, " you are full of words. You have freed the soul of your son with your tale ; and if you tell me a harder case than that you will get your second youngest son, and then you will have two sons."

" Well then," said Conall, " on condition that thou dost that, I will tell thee how I was once in a harder case than to be in thy power in prison to-night."

" Let's hear," said the king.

" I was then," said Conall, " quite a young lad, and I went out hunting, and my father's land was beside the sea, and it was rough with rocks, caves, and rifts. When I was going on the top of the shore, I saw as if there were a smoke coming up between two rocks, and I began to look what might be the meaning of the smoke coming up there. When I was looking, what should I do but fall ; and the place was so full of heather, that neither bone nor skin was broken. I knew not how I should get out of this. I was not looking before me, but I kept looking overhead the way I came—and thinking that the day would never come that I could get up there. It was terrible for me to be there till I should die. I heard a great clattering coming, and what was there but a great giant and two dozen of goats with him, and a buck at their head. And when the giant had tied the goats, he came up and he said to me, ' Hao O ! Conall, it's long since my knife has been rusting in my pouch waiting for thy tender flesh.' ' Och !' said I, ' it's not much you will be bettered by me, though you should tear me asunder ; I will make but one meal for you. But I see that you are one-eyed. I am a good leech, and I will give you the sight of the other eye.' The giant went and he drew the great caldron on the site of the fire. I myself was telling him how he should heat the water, so that I should give its sight to the other eye. I got heather and I made a rubber of it, and I set him upright in the caldron. I began at the eye that was well, pretending to him that I would give its sight to the other one, till I left them as bad as each other; and surely it was easier to spoil the one that was well than to give sight to the other.

"When he saw that he could not see a glimpse, and when I myself said to him that I would get out in spite of him, he gave a spring out of the water, and he stood in the mouth of the cave, and he said that he would have revenge for the sight of his eye. I had but to stay there crouched the length of the night, holding in my breath in such a way that he might not find out where I was.

"When he felt the birds calling in the morning, and knew that the day was, he said—'Art thou sleeping? Awake and let out my lot of goats.' I killed the buck. He cried, 'I do believe that thou art killing my buck.'

"'I am not,' said I, 'but the ropes are so tight that I take long to loose them.' I let out one of the goats, and there he was caressing her, and he said to her, 'There thou art thou shaggy, hairy white goat, and thou seest me, but I see thee not.' I kept letting them out by the way of one and one, as I flayed the buck, and before the last one was out I had him flayed bag-wise. Then I went and I put my legs in place of his legs, and my hands in place of his forelegs, and my head in place of his head, and the horns on top of my head, so that the brute might think that it was the buck. I went out. When I was going out the giant laid his hand on me, and he said, 'There thou art, thou pretty buck; thou seest me, but I see thee not.' When I myself got out,

THERE THOU ART THOU PRETTY BUCK · THOU SEEST ME BUT I SEE THEE NOT

and I saw the world about me, surely, oh, king! joy was on me. When I was out and had shaken the skin off me, I said to the brute, ' I am out now in spite of you.'

"'Aha!' said he, ' hast thou done this to me. Since thou wert so stalwart that thou hast got out, I will give thee a ring that I have here ; keep the ring, and it will do thee good.'

"' I will not take the ring from you,' said I, ' but throw it, and I will take it with me.' He threw the ring on the flat ground, I went myself and I lifted the ring, and I put it on my finger. When he said me then, ' Is the ring fitting thee ?' I said to him, 'It is.' Then he said, 'Where art thou, ring ?' And the ring said, ' I am here.' The brute went and went towards where the ring was speaking, and now I saw that I was in a harder case than ever I was. I drew a dirk. I cut the finger from off me, and I threw it from me as far as I could out on the loch, and there was a great depth in the place. He shouted, ' Where art thou, ring ?' And the ring said, ' I am here,' though it was on the bed of ocean. He gave a spring after the ring, and out he went in the sea. And I was as pleased then when I saw him drowning, as though you should grant my own life and the life of my two sons with me, and not lay any more trouble on me.

" When the giant was drowned I went in, and I took with me all he had of gold and silver, and I went home, and surely great joy was on my people when I arrived. And as a sign now look, the finger is off me."

" Yes, indeed, Conall, you are wordy and wise," said the king. " I see the finger is off you. You have freed your two sons, but tell me a case in which you ever were that is

harder than to be looking on your son being hanged to-
morrow, and you shall get the soul of your eldest son."

"Then went my father," said Conall, "and he got me a
wife, and I was married. I went to hunt. I was going
beside the sea, and I saw an island over in the midst of the
loch, and I came there where a boat was with a rope before
her, and a rope behind her, and many precious things within
her. I looked myself on the boat to see how I might get part of
them. I put in the one foot, and the other foot was on the
ground, and when I raised my head what was it but the boat
over in the middle of the loch, and she never stopped till she
reached the island. When I went out of the boat the boat
returned where she was before. I did not know now what I
should do. The place was without meat or clothing, without
the appearance of a house on it. I came out on the top of a
hill. Then I came to a glen ; I saw in it, at the bottom of a
hollow, a woman with a child, and the child was naked on
her knee, and she had a knife in her hand. She tried to
put the knife to the throat of the babe, and the babe began
to laugh in her face, and she began to cry, and she threw
the knife behind her. I thought to myself that I was near
my foe and far from my friends, and I called to the woman,
'What are you doing here ?' And she said to me, 'What
brought you here ?' I told her myself word upon word
how I came. 'Well then,' said she, 'it was so I came
also.' She showed me to the place where I should come
in where she was. I went in, and I said to her, 'What
was the matter that you were putting the knife on the neck
of the child ?' 'It is that he must be cooked for the giant
who is here, or else no more of my world will be before
me.' Just then we could be hearing the footsteps of the

giant, 'What shall I do? what shall I do?' cried the
woman. I went to the caldron, and by luck it was not
hot, so in it I got just as the brute came in. 'Hast thou
boiled that youngster for me?' he cried. 'He's not done
yet,' said she, and I cried out from the caldron, 'Mammy,
mammy, it's boiling I am.' Then the giant laughed out
HAI, HAW, HOGARAICH, and heaped on wood under
the caldron.

"And now I was sure I would scald before I could
get out of that. As fortune favoured me, the brute slept
beside the caldron. There I was scalded by the bottom of
the caldron. When she perceived that he was asleep, she
set her mouth quietly to the hole that was in the lid, and
she said to me 'was I alive?' I said I was. I put up my
head, and the hole in the lid was so large, that my head
went through easily. Everything was coming easily with
me till I began to bring up my hips. I left the skin of my
hips behind me, but I came out. When I got out of the
caldron I knew not what to do ; and she said to me that
there was no weapon that would kill him but his own
weapon. I began to draw his spear and every breath that
he drew I thought I would be down his throat, and when
his breath came out I was back again just as far. But with
every ill that befell me I got the spear loosed from him.
Then I was as one under a bundle of straw in a great wind
for I could not manage the spear. And it was fearful to
look on the brute, who had but one eye in the midst of his
face ; and it was not agreeable for the like of me to attack
him. I drew the dart as best I could, and I set it in his
eye. When he felt this he gave his head a lift, and he
struck the other end of the dart on the top of the cave, and

it went through to the back of his head. And he fell cold dead where he was ; and you may be sure, oh king, that joy was on me. I myself and the woman went out on clear ground, and we passed the night there. I went and got the boat with which I came, and she was no way lightened, and took the woman and the child over on dry land ; and I returned home."

The king of Lochlann's mother was putting on a fire at this time, and listening to Conall telling the tale about the child.

" Is it you," said she, " that were there ? "

" Well then," said he, " 'twas I."

" Och ! och ! " said she, " 'twas I that was there, and the king is the child whose life you saved ; and it is to you that life thanks should be given." Then they took great joy.

The king said, " Oh, Conall, you came through great hardships. And now the brown horse is yours, and his sack full of the most precious things that are in my treasury."

They lay down that night, and if it was early that Conall rose, it was earlier than that that the queen was on foot making ready. He got the brown horse and his sack full of gold and silver and stones of great price, and then Conall and his three sons went away, and they returned home to the Erin realm of gladness. He left the gold and silver in his house, and he went with the horse to the king. They were good friends evermore. He returned home to his wife, and they set in order a feast ; and that was a feast if ever there was one, oh son and brother.

Hudden and Dudden and
Donald O'Neary

HERE was once upon a time two farmers, and their names were Hudden and Dudden. They had poultry in their yards, sheep on the uplands, and scores of cattle in the meadow-land alongside the river. But for all that they weren't happy. For just between their two farms there lived a poor man by the name of Donald O'Neary. He had a hovel over his head and a strip of grass that was barely enough to keep his one cow, Daisy, from starving, and, though she did her best, it was but seldom that Donald got a drink of milk or a roll of butter from Daisy. You would think there was little here to make

Hudden and Dudden jealous, but so it is, the more one has
the more one wants, and Donald's neighbours lay awake of
nights scheming how they might get hold of his little strip
of grass-land.   Daisy, poor thing, they never thought of ;
she was just a bag of bones.

One day Hudden met Dudden, and they were soon grum-
bling as usual, and all to the tune of " If only we could get
that vagabond Donald O'Neary out of the country."

" Let's kill Daisy," said Hudden at last ; " if that doesn't
make him clear out, nothing will."

No sooner said than agreed, and it wasn't dark before
Hudden and Dudden crept up to the little shed where lay
poor Daisy trying her best to chew the cud, though she
hadn't had as much grass in the day as would cover your
hand.   And when Donald came to see if Daisy was all snug
for the night, the poor beast had only time to lick his hand
once before she died.

Well, Donald was a shrewd fellow, and downhearted
though he was, began to think if he could get any good out
of Daisy's death.   He thought and he thought, and the
next day you could have seen him trudging off early to the
fair, Daisy's hide over his shoulder, every penny he had
jingling in his pockets.   Just before he got to the fair, he
made several slits in the hide, put a penny in each slit,
walked into the best inn of the town as bold as if it belonged
to him, and, hanging the hide up to a nail in the wall, sat
down.

" Some of your best whisky," says he to the landlord.
But the landlord didn't like his looks.   " Is it fearing I
won't pay you, you are ? " says Donald ; " why I have a
hide here that gives me all the money I want."   And with

that he hit it a whack with his stick and out hopped a penny. The landlord opened his eyes, as you may fancy.

" What'll you take for that hide ? "

" It's not for sale, my good man."

" Will you take a gold piece ? "

" It's not for sale, I tell you. Hasn't it kept me and mine for years ? " and with that Donald hit the hide another whack and out jumped a second penny.

Well, the long and the short of it was that Donald let the hide go, and, that very evening, who but he should walk up to Hudden's door ?

" Good-evening, Hudden. Will you lend me your best pair of scales ? "

Hudden stared and Hudden scratched his head, but he lent the scales.

When Donald was safe at home, he pulled out his pocketful of bright gold and began to weigh each piece in the scales. But Hudden had put a lump of butter at the bottom, and so the last piece of gold stuck fast to the scales when he took them back to Hudden.

If Hudden had stared before, he stared ten times more now, and no sooner was Donald's back turned, than he was off as hard as he could pelt to Dudden's.

" Good-evening, Dudden. That vagabond, bad luck to him ——"

" You mean Donald O'Neary ? "

" And who else should I mean ? He's back here weighing out sackfuls of gold."

" How do you know that ? "

" Here are my scales that he borrowed, and here's a gold piece still sticking to them."

Off they went together, and they came to Donald's door. Donald had finished making the last pile of ten gold pieces. And he couldn't finish because a piece had stuck to the scales.

In they walked without an " If you please " or " By your leave."

" Well, *I* never !" that was all *they* could say.

" Good-evening, Hudden ; good-evening, Dudden. Ah ! you thought you had played me a fine trick, but you never did me a better turn in all your lives. When I found poor Daisy dead, I thought to myself, ' Well, her hide may fetch something ; ' and it did. Hides are worth their weight in gold in the market just now."

Hudden nudged Dudden, and Dudden winked at Hudden.

" Good-evening, Donald O'Neary."

" Good-evening, kind friends."

The next day there wasn't a cow or a calf that belonged to Hudden or Dudden but her hide was going to the fair in Hudden's biggest cart drawn by Dudden's strongest pair of horses.

When they came to the fair, each one took a hide over his arm, and there they were walking through the fair, bawling out at the top of their voices : ' Hides to sell ! hides to sell ! "

Out came the tanner :

" How much for your hides, my good men ?"

" Their weight in gold."

" It's early in the day to come out of the tavern." That was all the tanner said, and back he went to his yard.

" Hides to sell !   Fine fresh hides to sell !"

Out came the cobbler.

" How much for your hides, my men ? "

" Their weight in gold."

" Is it making game of me you are ! Take that for your pains," and the cobbler dealt Hudden a blow that made him stagger.

Up the people came running from one end of the fair to the other.   " What's the matter ?   What's the matter ?" cried they.

" Here are a couple of vagabonds selling hides at their weight in gold," said the cobbler.

" Hold 'em fast ; hold 'em fast ! " bawled the innkeeper, who was the last to come up, he was so fat.   " I'll **wager** it's one of the rogues who tricked me out of thirty gold pieces yesterday for a wretched hide."

It was more kicks than halfpence that Hudden and Dudden got before they were well on their way home again, and they didn't run the slower because all the dogs of the town were at their heels.

Well, as you may fancy, if they loved Donald little before, they loved him less now.

"What's the matter, friends?" said he, as he saw them tearing along, their hats knocked in, and their coats torn off, and their faces black and blue. "Is it fighting you've been? or mayhap you met the police, ill luck to them?"

"We'll police you, you vagabond. It's mighty smart you thought yourself, deluding us with your lying tales."

"Who deluded you? Didn't you see the gold with your own two eyes?"

But it was no use talking. Pay for it he must, and should. There was a meal-sack handy, and into it Hudden and Dudden popped Donald O'Neary, tied him up tight, ran a pole through the knot, and off they started for the Brown Lake of the Bog, each with a pole-end on his shoulder, and Donald O'Neary between.

But the Brown Lake was far, the road was dusty, Hudden and Dudden were sore and weary, and parched with thirst. There was an inn by the roadside.

"Let's go in," said Hudden; "I'm dead beat. It's heavy he is for the little he had to eat."

If Hudden was willing, so was Dudden. As for Donald, you may be sure his leave wasn't asked, but he was lumped down at the inn door for all the world as if he had been a sack of potatoes.

"Sit still, you vagabond," said Dudden; "if we don't mind waiting, you needn't."

Donald held his peace, but after a while he heard the glasses clink, and Hudden singing away at the top of his voice.

"I won't have her, I tell you ; I won't have her!" said Donald. But nobody heeded what he said.

"I won't have her, I tell you ; I won't have her!" said Donald, and this time he said it louder ; but nobody heeded what he said.

"I won't have her, I tell you ; I won't have her!" said Donald ; and this time he said it as loud as he could.

"And who won't you have, may I be so bold as to ask?" said a farmer, who had just come up with a drove of cattle, and was turning in for a glass.

"It's the king's daughter. They are bothering the life out of me to marry her."

"You're the lucky fellow. I'd give something to be in your shoes."

"Do you see that now! Wouldn't it be a fine thing for a farmer to be marrying a princess, all dressed in gold and jewels ?"

"Jewels, do you say ? Ah, now, couldn't you take me with you ?"

"Well, you're an honest fellow, and as I don't care for the king's daughter, though she's as beautiful as the day, and is covered with jewels from top to toe, you shall have her. Just undo the cord, and let me out ; they tied me up tight, as they knew I'd run away from her."

Out crawled Donald ; in crept the farmer.

"Now lie still, and don't mind the shaking ; it's only rumbling over the palace steps you'll be. And maybe they'll abuse you for a vagabond, who won't have the king's daughter ; but you needn't mind that. Ah ! it's a deal I'm giving up for you, sure as it is that I don't care for the princess."

"Take my cattle in exchange," said the farmer ; and you may guess it wasn't long before Donald was at their tails driving them homewards.

Out came Hudden and Dudden, and the one took one end of the pole, and the other the other.

"I'm thinking he's heavier," said Hudden.

"Ah, never mind," said Dudden ; "it's only a step now to the Brown Lake."

"I'll have her now ! I'll have her now !" bawled the farmer, from inside the sack.

"By my faith, and you shall though," said Hudden, and he laid his stick across the sack.

"I'll have her ! I'll have her !" bawled the farmer, louder than ever.

"Well, here you are," said Dudden, for they were now come to the Brown Lake, and, unslinging the sack, they pitched it plump into the lake.

"You'll not be playing your tricks on us any longer," said Hudden.

"True for you," said Dudden. "Ah, Donald, my boy, it was an ill day when you borrowed my scales."

Off they went, with a light step and an easy heart, but when they were near home, who should they see but Donald O'Neary, and all around him the cows were grazing, and the calves were kicking up their heels and butting their heads together.

"Is it you, Donald ?" said Dudden. "Faith, you've been quicker than we have."

"True for you, Dudden, and let me thank you kindly; the turn was good, if the will was ill.   You'll have heard, like me, that the Brown Lake leads to the Land of Promise. I always put it down as lies, but it is just as true as my word.   Look at the cattle."

Hudden stared, and Dudden gaped; but they couldn't get over the cattle; fine fat cattle they were too.

"It's only the worst I could bring up with me," said Donald O'Neary; "the others were so fat, there was no driving them.   Faith, too, it's little wonder they didn't care to leave, with grass as far as you could see, and as sweet and juicy as fresh butter."

"Ah, now, Donald, we haven't always been friends," said Dudden, "but, as I was just saying, you were ever a decent lad, and you'll show us the way, won't you?"

"I don't see that I'm called upon to do that; there is a power more cattle down there.   Why shouldn't I have them all to myself?"

"Faith, they may well say, the richer you get, the harder the heart.   You always were a neighbourly lad, Donald. You wouldn't wish to keep the luck all to yourself?"

"True for you, Hudden, though 'tis a bad example you set me.   But I'll not be thinking of old times.   There is plenty for all there, so come along with me."

Off they trudged, with a light heart and an eager step. When they came to the Brown Lake, the sky was full of little white clouds, and, if the sky was full, the lake was as full.

"Ah! now, look, there they are," cried Donald, as he pointed to the clouds in the lake.

"Where? where?" cried Hudden, and "Don't be greedy!"

cried Dudden, as he jumped his hardest to be up first with
the fat cattle.   But if he jumped first, Hudden wasn't long
behind.

They never came back.   Maybe they got too fat, like
the cattle.   As for Donald O'Neary, he had cattle and sheep
all his days to his heart's content.

The Shepherd of Myddvai

 P in the Black Mountains in Caermarthenshire lies the lake known as Lyn y Van Vach. To the margin of this lake the shepherd of Myddvai once led his lambs, and lay there whilst they sought pasture. Suddenly, from the dark waters of the lake, he saw three maidens rise. Shaking the bright drops from their hair and gliding to the shore, they wandered about amongst his flock. They had more than mortal beauty, and he was filled with love for her that came nearest to him. He offered her the bread he had with him, and she took it and tried it, but then sang to him :

> Hard-baked is thy bread,
> 'Tis not easy to catch me,

and then ran off laughing to the lake.

Next day he took with him bread not so well done, and watched for the maidens. When they came ashore he offered his bread as before, and the maiden tasted it and sang :

> Unbaked is thy bread,
> I will not have thee,

and again disappeared in the waves.

A third time did the shepherd of Myddvai try to attract the maiden, and this time he offered her bread that he had found floating about near the shore. This pleased her, and she promised to become his wife if he were able to pick her out from among her sisters on the following day. When the time came the shepherd knew his love by the strap of her sandal. Then she told him she would be as good a wife to him as any earthly maiden could be unless he should strike her three times without cause. Of course he deemed that this could never be ; and she, summoning from the lake three cows, two oxen, and a bull, as her marriage portion, was led homeward by him as his bride.

The years passed happily, and three children were born to the shepherd and the lake-maiden. But one day here were going to a christening, and she said to her husband it was far to walk, so he told her to go for the horses.

" I will," said she, " if you bring me my gloves which I've left in the house."

But when he came back with the gloves, he found she had not gone for the horses ; so he tapped her lightly on the shoulder with the gloves, and said, "Go, go."

" That's one," said she.

Another time they were at a wedding, when suddenly the lake-maiden fell a-sobbing and a-weeping, amid the joy and mirth of all around her.

Her husband tapped her on the shoulder, and asked her, " Why do you weep ? "

" Because they are entering into trouble ; and trouble is upon you ; for that is the second causeless blow you have given me. Be careful ; the third is the last."

The husband was careful never to strike her again. But one day at a funeral she suddenly burst out into fits of laughter. Her husband forgot, and touched her rather roughly on the shoulder, saying, " Is this a time for laughter ? "

" I laugh," she said, " because those that die go out of trouble, but your trouble has come. The last blow has been struck ; our marriage is at an end, and so farewell." And with that she rose up and left the house and went to their home.

Then she, looking round upon her home, called to the cattle she had brought with her :

> Brindle cow, white speckled,
> Spotted cow, bold freckled,
> Old white face, and gray Geringer,
> And the white bull from the king's coast,
> Grey ox, and black calf,
> All, all, follow me home,

Now the black calf had just been slaughtered, and was hanging on the hook ; but it got off the hook alive and well and followed her ; and the oxen, though they were ploughing, trailed the plough with them and did her bidding. So she fled to the lake again, they following her, and with them plunged into the dark waters. And to this day is the furrow seen which the plough left as it was dragged across the mountains to the tarn.

Only once did she come again, when her sons were grown to manhood, and then she gave them gifts of healing by which they won the name of Meddygon Myddvai, the physicians of Myddvai.

The Sprightly Tailor

 SPRIGHTLY tailor was employed by the great Macdonald, in his castle at Saddell, in order to make the laird a pair of trews, used in olden time.   And trews being the vest and breeches united in one piece, and ornamented with fringes, were very comfortable, and suitable to be worn in walkin or dancing.   And Macdonald had said to the tailor, that if he would make the trews by night in the church, he would get a handsome reward. For it was thought that the old ruined church was haunted, and that fearsome things were to be seen there at night.

The tailor was well aware of this ; but he was a sprightly man, and when the laird dared him to make the trews by

Keep your eyes where you belong.

night in the church, the tailor was not to be daunted, but took it in hand to gain the prize. So, when night came, away he went up the glen, about half a mile distance from the castle, till he came to the old church. Then he chose him a nice gravestone for a seat and he lighted his candle, and put on his thimble, and set to work at the trews ; plying his needle nimbly, and thinking about the hire that the laird would have to give him.

For some time he got on pretty well, until he felt the floor all of a tremble under his feet ; and looking about him, but keeping his fingers at work, he saw the appearance of a great human head rising up through the stone pavement of the church. And when the head had risen above the surface, there came from it a great, great voice. And the voice said : " Do you see this great head of mine ? "

" I see that, but I'll sew this ! " replied the sprightly tailor ; and he stitched away at the trews.

Then the head rose higher up through the pavement, until its neck appeared. And when its neck was shown, the thundering voice came again and said : " Do you see this great neck of mine ? "

" I see that, but I'll sew this ! " said the sprightly tailor ; and he stitched away at his trews.

Then the head and neck rose higher still, until the great shoulders and chest were shown above the ground. And again the mighty voice thundered : " Do you see this great chest of mine ? "

And again the sprightly tailor replied : " I see that, but I'll sew this ! " and stitched away at his trews.

And still it kept rising through the pavement, until it

shook a great pair of arms in the tailor's face, and said :
" Do you see these great arms of mine ? "

" I see those, but I'll sew this ! " answered the tailor ;
and he stitched hard at his trews, for he knew that he had
no time to lose.

The sprightly tailor was taking the long stitches, when he
saw it gradually rising and rising through the floor, until it
lifted out a great leg, and stamping with it upon the pavement, said in a roaring voice : " Do you see this great leg
of mine ? "

" Aye, aye : I see that, but I'll sew this ! " cried the
tailor ; and his fingers flew with the needle, and he took
such long stitches, that he was just come to the end of the
trews, when it was taking up its other leg. But before it
could pull it out of the pavement, the sprightly tailor had
finished his task ; and, blowing out his candle, and springing
from off his gravestone, he buckled up, and ran out of the
church with the trews under his arm. Then the fearsome
thing gave a loud roar, and stamped with both his feet upon
the pavement, and out of the church he went after the
sprightly tailor.

Down the glen they ran, faster than the stream when the
flood rides it ; but the tailor had got the start and a nimble
pair of legs, and he did not choose to lose the laird's reward.
And though the thing roared to him to stop, yet the
sprightly tailor was not the man to be beholden to a
monster. So he held his trews tight, and let no darkness
grow under his feet, until he had reached Saddell Castle.
He had no sooner got inside the gate, and shut it, than the
apparition came up to it ; and, enraged at losing his prize,
struck the wall above the gate, and left there the mark of

borrowing of idea (ROMAN)

his five great fingers. Ye may see them plainly to this day, if ye'll only peer close enough.

But the sprightly tailor gained his reward : for Macdonald paid him handsomely for the trews, and never discovered that a few of the stitches were somewhat long.

The Story of Deirdre

THERE was a man in Ireland once who was called Malcolm Harper. The man was a right good man, and he had a goodly share of this world's goods. He had a wife, but no family. What did Malcolm hear but that a soothsayer had come home to the place, and as the man was a right good man, he wished that the soothsayer might come near them. Whether it was that he was invited or that he came of himself, the soothsayer came to the house of Malcolm.

" Are you doing any soothsaying ? " says Malcolm.

" Yes, I am doing a little. Are you in need of sooth-saying ? "

" Well, I do not mind taking soothsaying from you, if you had soothsaying for me, and you would be willing to do it."

" Well, I will do soothsaying for you. What kind of soothsaying do you want ? "

" Well, the soothsaying I wanted was that you would tell me my lot or what will happen to me, if you can give me knowledge of it."

" Well, I am going out, and when I return, I will tell you."

And the soothsayer went forth out of the house and he was not long outside when he returned.

" Well," said the soothsayer, " I saw in my second sight that it is on account of a daughter of yours that the greatest amount of blood shall be shed that has ever been shed in Erin since time and race began. And the three most famous heroes that ever were found will lose their heads on her account."

After a time a daughter was born to Malcolm, he did not allow a living being to come to his house, only himself and the nurse. He asked this woman, " Will you yourself bring up the child to keep her in hiding far away where eye will not see a sight of her nor ear hear a word about her?"

The woman said she would, so Malcolm got three men, and he took them away to a large mountain, distant and far from reach, without the knowledge or notice of any one. He caused there a hillock, round and green, to be dug out of the middle, and the hole thus made to be covered carefully over so that a little company could dwell there together. This was done.

Deirdre and her foster-mother dwelt in the bothy mid the hills without the knowledge or the suspicion of any living person about them and without anything occurring, until Deirdre was sixteen years of age. Deirdre grew like the white sapling, straight and trim as the rash on the moss. She was the creature of fairest form, of loveliest aspect, and of gentlest nature that existed between earth and heaven in all Ireland—whatever colour of hue she had before, there was nobody that looked into her face but she would blush fiery red over it.

The woman that had charge of her, gave Deirdre every information and skill of which she herself had knowledge and skill. There was not a blade of grass growing from root, nor a bird singing in the wood, nor a star shining from heaven but Deirdre had a name for it. But one thing, she did not wish her to have either part or parley with any single living man of the rest of the world. But on a gloomy winter night, with black, scowling clouds, a hunter of game was wearily travelling the hills, and what happened but that he missed the trail of the hunt, and lost his course and companions. A drowsiness came upon the man as he wearily wandered over the hills, and he lay down by the side of the beautiful green knoll in which Deirdre lived, and he slept. The man was faint from hunger and wandering, and benumbed with cold, and a deep sleep fell upon him. When he lay down beside the green hill where Deirdre was, a troubled dream came to the man, and he thought that he enjoyed the warmth of a fairy broch, the fairies being inside playing music. The hunter shouted out in his dream, if there was any one in the broch, to let him in for the Holy One's sake. Deirdre heard the voice and said to her foster-mother: "O foster-mother, what cry is that ?" "It is nothing at all, Deirdre—merely the birds of the air astray and seeking each other. But let them go past to the bosky glade. There is no shelter or house for them here." "Oh, foster-mother, the bird asked to get inside for the sake of the God of the Elements, and you yourself tell me that anything that is asked in His name we ought to do. If you will not allow the bird that is being benumbed with cold, and done to death with hunger, to be let in, I do not think much of your language or your faith. But since I give credence to your language and to your faith, which you taught me, I will myself let in the bird." And Deirdre arose and drew the bolt from the leaf of the door, and she let in the hunter. She placed a seat in the place for sitting, food in the place for eating, and drink in the place for drinking for the man who came to the house. "Oh, for this life and raiment, you man that came in, keep restraint on your tongue !" said the old woman. "It is not a great thing for you to keep your mouth shut and your tongue quiet when you get a home and shelter of a hearth on a gloomy winter's night." "Well," said the hunter, "I may do that—keep my mouth shut and my tongue quiet, since I came to the house and received hospitality from you ; but by the hand of thy father and grandfather, and by your own two hands, if some other of the people of the world saw this beauteous creature you have here hid away, they would not long leave her with you, I swear."

"What men are these you refer to ?" said Deirdre.

"Well, I will tell you, young woman," said the hunter.

DEIRDRE.
O NURSE WHAT
CRY IS THAT?

ONLY THE BIRDS OF THE AIR
CALLING ONE TO THE OTHER.—
THERE IS NO HOME FOR THEM HERE
LET THEM GO BY TO THE THICKET.

"They are Naois, son of Uisnech, and Allen and Arden his two brothers."

"What like are these men when seen, if we were to see them?" said Deirdre.

"Why, the aspect and form of the men when seen are these," said the hunter: "they have the colour of the raven on their hair, their skin like swan on the wave in whiteness, and their cheeks as the blood of the brindled red calf, and their speed and their leap are those of the salmon of the torrent and the deer of the grey mountain side. And Naois is head and shoulders over the rest of the people of Erin."

"However they are," said the nurse, "be you off from here and take another road. And, King of Light and Sun! in good sooth and certainty, little are my thanks for yourself or for her that let you in!"

The hunter went away, and went straight to the palace of King Connachar. He sent word in to the king that he wished to speak to him if he pleased. The king answered the message and came out to speak to the man. "What is the reason of your journey?" said the king to the hunter.

"I have only to tell you, O king," said the hunter, "that I saw the fairest creature that ever was born in Erin, and I came to tell you of it."

"Who is this beauty and where is she to be seen, when she was not seen before till you saw her, if you did see her?"

"Well, I did see her," said the hunter. "But, if I did, no man else can see her unless he get directions from me as to where she is dwelling."

"And will you direct me to where she dwells? and the

reward of your directing me will be as good as the reward of your message," said the king.

"Well, I will direct you, O king, although it is likely that this will not be what they want," said the hunter.

Connachar, King of Ulster, sent for his nearest kinsmen, and he told them of his intent. Though early rose the song of the birds mid the rocky caves and the music of the birds in the grove, earlier than that did Connachar, King of Ulster, arise, with his little troop of dear friends, in the delightful twilight of the fresh and gentle May ; the dew was heavy on each bush and flower and stem, as they went to bring Deirdre forth from the green knoll where she stayed. Many a youth was there who had a lithe leaping and lissom step when they started whose step was faint, failing, and faltering when they reached the bothy on account of the length of the way and roughness of the road. " Yonder, now, down in the bottom of the glen is the bothy where the woman dwells, but I will not go nearer than this to the old woman," said the hunter.

Connachar with his band of kinsfolk went down to the green knoll where Deirdre dwelt and he knocked at the door of the bothy. The nurse replied, " No less than a king's command and a king's army could put me out of my bothy to-night. And I should be obliged to you, were you to tell who it is that wants me to open my bothy door." " It is I, Connachar, King of Ulster." When the poor woman heard who was at the door, she rose with haste and let in the king and all that could get in of his retinue.

When the king saw the woman that was before him that he had been in quest of, he thought he never saw in the course of the day nor in the dream of night a creature so

fair as Deirdre and he gave his full heart's weight of love
to her. Deirdre was raised on the topmost of the heroes'
shoulders and she and her foster-mother were brought to
the Court of King Connachar of Ulster.

With the love that Connachar had for her, he wanted to
marry Deirdre right off there and then, will she nill she
marry him. But she said to him, " I would be obliged to
you if you will give me the respite of a year and a day."
He said " I will grant you that, hard though it is, if you
will give me your unfailing promise that you will marry me
at the year's end." And she gave the promise. Connachar
got for her a woman-teacher and merry modest maidens fair
that would lie down and rise with her, that would play and
speak with her. Deirdre was clever in maidenly duties and
wifely understanding, and Connachar thought he never saw
with bodily eye a creature that pleased him more.

Deirdre and her women companions were one day out on
the hillock behind the house enjoying the scene, and drinking
in the sun's heat. What did they see coming but three
men a-journeying. Deirdre was looking at the men that
were coming, and wondering at them. When the men
neared them, Deirdre remembered the language of the
huntsman, and she said to herself that these were the three
sons of Uisnech, and that this was Naois, he having what
was above the bend of the two shoulders above the men of
Erin all. The three brothers went past without taking any
notice of them, without even glancing at the young girls on
the hillock. What happened but that love for Naois struck
the heart of Deirdre, so that she could not but follow after
him. She girded up her raiment and went after the men
that went past the base of the knoll, leaving her women

attendants there. Allen and Arden had heard of the woman that Connachar, King of Ulster, had with him, and they thought that, if Naois, their brother, saw her, he would have her himself, more especially as she was not married to the King. They perceived the woman coming, and called on one another to hasten their step as they had a long distance to travel, and the dusk of night was coming on. They did so. She cried : "Naois, son of Uisnech, will you leave me ? " " What piercing, shrill cry is that—the most melodious my ear ever heard, and the shrillest that ever struck my heart of all the cries I ever heard ? " " It is anything else but the wail of the wave-swans of Connachar," said his brothers. "No! yonder is a woman's cry of distress," said Naois, and he swore he would not go further until he saw from whom the cry came, and Naois turned back. Naois and Deirdre met, and Deirdre kissed Naois three times, and a kiss each to his brothers. With the confusion that she was in, Deirdre went into a crimson blaze of fire, and her colour came and went as rapidly as the movement of the aspen by the stream side. Naois thought he never saw a fairer creature, and Naois gave Deirdre the love that he never gave to thing, to vision, or to creature but to herself.

Then Naois placed Deirdre on the topmost height of his shoulder, and told his brothers to keep up their pace, and they kept up their pace. Naois thought that it would not be well for him to remain in Erin on account of the way in which Connachar, King of Ulster, his uncle's son, had gone against him because of the woman, though he had not married her ; and he turned back to Alba, that is, Scotland. He reached the side of Loch-Ness and made his habitation there. He could kill the salmon of the torrent from out his own door, and the deer of the grey gorge from out his window. Naois and Deirdre and Allen and Arden dwelt in a tower, and they were happy so long a time as they were there.

By this time the end of the period came at which Deirdre had to marry Connachar, King of Ulster. Connachar made up his mind to take Deirdre away by the sword whether she was married to Naois or not. So he prepared a great and gleeful feast. He sent word far and wide through Erin all to his kinspeople to come to the feast. Connachar thought to himself that Naois would not come though he should bid him ; and the scheme that arose in his mind was to send for his father's brother, Ferchar Mac Ro, and to send him on an embassy to Naois. He did so ; and Connachar said to Ferchar, " Tell Naois, son of Uisnech, that I am setting forth a great and gleeful feast to my friends and kinspeople throughout the wide extent of Erin all, and that I shall not have rest by day nor sleep by night if he and Allen and Arden be not partakers of the feast."

Ferchar Mac Ro and his three sons went on their journey, and reached the tower where Naois was dwelling by the side of Loch Etive. The sons of Uisnech gave a cordial kindly welcome to Ferchar Mac Ro and his three sons, and asked of him the news of Erin. " The best news that I have for you," said the hardy hero, " is that Connachar, King of Ulster, is setting forth a great sumptuous feast to his friends and kinspeople throughout the wide extent of Erin all, and he has vowed by the earth beneath him, by the high heaven above him, and by the sun that wends to the west, that he will have no rest by day nor sleep by night if the sons of Uisnech, the sons of his own father's brother, will not come back to the land of their home and the soil of their nativity, and to the feast likewise, and he has sent us on embassy to invite you."

" We will go with you," said Naois.

" We will," said his brothers.

But Deirdre did not wish to go with Ferchar Mac Ro, and she tried every prayer to turn Naois from going with him——she said :

" I saw a vision, Naois, and do you interpret it to me," said Deirdre——then she sang :

> O Naois, son of Uisnech, hear
> What was shown in a dream to me.
>
> There came three white doves out of the South
> Flying over the sea,
> And drops of honey were in their mouth
> From the hive of the honey-bee.
>
> O Naois, son of Uisnech, hear,
> What was shown in a dream to me.
>
> I saw three grey hawks out of the south
> Come flying over the sea,
> And the red red drops they bare in their mouth
> They were dearer than life to me.

Said Naois :——

> It is nought but the fear of woman's heart,
> And a dream of the night, Deirdre.

" The day that Connachar sent the invitation to his feast will be unlucky for us if we don't go, O Deirdre."

" You will go there," said Ferchar Mac Ro ; " and if Connachar show kindness to you, show ye kindness to him ; and if he will display wrath towards you display ye wrath towards him, and I and my three sons will be with you."

"We will," said Daring Drop. "We will," said Hardy Holly. "We will," said Fiallan the Fair.

"I have three sons, and they are three heroes, and in any harm or danger that may befall you, they will be with you, and I myself will be along with them." And Ferchar Mac Ro gave his vow and his word in presence of his arms that, in any harm or danger that came in the way of the sons of Uisnech, he and his three sons would not leave head on live body in Erin, despite sword or helmet, spear or shield, blade or mail, be they ever so good.

Deirdre was unwilling to leave Alba, but she went with Naois. Deirdre wept tears in showers and she sang :

> Dear is the land, the land over there,
> Alba full of woods and lakes ;
> Bitter to my heart is leaving thee,
> But I go away with Naois.

Ferchar Mac Ro did not stop till he got the sons of Uisnech away with him, despite the suspicion of Deirdre.

> The coracle was put to sea,
> The sail was hoisted to it ;
> And the second morrow they arrived
> On the white shores of Erin.

As soon as the sons of Uisnech landed in Erin, Ferchar Mac Ro sent word to Connachar, king of Ulster, that the men whom he wanted were come, and let him now show kindness to them. "Well," said Connachar, "I did not expect that the sons of Uisnech would come, though I sent for them, and I am not quite ready to receive them. But there is a house down yonder where I keep strangers, and let them go down to it to-day, and my house will be ready before them to-morrow."

But he that was up in the palace felt it long that he was not getting word as to how matters were going on for those down in the house of the strangers. " Go you, Gelban Grednach, son of Lochlin's King, go you down and bring me information as to whether her former hue and complexion are on Deirdre. If they be, I will take her out with edge of blade and point of sword, and if not, let Naois, son of Uisnech, have her for himself," said Connachar.

Gelban, the cheering and charming son of Lochlin's King, went down to the place of the strangers, where the sons of Uisnech and Deirdre were staying. He looked in through the bicker-hole on the door-leaf. Now she that he gazed upon used to go into a crimson blaze of blushes when any one looked at her. Naois looked at Deirdre and knew that some one was looking at her from the back of the door-leaf. He seized one of the dice on the table before him and fired it through the bicker-hole, and knocked the eye out of Gelban Grednach the Cheerful and Charming, right through the back of his head. Gelban returned back to the palace of King Connachar.

" You were cheerful, charming, going away, but you are cheerless, charmless, returning. What has happened to you, Gelban ? But have you seen her, and are Deirdre's hue and complexion as before ? " said Connachar.

" Well, I have seen Deirdre, and I saw her also truly, and while I was looking at her through the bicker-hole on the door, Naois, son of Uisnech, knocked out my eye with one of the dice in his hand. But of a truth and verity, although he put out even my eye, it were my desire still to remain looking at her with the other eye, were it not for the hurry you told me to be in," said Gelban.

"That is true," said Connachar; "let three hundred brave heroes go down to the abode of the strangers, and let them bring hither to me Deirdre, and kill the rest."

Connachar ordered three hundred active heroes to go down to the abode of the strangers and to take Deirdre up with them and kill the rest. "The pursuit is coming," said Deirdre.

"Yoo, but I will myself go out and stop the pursuit," said Naois.

"It is not you, but we that will go," said Daring Drop, and Hardy Holly, and Fiallan the Fair; "it is to us that our father entrusted your defence from harm and danger when he himself left for home." And the gallant youths, full noble, full manly, full handsome, with beauteous brown locks, went forth girt with battle arms fit for fierce fight and clothed with combat dress for fierce contest fit, which was burnished, bright, brilliant, bladed, blazing, on which were many pictures of beasts and birds and creeping things, lions and lithe-limbed tigers, brown eagle and harrying hawk and adder fierce; and the young heroes laid low three-thirds of the company.

Connachar came out in haste and cried with wrath: "Who is there on the floor of fight, slaughtering my men?"

"We, the three sons of Ferchar Mac Ro."

"Well," said the king, "I will give a free bridge to your grandfather, a free bridge to your father, and a free bridge each to you three brothers, if you come over to my side to-night."

" Well, Connachar, we will not accept that offer from you nor thank you for it.   Greater by far do we prefer to go home to our father and tell the deeds of heroism we have done, than accept anything on these terms from you. Naois, son of Uisnech, and Allen and Arden are as nearly related to yourself as they are to us, though you are so keen to shed their blood, and you would shed our blood also, Connachar."   And the noble, manly, handsome youths with beauteous, brown locks returned inside.   " We are now," said they, " going home to tell our father that you are now safe from the hands of the king."   And the youths all fresh and tall and lithe and beautiful, went home to their father to tell that the sons of Uisnech were safe.   This happened at the parting of the day and night in the morning twilight time, and Naois said they must go away, leave that house, and return to Alba.

Naois and Deirdre, Allan and Arden started to return to Alba.   Word came to the king that the company he was in pursuit of were gone.   The king then sent for Duanan Gacha Druid, the best magician he had, and he spoke to him as follows :—" Much wealth have I expended on you, Duanan Gacha Druid, to give schooling and learning and magic mystery to you, if these people get away from me to-day without care, without consideration or regard for me, without chance of overtaking them, and without power to stop them."

" Well, I will stop them," said the magician, " until the company you send in pursuit return."   And the magician placed a wood before them through which no man could go, but the sons of Uisnech marched through the wood without halt or hesitation, and Deirdre held on to Naois's hand.

" What is the good of that ? that will not do yet," said Connachar. " They are off without bending of their feet or stopping of their step, without heed or respect to me, and I am without power to keep up to them or opportunity to turn them back this night."

" I will try another plan on them," said the druid ; and he placed before them a grey sea instead of a green plain. The three heroes stripped and tied their clothes behind their heads, and Naois placed Deirdre on the top of his shoulder.

> They stretched their sides to the stream,
>   And sea and land were to them the same,
> The rough grey ocean was the same
>   As meadow-land green and plain.

" Though that be good, O Duanan, it will not make the heroes return," said Connachar ; " they are gone without regard for me, and without honour to me, and without power on my part to pursue them or to force them to return this night."

" We shall try another method on them, since yon one did not stop them," said the druid. And the druid froze the grey ridged sea into hard rocky knobs, the sharpness of sword being on the one edge and the poison power of adders on the other. Then Arden cried that he was getting tired, and nearly giving over. " Come you, Arden, and sit on my right shoulder," said Naois. Arden came and sat on Naois's shoulder. Arden was long in this posture when he died ; but though he was dead Naois would not let him go. Allen then cried out that he was getting faint and nigh-well giving up. When Naois heard his prayer, he gave forth the piercing sigh of death, and asked Allen to lay hold of him and he would bring him to land.

Allen was not long when the weakness of death came on him and his hold failed. Naois looked around, and when he saw his two well-beloved brothers dead, he cared not

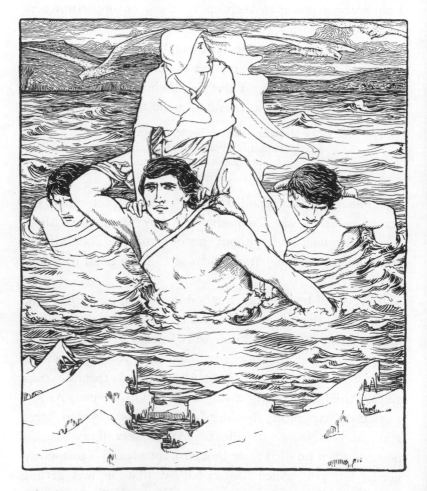

whether he lived or died, and he gave forth the bitter sigh of death, and his heart burst.

"They are gone," said Duanan Gacha Druid to the king,

" and I have done what you desired me. The sons of
Uisnech are dead and they will trouble you no more ; and
you have your wife hale and whole to yourself."

" Blessings for that upon you and may the good results
accrue to me, Duanan. I count it no loss what I spent in
the schooling and teaching of you. Now dry up the
flood, and let me see if I can behold Deirdre," said
Connachar. And Duanan Gacha Druid dried up the flood
from the plain and the three sons of Uisnech were lying
together dead, without breath of life, side by side on the
green meadow plain and Deirdre bending above showering
down her tears.

Then Deirdre said this lament : " Fair one, loved one,
flower of beauty ; beloved upright and strong ; beloved
noble and modest warrior. Fair one, blue-eyed, beloved of
thy wife ; lovely to me at the trysting-place came thy clear
voice through the woods of Ireland. I cannot eat or smile
henceforth. Break not to-day, my heart : soon enough
shall I lie within my grave. Strong are the waves of sorrow,
but stronger is sorrow's self, Connachar."

The people then gathered round the heroes' bodies and
asked Connachar what was to be done with the bodies.
The order that he gave was that they should dig a pit
and put the three brothers in it side by side.

Deirdre kept sitting on the brink of the grave, constantly
asking the gravediggers to dig the pit wide and free. When
the bodies of the brothers were put in the grave, Deirdre
said :—

> Come over hither, Naois, my love,
> Let Arden close to Allen lie ;
> If the dead had any sense to feel,
> Ye would have made a place for Deirdre.

The men did as she told them.   She jumped into the grave and lay down by Naois, and she was dead by his side.

The king ordered the body to be raised from out the grave and to be buried on the other side of the loch. It was done as the king bade, and the pit closed. Thereupon a fir shoot grew out of the grave of Deirdre and a fir shoot from the grave of Naois, and the two shoots united in a knot above the loch. The king ordered the shoots to be cut down, and this was done twice, until, at the third time, the wife whom the king had married caused him to stop this work of evil and his vengeance on the remains of the dead.

Munachar and Manachar

HERE once lived a Munachar and a Manachar, a long time ago, and it is a long time since it was, and if they were alive now they would not be alive then. They went out together to pick raspberries, and as many as Munachar used to pick Manachar used to eat. Munachar said he must go look for a rod to make a gad to hang Manachar, who ate his raspberries every one ; and he came to the rod. "What news the day ?" said the rod. " It is my own news that I'm seeking. Going looking for a rod, a rod to make a gad, a gad to hang Manachar, who ate my raspberries every one."

"You will not get me," said the rod, "until you get an axe to cut me." He came to the axe. "What news to-day ?" said the axe. " It's my own news I'm seeking. Going looking for an axe, an axe to cut a rod, a rod to make a gad, a gad to hang Manachar, who ate my raspberries every one."

"You will not get me," said the axe, " until you get a

flag to edge me." He came to the flag. "What news to-day?" says the flag. "It's my own news I'm seeking. Going looking for a flag, flag to edge axe, axe to cut a rod, a rod to make a gad, a gad to hang Manachar, who ate my raspberries every one."

"You will not get me," says the flag, "till you get water to wet me." He came to the water. "What news to-day?" says the water. "It's my own news that I'm seeking. Going looking for water, water to wet flag to edge axe, axe to cut a rod, a rod to make a gad, a gad to hang Manachar, who ate my raspberries every one."

"You will not get me," said the water, "until you get a deer who will swim me." He came to the deer. "What news to-day?" says the deer. "It's my own news I'm seeking. Going looking for a deer, deer to swim water, water to wet flag, flag to edge axe, axe to cut a rod, a rod to make a gad, a gad to hang Manachar, who ate my raspberries every one."

"You will not get me," said the deer, "until you get a hound who will hunt me." He came to the hound. "What news to-day?" says the hound. "It's my own news I'm seeking. Going looking for a hound, hound to hunt deer, deer to swim water, water to wet flag, flag to edge axe, axe to cut a rod, a rod to make a gad, a gad to hang Manachar, who ate my raspberries every one."

"You will not get me," said the hound, "until you get a bit of butter to put in my claw." He came to the butter. "What news to-day?" says the butter. "It's my own news I'm seeking. Going looking for butter, butter to go in claw of hound, hound to hunt deer, deer to swim water, water to wet flag, flag to edge axe, axe to cut a rod, a rod to make a gad, a gad to hang Manachar, who ate my raspberries every one."

"You will not get me," said the butter, "until you get a cat who shall scrape me." He came to the cat. "What news to-day?" said the cat. "It's my own news I'm seeking. Going looking for a cat, cat to scrape butter, butter to go in claw of hound, hound to hunt deer, deer to swim water, water to wet flag, flag to edge axe, axe to cut a rod, a rod to make a gad, gad to hang Manachar, who ate my raspberries every one."

"You will not get me," said the cat, "until you will get milk which you will give me." He came to the cow. "What news to-day?" said the cow. "It's my own news I'm seeking. Going looking for a cow, cow to give me milk, milk I will give to the cat, cat to scrape butter, butter to go in claw of hound, hound to hunt deer, deer to swim water, water to wet flag, flag to edge axe, axe to cut a rod, a rod to make a gad, a gad to hang Manachar, who ate my raspberries every one."

"You will not get any milk from me," said the cow, "until you bring me a whisp of straw from those threshers yonder." He came to the threshers. "What news to-day?" said the threshers. "It's my own news I'm seeking. Going looking for a whisp of straw from ye to give to the cow, the cow to give me milk, milk I will give to the cat, cat to scrape butter, butter to go in claw of hound, hound to hunt deer, deer to swim water, water to wet flag, flag to edge axe, axe to cut a rod, a rod to make a gad, a gad to hang Manachar, who ate my raspberries every one."

"You will not get any whisp of straw from us," said the

threshers, " until you bring us the makings of a cake from the miller over yonder." He came to the miller. " What news to-day ? " said the miller. " It's my own news I'm seeking. Going looking for the makings of a cake which I will give to the threshers, the threshers to give me a whisp of straw, the whisp of straw I will give to the cow, the cow to give me milk, milk I will give to the cat, cat to scrape butter, butter to go in claw of hound, hound to hunt deer, deer to swim water, water to wet flag, flag to edge axe, axe to cut a rod, a rod to make a gad, a gad to hang Manachar, who ate my raspberries every one."

" You will not get any makings of a cake from me," said the miller, " till you bring me the full of that sieve of water from the river over there."

He took the sieve in his hand and went over to the river, but as often as ever he would stoop and fill it with water, the moment he raised it the water would run out of it again, and sure, if he had been there from that day till this, he never could have filled it. A crow went flying by him, over his head. " Daub ! daub !" said the crow. " My blessings on ye, then," said Munachar, " but it's the good advice you have," and he took the red clay and the daub that was by the brink, and he rubbed it to the bottom of the sieve, until all the holes were filled, and then the sieve held the water, and he brought the water to the miller, and the miller gave him the makings of a cake, and he gave the makings of the cake to the threshers, and the threshers gave him a whisp of straw, and he gave the whisp of straw to the cow, and the cow gave him milk, the milk he gave to the cat, the cat scraped the butter, the butter went into the claw of the hound, the hound hunted the deer, the deer swam the water, the water wet the flag, the flag sharpened the axe, the axe cut the rod, and the rod made a gad, and when he had it ready to hang Manachar he found that Manachar had BURST.

Gold-Tree and Silver-Tree

NCE upon a time there was a king who had a wife, whose name was Silver-tree, and a daughter, whose name was Gold-tree. On a certain day of the days, Gold-tree and Silver-tree went to a glen, where there was a well, and in it there was a trout.

Said Silver-tree, " Troutie, bonny little fellow, am not I the most beautiful queen in the world ?"

" Oh ! indeed you are not."

" Who then ?"

" Why, Gold-tree, your daughter."

Silver-tree went home, blind with rage. She lay down on the bed, and vowed she would never be well until she could get the heart and the liver of Gold-tree, her daughter, to eat.

At nightfall the king came home, and it was told him

that Silver-tree, his wife, was very ill. He went where she was, and asked her what was wrong with her.

" Oh! only a thing which you may heal if you like."

" Oh! indeed there is nothing at all which I could do for you that I would not do."

" If I get the heart and the liver of Gold-tree, my daughter, to eat, I shall be well."

Now it happened about this time that the son of a great king had come from abroad to ask Gold-tree for marrying. The king now agreed to this, and they went abroad.

The king then went and sent his lads to the hunting-hill for a he-goat, and he gave its heart and its liver to his wife to eat ; and she rose well and healthy.

A year after this Silver-tree went to the glen, where there was the well in which there was the trout.

" Troutie, bonny little fellow," said she, " am not I the most beautiful queen in the world ?"

" Oh! indeed you are not."

" Who then ?"

" Why, Gold-tree, your daughter."

" Oh! well, it is long since she was living. It is a year since I ate her heart and liver."

" Oh! indeed she is not dead. She is married to a great prince abroad."

Silver-tree went home, and begged the king to put the long-ship in order, and said, " I am going to see my dear Gold-tree, for it is so long since I saw her." The long-ship was put in order, and they went away.

It was Silver-tree herself that was at the helm, and she steered the ship so well that they were not long at all before they arrived.

The prince was out hunting on the hills.   Gold-tree knew the long-ship of her father coming.

"Oh!" said she to the servants, "my mother is coming, and she will kill me."

"She shall not kill you at all; we will lock you in a room where she cannot get near you."

This is how it was done; and when Silver-tree came ashore, she began to cry out:

"Come to meet your own mother, when she comes to see you," Gold-tree said that she could not, that she was locked in the room, and that she could not get out of it.

"Will you not put out," said Silver-tree, "your little finger through the key-hole, so that your own mother may give a kiss to it?"

She put out her little finger, and Silver-tree went and put a poisoned stab in it, and Gold-tree fell dead.

When the prince came home, and found Gold-tree dead, he was in great sorrow, and when he saw how beautiful she was, he did not bury her at all, but he locked her in a room where nobody would get near her.

In the course of time he married again, and the whole house was under the hand of this wife but one room, and he himself always kept the key of that room. On a certain day of the days he forgot to take the key with him, and the second wife got into the room. What did she see there but the most beautiful woman that she ever saw.

She began to turn and try to wake her, and she noticed the poisoned stab in her finger. She took the stab out, and Gold-tree rose alive, as beautiful as she was ever.

At the fall of night the prince came home from the hunting-hill, looking very downcast.

"What gift," said his wife, "would you give me that I could make you laugh?"

"Oh! indeed, nothing could make me laugh, except Gold-tree were to come alive again."

"Well, you'll find her alive down there in the room."

When the prince saw Gold-tree alive he made great rejoicings, and he began to kiss her, and kiss her, and kiss her. Said the second wife, "Since she is the first one you had it is better for you to stick to her, and I will go away."

"Oh! indeed you shall not go away, but I shall have both of you."

At the end of the year, Silver-tree went to the glen, where there was the well, in which there was the trout.

"Troutie, bonny little fellow," said she, "am not I the most beautiful queen in the world?"

"Oh! indeed you are not."

"Who then?"

"Why, Gold-tree, your daughter."

"Oh! well, she is not alive. It is a year since I put the poisoned stab into her finger."

"Oh! indeed she is not dead at all, at all."

Silver-tree went home, and begged the king to put the long-ship in order, for that she was going to see her dear Gold-tree, as it was so long since she saw her. The long-ship was put in order, and they went away. It was Silver-tree herself that was at the helm, and she steered the ship so well that they were not long at all before they arrived.

The prince was out hunting on the hills. Gold-tree knew her father's ship coming.

"Oh!" said she, "my mother is coming, and she will kill me."

"Not at all," said the second wife; "we will go down to meet her."

Silver-tree came ashore. "Come down, Gold-tree, love," said she, "for your own mother has come to you with a precious drink."

"It is a custom in this country," said the second wife, "that the person who offers a drink takes a draught out of it first."

Silver-tree put her mouth to it, and the second wife went and struck it so that some of it went down her throat, and she fell dead. They had only to carry her home a dead corpse and bury her.

The prince and his two wives were long alive after this, pleased and peaceful.

I left them there.

King O'Toole and His Goose

CH, I thought all the world, far and near, had heerd o' King O'Toole—well, well, but the darkness of mankind is untellible! Well, sir, you must know, as you didn't hear it afore, that there was a king, called King O'Toole, who was a fine old king in the old ancient times, long ago ; and it was he that owned the churches in the early days. The king, you see, was the right sort ; he was the real boy, and loved sport as he loved his life, and hunting in particular ; and from the rising o' the sun, up he got, and away he went over the mountains after the deer ; and fine times they were.

Well, it was all mighty good, as long as the king had his health ; but, you see, in course of time the king grew old, by raison he was stiff in his limbs, and when he got stricken in years, his heart failed him, and he was lost entirely for want o' diversion, because he couldn't go a-hunting no longer ; and, by dad, the poor king was obliged at last to get a goose to divert him.   Oh, you may laugh, if you like, but it's truth I'm telling you ; and the way the goose diverted him was this-a-way : You see, the goose used to swim across the lake, and go diving for trout, and catch fish on a Friday for the king, and flew every other day round about the lake, diverting the poor king. All went on mighty well until, by dad, the goose got stricken in years like her master, and couldn't divert him no longer, and then it was that the poor king was lost entirely. The king was walkin' one mornin' by the edge of the lake, lamentin' his

cruel fate, and thinking of drowning himself, that could get no diversion in life, when all of a sudden, turning round the corner, who should he meet but a mighty decent young man coming up to him.

"God save you," says the king to the young man.

"God save you kindly, King O'Toole," says the young man.

"True for you," says the king. "I am King O'Toole," says he, "prince and plennypennytinchery of these parts," says he ; "but how came ye to know that ?" says he.

" Oh, never mind," says St. Kavin.

You see it was Saint Kavin, sure enough—the saint himself in disguise, and nobody else. " Oh, never mind," says he, " I know more than that. May I make bold to ask how is your goose, King O'Toole ? " says he.

" Blur-an-agers, how came ye to know about my goose ? " says the king.

" Oh, no matter ; I was given to understand it," says Saint Kavin.

After some more talk the king says, " What are you ? "

" I'm an honest man," says Saint Kavin.

" Well, honest man," says the king, " and how is it you make your money so aisy ? "

" By makin' old things as good as new," says Saint Kavin.

" Is it a tinker you are ? " says the king.

" No," says the saint ; " I'm no tinker by trade, King O'Toole ; I've a better trade than a tinker," says he— " what would you say," says he, " if I made your old goose as good as new ? "

My dear, at the word of making his goose as good as new, you'd think the poor old king's eyes were ready to jump out of his head. With that the king whistled, and down came the poor goose, just like a hound, waddling up to the poor cripple, her master, and as like him as two peas. The minute the saint clapt his eyes on the goose, " I'll do the job for you," says he, " King O'Toole."

" By *Jaminee !* " says King O'Toole, " if you do, I'll say you're the cleverest fellow in the seven parishes."

" Oh, by dad," says St. Kavin, " you must say more nor that—my horn's not so soft all out," says he, " as to repair your old goose for nothing ; what'll you gi' me if I do the job for you ?—that's the chat," says St. Kavin.

"I'll give you whatever you ask," says the king ; "isn't that fair ?"

"Divil a fairer," says the saint ; "that's the way to do business. Now," says he, "this is the bargain I'll make with you, King O'Toole : will you gi' me all the ground the goose flies over, the first offer, after I make her as good as new ?"

"I will," says the king.

"You won't go back o' your word ?" says St. Kavin.

"Honour bright !" says King O'Toole, holding out his fist.

"Honour bright !" says St. Kavin, back agin, "it's a bargain. Come here !" says he to the poor old goose—"come here, you unfortunate ould cripple, and it's I that'll make you the sporting bird." With that, my dear, he took up the goose by the two wings—"Criss o' my cross an you," says he, markin' her to grace with the blessed sign at the same minute—and throwing her up in the air, "whew," says he, jist givin' her a blast to help her ; and with that, my jewel, she took to her heels, flyin' like one o' the eagles themselves, and cutting as many capers as a swallow before a shower of rain.

Well, my dear, it was a beautiful sight to see the king standing with his mouth open, looking at his poor old goose flying as light as a lark, and better than ever she was : and when she lit at his feet, patted her on the head, and "Ma vourneen," says he, "but you are the *darlint* o' the world."

"And what do you say to me," says Saint Kavin, "for making her the like ?"

" By Jabers," says the king, " I say nothing beats the art
o' man, barring the bees."

"And do you say no more nor that ?" says Saint
Kavin.

" And that I'm beholden to you," says the king.

"But will you gi'e me all the ground the goose flew
over ?" says Saint Kavin.

"I will," says King O'Toole, "and you're welcome to it,"
says he, " though it's the last acre I have to give."

" But you'll keep your word true ?" says the saint.

" As true as the sun," says the king.

" It's well for you, King O'Toole, that you said that

word," says he ; " for if you didn't say that word, the
devil the bit o' your goose would ever fly agin."

When the king was as good as his word, Saint Kavin
was pleased with him, and then it was that he made himself
known to the king. "And," says he, "King O'Toole,
you're a decent man, for I only came here to try you.
You don't know me," says he, "because I'm disguised."

" Musha ! then," says the king, " who are you ?"

" I'm Saint Kavin," said the saint, blessing himself.

" Oh, queen of heaven !" says the king, making the sign
of the cross between his eyes, and falling down on his
knees before the saint ; "is it the great Saint Kavin,"
says he, "that I've been discoursing all this time without
knowing it," says he, " all as one as if he was a lump of
a *gossoon ?*—and so you're a saint ?" says the king.

" I am," says Saint Kavin.

" By Jabers, I thought I was only talking to a dacent
boy," says the king.

" Well, you know the difference now," says the saint.
"I'm Saint Kavin," says he, "the greatest of all the saints."

And so the king had his goose as good as new, to divert
him as long as he lived : and the saint supported him after
he came into his property, as I told you, until the day of
his death—and that was soon after ; for the poor goose
thought he was catching a trout one Friday ; but, my
jewel, it was a mistake he made—and instead of a trout,
it was a thieving horse-eel ; and instead of the goose killing a trout for the king's supper—by dad, the eel killed
the king's goose—and small blame to him ; but he didn't ate
her, because he darn't ate what Saint Kavin had laid his
blessed hands on.

The Wooing of Olwen

HORTLY after the birth of Kilhuch, the son of King Kilyth, his mother died. Before her death she charged the king that he should not take a wife again until he saw a briar with two blossoms upon her grave, and the king sent every morning to see if anything were growing thereon. After many years the briar appeared, and he took to wife the widow of King Doged. She foretold to her stepson, Kilhuch, that it was his destiny to marry a maiden named Olwen, or none other, and he, at his father's bidding, went to the court of his cousin, King Arthur, to ask as a boon the hand of the maiden. He rode upon a grey steed with shell-formed hoofs, having a bridle of linked gold, and a saddle also of gold. In his hand were two spears of silver, well-tempered, headed with steel, of an edge to wound the wind and cause blood to flow, and swifter than the fall of the dew-drop from the blade of reed grass upon the earth when the dew of June is at its heaviest. A gold-hilted sword was on his thigh, and the blade was of gold, having inlaid upon it a cross of the hue of the lightning of heaven. Two brindled, white-breasted greyhounds,

with strong collars of rubies, sported round him, and his courser cast up four sods with its four hoofs like four swallows about his head. Upon the steed was a four-cornered cloth of purple, and an apple of gold was at each corner. Precious gold was upon the stirrups and shoes, and the blade of grass bent not beneath them, so light was the courser's tread as he went towards the gate of King Arthur's palace.

Arthur received him with great ceremony, and asked him to remain at the palace ; but the youth replied that he came not to consume meat and drink, but to ask a boon of the king.

Then said Arthur, " Since thou wilt not remain here, chieftain, thou shalt receive the boon, whatsoever thy tongue may name, as far as the wind dries and the rain moistens, and the sun revolves, and the sea encircles, and the earth extends, save only my ships and my mantle, my sword, my lance, my shield, my dagger, and Guinevere my wife."

So Kilhuch craved of him the hand of Olwen, the daughter of Yspathaden Penkawr, and also asked the favour and aid of all Arthur's court.

Then said Arthur, " O chieftain, I have never heard of the maiden of whom thou speakest, nor of her kindred, but I will gladly send messengers in search of her."

And the youth said, " I will willingly grant from this night to that at the end of the year to do so."

Then Arthur sent messengers to every land within his dominions to seek for the maiden ; and at the end of the year Arthur's messengers returned without having gained any knowledge or information concerning Olwen more than on the first day.

Then said Kilhuch, " Every one has received his boon, and I yet lack mine. I will depart and bear away thy honour with me."

Then said Kay, " Rash chieftain ! dost thou reproach Arthur ? Go with us, and we will not part until thou dost either confess that the maiden exists not in the world, or until we obtain her."

Thereupon Kay rose up.

Kay had this peculiarity, that his breath lasted nine nights and nine days under water, and he could exist nine nights and nine days without sleep. A wound from Kay's sword no physician could heal. Very subtle was Kay. When it pleased him he could render himself as tall as the highest tree in the forest. And he had another peculiarity— so great was the heat of his nature, that, when it rained hardest, whatever he carried remained dry for a handbreadth above and a handbreath below his hand ; and when his companions were coldest, it was to them as fuel with which to light their fire.

And Arthur called Bedwyr, who never shrank from any enterprise upon which Kay was bound. None was equal to him in swiftness throughout this island except Arthur and Drych Ail Kibthar. And although he was one-handed, three warriors could not shed blood faster than he on the field of battle. Another property he had ; his lance would produce a wound equal to those of nine opposing lances.

And Arthur called to Kynthelig the guide. " Go thou upon this expedition with the Chieftain." For as good a guide was he in a land which he had never seen as he was in his own.

He called Gwrhyr Gwalstawt Ieithoedd, because he knew all tongues.

He called Gwalchmai, the son of Gwyar, because he never returned home without achieving the adventure of which he went in quest.   He was the best of footmen and the best of knights.   He was nephew to Arthur, the son of his sister, and his cousin.

And Arthur called Menw, the son of Teirgwaeth, in order that if they went into a savage country, he might cast a charm and an illusion over them, so that none might see them whilst they could see every one.

They journeyed on till they came to a vast open plain, wherein they saw a great castle, which was the fairest in the world.   But so far away was it that at night it seemed no nearer, and they scarcely reached it on the third day. When they came before the castle they beheld a vast flock of sheep, boundless and without end.   They told their errand to the herdsman, who endeavoured to dissuade them, since none who had come thither on that quest had returned alive.   They gave to him a gold ring, which he conveyed to his wife, telling her who the visitors were.

On the approach of the latter, she ran out with joy to greet them, and sought to throw her arms about their necks. But Kay, snatching a billet out of the pile, placed the log between her two hands, and she squeezed it so that it became a twisted coil.

" O woman," said Kay, " if thou hadst squeezed me thus, none could ever again have set their affections on me.   Evil love were this."

They entered the house, and after meat she told them that the maiden Olwen came there every Saturday to wash.

They pledged their faith that they would not harm her, and a message was sent to her. So Olwen came, clothed in a robe of flame-coloured silk, and with a collar of ruddy gold, in which were emeralds and rubies, about her neck. More golden was her hair than the flower of the broom, and her skin was whiter than the foam of the wave, and fairer were her hands and her fingers than the blossoms of the wood anemone amidst the spray of the meadow fountain. Brighter were her glances than those of a falcon ; her bosom was more snowy than the breast of the white swan, her cheek redder than the reddest roses. Whoso beheld was filled with her love. Four white trefoils sprang up wherever she trod, and therefore was she called Olwen.

Then Kilhuch, sitting beside her on a bench, told her his love, and she said that he would win her as his bride if he granted whatever her father asked.

Accordingly they went up to the castle and laid their request before him.

" Raise up the forks beneath my two eyebrows which have fallen over my eyes," said Yspathaden Penkawr, " that I may see the fashion of my son-in-law."

They did so, and he promised them an answer on the morrow. But as they were going forth, Yspathaden seized one of the three poisoned darts that lay beside him and threw it back after them.

And Bedwyr caught it and flung it back, wounding Yspathaden in the knee.

Then said he, " A cursed ungentle son-in-law, truly. I shall ever walk the worse for his rudeness. This poisoned iron pains me like the bite of a gad-fly. Cursed be the smith who forged it, and the anvil whereon it was wrought."

The knights rested in the house of Custennin the herdsman, but the next day at dawn they returned to the castle
and renewed their request.

Yspathaden said it was necessary that he should consult

Olwen's four great-grandmothers and her four great-grand-
sires.

The knights again withdrew, and as they were going he
took the second dart and cast it after them.

But Menw caught it and flung it back, piercing Yspathaden's breast with it, so that it came out at the small of
his back.

" A cursed ungentle son-in-law, truly," says he, " the
hard iron pains me like the bite of a horse-leech. Cursed
be the hearth whereon it was heated ! Henceforth whenever

I go up a hill, I shall have a scant in my breath and a pain in my chest."

On the third day the knights returned once more to the palace, and Yspathaden took the third dart and cast it at them.

But Kilhuch caught it and threw it vigorously, and wounded him through the eyeball, so that the dart came out at the back of his head.

" A cursed ungentle son-in-law, truly. As long as I remain alive my eyesight will be the worse. Whenever I go against the wind my eyes will water, and peradventure my head will burn, and I shall have a giddiness every new moon. Cursed be the fire in which it was forged. Like the bite of a mad dog is the stroke of this poisoned iron."

And they went to meat.

Said Yspathaden Penkawr, " Is it thou that seekest my daughter ? "

" It is I," answered Kilhuch.

" I must have thy pledge that thou wilt not do towards me otherwise than is just, and when I have gotten that which I shall name, my daughter thou shalt have."

" I promise thee that willingly," said Kilhuch, " name what thou wilt."

" I will do so," said he.

" Throughout the world there is not a comb or scissors with which I can arrange my hair, on account of its rankness, except the comb and scissors that are between the two ears of Turch Truith, the son of Prince Tared. He will not give them of his own free will, and thou wilt not be able to compel him."

" It will be easy for me to compass this, although thou mayest think that it will not be easy."

" Though thou get this, there is yet that which thou wilt not get. It will not be possible to hunt Turch Truith without Drudwyn the whelp of Greid, the son of Eri, and know that throughout the world there is not a huntsman who can hunt with this dog, except Mabon the son of Modron. He was taken from his mother when three nights old, and it is not known where he now is, nor whether he is living or dead."

" It will be easy for me to compass this, although thou mayest think that it will not be easy."

" Though thou get this, there is yet that which thou wilt not get. Thou wilt not get Mabon, for it is not known where he is, unless thou find Eidoel, his kinsman in blood, the son of Aer. For it would be useless to seek for him. He is his cousin."

" It will be easy for me to compass this, although thou mayest think that it will not be easy. Horses shall I have, and chivalry ; and my lord and kinsman Arthur will obtain for me all these things. And I shall gain thy daughter, and thou shalt lose thy life."

" Go forward. And thou shalt not be chargeable for food or raiment for my daughter while thou art seeking these things ; and when thou hast compassed all these marvels, thou shalt have my daughter for wife."

Now, when they told Arthur how they had sped, Arthur said, " Which of these marvels will it be best for us to seek first ? "

" It will be best," said they, " to seek Mabon the son of Modron ; and he will not be found unless we first find Eidoel, the son of Aer, his kinsman."

Then Arthur rose up, and the warriors of the Islands of Britain with him, to seek for Eidoel ; and they proceeded until they came before the castle of Glivi, where Eidoel was imprisoned.

Glivi stood on the summit of his castle, and said, " Arthur, what requirest thou of me, since nothing remains to me in this fortress, and I have neither joy nor pleasure in it ; neither wheat nor oats ? "

Said Arthur, " Not to injure thee came I hither, but to seek for the prisoner that is with thee."

" I will give thee my prisoner, though I had not thought to give him up to any one ; and therewith shalt thou have my support and my aid."

His followers then said unto Arthur, " Lord, go thou home, thou canst not proceed with thy host in quest of such small adventures as these."

Then said Arthur, " It were well for thee, Gwrhyr Gwalstawt Ieithoedd, to go upon this quest, for thou knowest all languages, and art familiar with those of the birds and the beasts. Go, Eidoel, likewise with my men in search of thy cousin. And as for you, Kay and Bedwyr, I have hope of whatever adventure ye are in quest of, that ye will achieve it. Achieve ye this adventure for me."

These went forward until they came to the Ousel of Cilgwri, and Gwrhyr adjured her for the sake of Heaven, saying, " Tell me if thou knowest aught of Mabon, the son of Modron, who was taken when three nights old from between his mother and the wall.

And the Ousel answered, "When I first came here there was a smith's anvil in this place, and I was then a young bird, and from that time no work has been done upon it, save the pecking of my beak every evening, and now there is not so much as the size of a nut remaining thereof ; yet the vengeance of Heaven be upon me if during all that time I have ever heard of the man for whom you inquire. Nevertheless, there is a race of animals who were formed before me, and I will be your guide to them."

So they proceeded to the place where was the Stag of Redynvre.

" Stag of Redynvre, behold we are come to thee, an embassy from Arthur, for we have not heard of any animal older than thou. Say, knowest thou aught of Mabon ? "

The stag said, " When first I came hither, there was a plain all around me, without any trees save one oak sapling, which grew up to be an oak with an hundred branches. And that oak has since perished, so that now nothing remains of it but the withered stump ; and from that day to this I have been here, yet have I never heard of the man for whom you inquire. Nevertheless, I will be your guide to the place where there is an animal which was formed before I was."

So they proceeded to the place where was the Owl of Cwm Cawlwyd, to inquire of him concerning Mabon.

And the owl said, " If I knew I would tell you. When first I came hither, the wide valley you see was a wooded glen. And a race of men came and rooted it up. And there grew there a second wood, and this wood is the third. My wings, are they not withered stumps ? Yet all this time, even until to-day, I have never heard of the man for whom you inquire. Nevertheless, I will be the guide of Arthur's embassy until you come to the place where is the oldest

Gwrhyr and Eidoel talk with the Eagle of Gwern Abwy ❧

animal in this world, and the one who has travelled most, the eagle of Gwern Abwy."

When they came to the eagle, Gwrhyr asked it the same question ; but it replied, " I have been here for a great space of time, and when I first came hither there was a rock here, from the top of which I pecked at the stars every evening, and now it is not so much as a span high. From that day to this I have been here, and I have never heard of the man for whom you inquire, except once when I went in search of food as far as Llyn Llyw. And when I came there, I struck my talons into a salmon, thinking he would serve me as food for a long time. But he drew me into the deep, and I was scarcely able to escape from him. After that I went with my whole kindred to attack him and to try to destroy him, but he sent messengers and made peace with me, and came and besought me to take fifty fish-spears out of his back. Unless he know something of him whom you seek, I cannot tell you who may. However, I will guide you to the place where he is."

So they went thither, and the eagle said, " Salmon of Llyn Llyw, I have come to thee with an embassy from Arthur to ask thee if thou knowest aught concerning Mabon, the son of Modron, who was taken away at three nights old from between his mother and the wall."

And the salmon answered, " As much as I know I will tell thee. With every tide I go along the river upwards, until I come near to the walls of Gloucester, and there have I found such wrong as I never found elsewhere ; and to the end that ye may give credence thereto, let one of you go thither upon each of my two shoulders."

So Kay and Gwrhyr went upon his shoulders, and they

proceeded till they came to the wall of the prison, and they heard a great wailing and lamenting from the dungeon.

Said Gwrhyr, " Who is it that laments in this house of stone ? "

And the voice replied, " Alas, it is Mabon, the son of Modron, who is here imprisoned ! "

Then they returned and told Arthur, who, summoning his warriors, attacked the castle.

And whilst the fight was going on, Kay and Bedwyr, mounting on the shoulders of the fish, broke into the dungeon, and brought away with them Mabon, the son of Modron.

Then Arthur summoned unto him all the warriors that were in the three islands of Britain and in the three islands adjacent ; and he went as far as Esgeir Oervel in Ireland where the Boar Truith was with his seven young pigs.   And the dogs were let loose upon him from all sides.   But he wasted the fifth part of Ireland, and then set forth through the sea to Wales.   Arthur and his hosts, and his horses, and his dogs followed hard after him.   But ever and awhile the boar made a stand, and many a champion of Arthur's did he slay.   Throughout all Wales did Arthur follow him, and one by one the young pigs were killed.   At length, when he would fain have crossed the Severn and escaped into Cornwall, Mabon the son of Modron came up with him, and Arthur fell upon him together with the champions of Britain.   On the one side Mabon the son of Modron spurred his steed and snatched his razor from him, whilst Kay came up with him on the other side and took from him the scissors.   But before they could obtain the comb he had regained the ground with his feet, and from the moment that he reached the shore, neither dog nor man nor horse could overtake him until he came to Cornwall. There Arthur and his hosts followed in his track until they overtook him in Cornwall. Hard had been their trouble before, but it was child's play to what they met in seeking the comb. Win it they did, and the Boar Truith they hunted into the deep sea, and it was never known whither he went.

Then Kilhuch set forward, and as many as wished ill to Yspathaden Penkawr. And they took the marvels with them to his court. And Kaw of North Britain came and shaved his beard, skin and flesh clean off to the very bone from ear to ear.

" Art thou shaved, man ? " said Kilhuch.

" I am shaved," answered he.

" Is thy daughter mine now ? "

" She is thine, but therefore needst thou not thank me, but Arthur who hath accomplished this for thee. By my free will thou shouldst never have had her, for with her I lose my life."

Then Goreu the son of Custennin seized him by the hair of his head and dragged him after him to the keep, and cut off his head and placed it on a stake on the citadel.

Thereafter the hosts of Arthur dispersed themselves each man to his own country.

Thus did Kilhuch son of Kelython win to wife Olwen, the daughter of Yspathaden Penkawr.

Jack and His Comrades

ONCE there was a poor widow, as often there has been, and she had one son. A very scarce summer came, and they didn't know how they'd live till the new potatoes would be fit for eating. So Jack said to his mother one evening, " Mother, bake my cake, and kill my hen, till I go seek my fortune ; and if I meet it, never fear but I'll soon be back to share it with you."

So she did as he asked her, and he set out at break of day on his journey. His mother came along with him to the yard gate, and says she, " Jack, which would you rather have, half the cake and half the hen with my blessing, or the whole of 'em with my curse ? "

" O musha, mother," says Jack, " why do you ax me that question ? sure you know I wouldn't have your curse and Damer's estate along with it."

" Well, then, Jack," says she, " here's the whole lot of 'em, with my thousand blessings along with them." So she stood on the yard fence and blessed him as far as her eyes could see him.

Well, he went along and along till he was tired, and

ne'er a farmer's house he went into wanted a boy. At last his road led by the side of a bog, and there was a poor ass up to his shoulders near a big bunch of grass he was striving to come at.

" Ah, then, Jack asthore," says he, " help me out or I'll be drowned."

" Never say't twice," says Jack, and he pitched in big stones and sods into the slob, till the ass got good ground under him.

" Thank you, Jack," says he, when he was out on the hard road ; " I'll do as much for you another time. Where are you going ? "

" Faith, I'm going to seek my fortune till harvest comes in, God bless it ! "

" And if you like," says the ass, " I'll go along with you ; who knows what luck we may have ! "

" With all my heart, it's getting late, let us be jogging."

Well, they were going through a village, and a whole army of gossoons were hunting a poor dog with a kettle tied to his tail. He ran up to Jack for protection, and the ass let such a roar out of him, that the little thieves took to their heels as if the ould boy was after them.

" More power to you, Jack," says the dog.

" I'm much obleeged to you : where is the baste and yourself going ? "

" We're going to seek our fortune till harvest comes in."

" And wouldn't I be proud to go with you ! " says the dog, " and get rid of them ill conducted boys ; purshuin' to 'em."

" Well, well, throw your tail over your arm, and come along."

They got outside the town, and sat down under an old
wall, and Jack pulled out his bread and meat, and shared
with the dog; and the ass made his dinner on a bunch
of thistles. While they were eating and chatting, what
should come by but a poor half-starved cat, and the
moll-row he gave out of him would make your heart ache.

"You look as if you saw the tops of nine houses since
breakfast," says Jack; "here's a bone and something on
it."

"May your child never know a hungry belly!" says
Tom; "it's myself that's in need of your kindness. May
I be so bold as to ask where yez are all going?"

"We're going to seek our fortune till the harvest comes
in, and you may join us if you like."

"And that I'll do with a heart and a half," says the cat,
"and thank'ee for asking me."'

Off they set again, and just as the shadows of the trees
were three times as long as themselves, they heard a great
cackling in a field inside the road, and out over the ditch
jumped a fox with a fine black cock in his mouth.

"Oh, you anointed villain!" says the ass, roaring like
thunder.

"At him, good dog!" says Jack, and the word wasn't
out of his mouth when Coley was in full sweep after the
Red Dog. Reynard dropped his prize like a hot potato,
and was off like shot, and the poor cock came back
fluttering and trembling to Jack and his comrades.

"O musha, naybours!" says he, "wasn't it the heigth
o' luck that threw you in my way! Maybe I won't
remember your kindness if ever I find you in hardship; and
where in the world are you all going?"

"We're going to seek our fortune till the harvest comes in ; you may join our party if you like, and sit on Neddy's crupper when your legs and wings are tired."

Well, the march began again, and just as the sun was gone down they looked around, and there was neither cabin nor farm house in sight.

"Well, well," says Jack, "the worse luck now the better another time, and it's only a summer night after all. We'll go into the wood, and make our bed on the long grass."

No sooner said than done. Jack stretched himself on a bunch of dry grass, the ass lay near him, the dog and cat lay in the ass's warm lap, and the cock went to roost in the next tree.

Well, the soundness of deep sleep was over them all, when the cock took a notion of crowing.

"Bother you, Black Cock!" says the ass : "you disturbed me from as nice a wisp of hay as ever I tasted. What's the matter?"

"It's daybreak that's the matter: don't you see light yonder?"

"I see a light indeed," says Jack, "but it's from a candle it's coming, and not from the sun. As you've roused us we may as well go over, and ask for lodging."

So they all shook themselves, and went on through grass, and rocks, and briars, till they got down into a hollow, and there was the light coming through the shadow, and along with it came singing, and laughing, and cursing.

"Easy, boys!" says Jack: "walk on your tippy toes till we see what sort of people we have to deal with."

So they crept near the window, and there they saw six robbers inside, with pistols, and blunderbushes, and cutlashes, sitting at a table, eating roast beef and pork, and drinking mulled beer, and wine, and whisky punch.

"Wasn't that a fine haul we made at the Lord of Dunlavin's!" says one ugly-looking thief with his mouth full, "and it's little we'd get only for the honest porter! here's his purty health!"

"The porter's purty health!" cried out every one of them, and Jack bent his finger at his comrades.

"Close your ranks, my men," says he in a whisper, "and let every one mind the word of command."

So the ass put his fore-hoofs on the sill of the window, the dog got on the ass's head, the cat on the dog's head, and the cock on the cat's head. Then Jack made a sign, and they all sung out like mad.

"Hee-haw, hee-haw!" roared the ass; "bow-wow!" barked the dog; "meaw-meaw!" cried the cat; "cock-a-doodle-doo!' crowed the cock.

"Level your pistols!" cried Jack, "and make smithereens of 'em. Don't leave a mother's son of 'em alive; present, fire!"

With that they gave another halloo, and smashed every pane in the window. The robbers were frightened out of

their lives.   They blew out the candles, threw down the
table, and skelped out at the back door as if they were in
earnest, and never drew rein till they were in the very heart
of the wood.

Jack and his party got into the room, closed the shutters,
lighted the candles, and ate and drank till hunger and thirst
were gone.   Then they lay down to rest ;—Jack in the bed,
the ass in the stable, the dog on the door-mat, the cat by
the fire, and the cock on the perch.

At first the robbers were very glad to find themselves
safe in the thick wood, but they soon began to get voxod.

" This damp grass is very different from our warm
room," says one.

" I was obliged to drop a fine pig's foot," says another.

" I didn't get a tayspoonful of my last tumbler," says
another.

" And all the Lord of Dunlavin's gold and silver that we
left behind ! " says the last.

" I think I'll venture back," says the captain, " and see
if we can recover anything."

" That's a good boy ! " said they all, and away he
went.

The lights were all out, and so he groped his way to the
fire, and there the cat flew in his face, and tore him with
teeth and claws.   He let a roar out of him, and made for
the room door, to look for a candle inside.   He trod on the
dog's tail, and if he did, he got the marks of his teeth in
his arms, and legs, and thighs.

" Thousand murders ! " cried he ; " I wish I was out of
this unlucky house."

When he got to the street door, the cock dropped down

upon him with his claws and bill, and what the cat and dog done to him was only a flay-bite to what he got from the cock.

"Oh, tattheration to you all, you unfeeling vagabones!" says he, when he recovered his breath; and he staggered and spun round and round till he reeled into the stable, back foremost, but the ass received him with a kick on the broadest part of his small clothes, and laid him comfortably on the dunghill.

When he came to himself, he scratched his head, and began to think what happened him; and as soon as he found that his legs were able to carry him, he crawled away, dragging one foot after another, till he reached the wood.

"Well, well," cried them all, when he came within hearing, "any chance of our property?"

"You may say chance," says he, "and it's itself is the poor chance all out. Ah, will any of you pull a bed of dry grass for me? All the sticking-plaster in Enniscorthy will be too little for the cuts and bruises I have on me. Ah, if you only knew what I have gone through for you! When I got to the kitchen fire, looking for a sod of lighted turf, what should be there but an old woman carding flax, and you may see the marks she left on my face with the cards. I made to the room door as fast as I could, and who should I stumble over but a cobbler and his seat, and if he did not work at me with his awls and his pinchers you may call me a rogue. Well, I got away from him somehow, but when I was passing through the door, it must be the divel himself that pounced down on me with his claws, and his teeth, that were equal to sixpenny nails, and his wings—ill luck be in his road! Well, at last I reached the stable, and there, by way of salute, I got a pelt from a sledge-hammer that sent me half a mile off. If you don't believe me, I'll give you leave to go and judge for yourselves."

"Oh, my poor captain," says they, "we believe you to the nines. Catch us, indeed, going within a hen's race of that unlucky cabin!"

Well, before the sun shook his doublet next morning, Jack and his comrades were up and about. They made a hearty breakfast on what was left the night before, and then they all agreed to set off to the castle of the Lord of Dunlavin, and give him back all his gold and silver. Jack put it all in the two ends of a sack and laid it across Neddy's back, and all took the road in their hands. Away they went, through bogs, up hills, down dales, and sometimes along the yellow high road, till they came to the hall-door of the Lord of Dunlavin, and who should be there, airing his powdered head, his white stockings, and his red breeches, but the thief of a porter.

He gave a cross look to the visitors, and says he to Jack, "What do you want here, my fine fellow? there isn't room for you all."

"We want," says Jack, "what I'm sure you haven't to give us—and that is, common civility."

"Come, be off, you lazy strollers!" says he, "while a cat 'ud be licking her ear, or I'll let the dogs at you."

"Would you tell a body," says the cock that was perched on the ass's head, "who was it that opened the door for the robbers the other night?"

Ah! maybe the porter's red face didn't turn the colour of his frill, and the Lord of Dunlavin and his pretty daughter, that were standing at the parlour window unknownst to the porter, put out their heads.

" I'd be glad, Barney," says the master, " to hear your answer to the gentleman with the red comb on him."

" Ah, my lord, don't believe the rascal ; sure I didn't open the door to the six robbers."

" And how did you know there were six, you poor innocent ? " said the lord.

" Never mind, sir," says Jack, " all your gold and silver is there in that sack, and I don't think you will begrudge us our supper and bed after our long march from the wood of Athsalach."

" Begrudge, indeed ! Not one of you will ever see a poor day if I can help it."

So all were welcomed to their heart's content, and the ass and the dog and the cock got the best posts in the farmyard, and the cat took possession of the kitchen. The lord took Jack in hands, dressed him from top to toe in broadcloth, and frills as white as snow, and turnpumps, and put a watch in his fob. When they sat down to dinner, the lady of the house said Jack had the air of a born gentleman about him, and the lord said he'd make him his steward. Jack brought his mother, and settled her comfortably near the castle, and all were as happy as you please.

The Shee an Gannon and the Gruagach Gaire

THE Shee an Gannon was born in the morning, named at noon, and went in the evening to ask his daughter of the king of Erin.

"I will give you my daughter in marriage," said the king of Erin; "you won't get her, though, unless you go and bring me back the tidings that I want, and tell me what it is that put a stop to the laughing of the Gruagach Gaire, who before this laughed always, and laughed so loud that the whole world heard him. There are twelve iron spikes out here in the garden behind my castle. On eleven of the spikes are the heads of kings' sons who came seeking my daughter in marriage, and all of them went away to get the knowledge I wanted. Not one was able to get it and tell me what stopped the Gruagach Gaire from laughing. I took the heads off them all when they came back without the tidings for which they went, and I'm greatly in dread that your head'll be on the twelfth spike, for I'll do the same to you that I did to the eleven kings' sons unless you tell what put a stop to the laughing of the Gruagach."

The Shee an Gannon made no answer, but left the king and pushed away to know could he find why the Gruagach was silent.

He took a glen at a step, a hill at a leap, and travelled all day till evening. Then he came to a house. The master of the house asked him what sort was he, and he said : " A young man looking for hire."

" Well," said the master of the house, " I was going to-morrow to look for a man to mind my cows. If you'll work for me, you'll have a good place, the best food a man could have to eat in this world, and a soft bed to lie on."

The Shee an Gannon took service, and ate his supper. Then the master of the house said : " I am the Gruagach Gaire ; now that you are my man and have eaten your supper, you'll have a bed of silk to sleep on."

Next morning after breakfast the Gruagach said to the Shee an Gannon : " Go out now and loosen my five golden cows and my bull without horns, and drive them to pasture ; but when you have them out on the grass, be careful you don't let them go near the land of the giant."

The new cowboy drove the cattle to pasture, and when near the land of the giant, he saw it was covered with woods and surrounded by a high wall. He went up, put his back against the wall, and threw in a great stretch of it ; then he went inside and threw out another great stretch of the wall, and put the five golden cows and the bull without horns on the land of the giant.

Then he climbed a tree, ate the sweet apples himself,

and threw the sour ones down to the cattle of the Gruagach Gaire.

Soon a great crashing was heard in the woods,—the noise of young trees bending, and old trees breaking. The cowboy looked around, and saw a five-headed giant pushing through the trees ; and soon he was before him.

" Poor miserable creature ! " said the giant ; " but weren't you impudent to come to my land and trouble me in this way ? You're too big for one bite, and too small for two. I don't know what to do but tear you to pieces."

" You nasty brute," said the cowboy, coming down to him from the tree, " 'tis little I care for you ;" and then they went at each other. So great was the noise between them that there was nothing in the world but what was looking on and listening to the combat.

They fought till late in the afternoon, when the giant was getting the upper hand ; and then the cowboy thought that if the giant should kill him, his father and mother would never find him or set eyes on him again, and he would never get the daughter of the king of Erin. The heart in his body grew strong at this thought. He sprang on the giant, and with the first squeeze and thrust he put him to his knees in the hard ground, with the second thrust to his waist, and with the third to his shoulders.

" I have you at last ; you're done for now ! " said the cowboy. Then he took out his knife, cut the five heads off the giant, and when he had them off he cut out the tongues and threw the heads over the wall.

Then he put the tongues in his pocket and drove home the cattle. That evening the Gruagach couldn't find vessels enough in all his place to hold the milk of the five golden cows.

But when the cowboy was on the way home with the cattle, the son of the king of Tisean came and took the giant's heads and claimed the princess in marriage when the Gruagach Gaire should laugh.

After supper the cowboy would give no talk to his master, but kept his mind to himself, and went to the bed of silk to sleep.

On the morning the cowboy rose before his master, and the first words he said to the Gruagach were:

"What keeps you from laughing, you who used to laugh so loud that the whole world heard you?"

"I'm sorry," said the Gruagach, "that the daughter of the king of Erin sent you here."

"If you don't tell me of your own will, I'll make you tell me," said the cowboy; and he put a face on himself that was terrible to look at, and running through the house like a madman, could find nothing that would give pain enough to the Gruagach but some ropes made of untanned sheepskin hanging on the wall.

He took these down, caught the Gruagach, fastened him by the three smalls, and tied him so that his little toes were whispering to his ears. When he was in this state the Gruagach said: "I'll tell you what stopped my laughing if you set me free."

So the cowboy unbound him, the two sat down together, and the Gruagach said:—

"I lived in this castle here with my twelve sons. We ate, drank, played cards, and enjoyed ourselves, till one day when my sons and I were playing, a slender brown hare came rushing in, jumped on to the hearth, tossed up the ashes to the rafters and ran away.

" On another day he came again ; but if he did, we were ready for him, my twelve sons and myself. As soon as he tossed up the ashes and ran off, we made after him, and followed him till nightfall, when he went into a glen. We saw a light before us. I ran on, and came to a house with a great apartment, where there was a man named Yellow Face with twelve daughters, and the hare was tied to the side of the room near the women.

" There was a large pot over the fire in the room, and a great stork boiling in the pot. The man of the house said to me : ' There are bundles of rushes at the end of the room, go there and sit down with your men ! '

" He went into the next room and brought out two pikes, one of wood, the other of iron, and asked me which of the pikes would I take. I said, ' I'll take the iron one ; ' for I thought in my heart that if an attack should come on me, I could defend myself better with the iron than the wooden pike.

" Yellow Face gave me the iron pike, and the first chance of taking what I could out of the pot on the point of the pike. I got but a small piece of the stork, and the man of the house took all the rest on his wooden pike. We had to fast that night ; and when the man and his twelve daughters ate the flesh of the stork, they hurled the bare bones in the faces of my sons and myself.

" We had to stop all night that way, beaten on the faces by the bones of the stork.

" Next morning, when we were going away, the man of the house asked me to stay a while ; and going into the next room, he brought out twelve loops of iron and one of wood, and said to me : ' Put the heads of your twelve sons into the iron loops, or your own head into the wooden one ; ' and I said : ' I'll put the twelve heads of my sons in the iron loops, and keep my own out of the wooden one.'

" He put the iron loops on the necks of my twelve sons, and put the wooden one on his own neck. Then he snapped the loops one after another, till he took the heads off my twelve sons and threw the heads and bodies out of the house ; but he did nothing to hurt his own neck.

" When he had killed my sons he took hold of me and stripped the skin and flesh from the small of my back down, and when he had done that he took the skin of a black sheep that had been hanging on the wall for seven years and clapped it on my body in place of my own flesh and skin ; and the sheepskin grew on me, and every year since then I shear myself, and every bit of wool I use for the stockings that I wear I clip off my own back."

When he had said this, the Gruagach showed the cowboy his back covered with thick black wool.

After what he had seen and heard, the cowboy said : " I know now why you don't laugh, and small blame to you.   But does that hare come here still ? "

" He does indeed," said the Gruagach.

Both went to the table to play, and they were not long playing cards when the hare ran in ; and before they could stop him he was out again.

But the cowboy made after the hare, and the Gruagach after the cowboy, and they ran as fast as ever their legs could carry them till nightfall ; and when the hare was entering the castle where the twelve sons of the Gruagach were

killed, the cowboy caught him by the two hind legs and
dashed out his brains against the wall ; and the skull of
the hare was knocked into the chief room of the castle, and
fell at the feet of the master of the place.

" Who has dared to interfere with my fighting pet ? "
screamed Yellow Face.

" I," said the cowboy ; " and if your pet had had manners,
he might be alive now."

The cowboy and the Gruagach stood by the fire. A
stork was boiling in the pot, as when the Gruagach came
the first time. The master of the house went into the next
room and brought out an iron and a wooden pike, and
asked the cowboy which would he choose.

" I'll take the wooden one," said the cowboy ; " and you
may keep the iron one for yourself."

So he took the wooden one ; and going to the pot, brought
out on the pike all the stork except a small bite, and he and
the Gruagach fell to eating, and they were eating the flesh
of the stork all night. The cowboy and the Gruagach
were at home in the place that time.

In the morning the master of the house went into the
next room, took down the twelve iron loops with a wooden
one, brought them out, and asked the cowboy which would
he take, the twelve iron or the one wooden loop.

" What could I do with the twelve iron ones for myself
or my master ? I'll take the wooden one."

He put it on, and taking the twelve iron loops, put
them on the necks of the twelve daughters of the house,
then snapped the twelve heads off them, and turning to
their father, said : " I'll do the same thing to you unless
you bring the twelve sons of my master to life, and make

them as well and strong as when you took their heads."

The master of the house went out and brought the twelve to life again ; and when the Gruagach saw all his

sons alive and as well as ever, he let a laugh out of himself, and all the Eastern world heard the laugh.

Then the cowboy said to the Gruagach : " It's a bad thing you have done to me, for the daughter of the king of Erin will be married the day after your laugh is heard."

" Oh ! then we must be there in time," said the Gruagach ; and they all made away from the place as fast as ever they could, the cowboy, the Gruagach, and his twelve sons.

They hurried on ; and when within three miles of the king's castle there was such a throng of people that no one could go a step ahead. "We must clear a road through this," said the cowboy.

"We must indeed," said the Gruagach ; and at it they went, threw the people some on one side and some on the other, and soon they had an opening for themselves to the king's castle.

As they went in, the daughter of the king of Erin and the son of the king of Tisean were on their knees just going to be married. The cowboy drew his hand on the bridegroom, and gave a blow that sent him spinning till he stopped under a table at the other side of the room.

"What scoundrel struck that blow ? " asked the king of Erin.

"It was I," said the cowboy.

"What reason had you to strike the man who won my daughter ? "

"It was I who won your daughter, not he ; and if you don't believe me, the Gruagach Gaire is here himself. He'll tell you the whole story from beginning to end, and show you the tongues of the giant."

So the Gruagach came up and told the king the whole story, how the Shee an Gannon had become his cowboy, had guarded the five golden cows and the bull without horns, cut off the heads of the five-headed giant, killed the wizard hare, and brought his own twelve sons to life. "And then," said the Gruagach, " he is the only man in the whole world I have ever told why I stopped laughing, and the only one who has ever seen my fleece of wool."

When the king of Erin heard what the Gruagach said,

and saw the tongues of the giant fitted in the head, he made the Shee an Gannon kneel down by his daughter, and they were married on the spot.

Then the son of the king of Tisean was thrown into prison, and the next day they put down a great fire, and the deceiver was burned to ashes.

The wedding lasted nine days, and the last day was better than the first.

The Story-Teller at Fault

T the time when the Tuatha De Dannan held the sovereignty of Ireland, there reigned in Leinster a king, who was remarkably fond of hearing stories. Like the other princes and chieftains of the island, he had a favourite story-teller, who held a large estate from his Majesty, on condition of telling him a new story every night of his life, before he went to sleep. Many indeed were the stories he knew, so that he had already reached a good old age without failing even for a single night in his task ; and such was the skill he displayed that whatever cares of state or other annoyances might prey upon the monarch's mind, his story-teller was sure to send him to sleep.

One morning the story-teller arose early, and as his custom was, strolled out into his garden turning over in his mind incidents which he might weave into a story for the king at night. But this morning he found himself quite at fault ; after pacing his whole demesne, he returned to his house without being able to think of anything new or strange. He found no difficulty in " there was once a king who had three sons " or " one day the king of all Ireland," but further than that he could not get. At length he went in to breakfast, and found his wife much perplexed at his delay.

" Why don't you come to breakfast, my dear?" said she.

" I have no mind to eat anything," replied the story-teller ; " long as I have been in the service of the king of Leinster, I never sat down to breakfast without having a new story ready for the evening, but this morning my mind is quite shut up, and I don't know what to do. I might as well lie down and die at once. I'll be disgraced for ever this evening, when the king calls for his story-teller."

Just at this moment the lady looked out of the window.

" Do you see that black thing at the end of the field ? " said she.

" I do," replied her husband.

They drew nigh, and saw a miserable looking old man lying on the ground with a wooden leg placed beside him.

" Who are you, my good man ? " asked the story-teller.

" Oh, then, 'tis little matter who I am. I'm a poor, old, lame, decrepit, miserable creature, sitting down here to rest awhile."

" An' what are you doing with that box and dice I see in your hand ? "

" I am waiting here to see if any one will play a game with me," replied the beggar man.

" Play with you ! Why what has a poor old man like you to play for ? "

" I have one hundred pieces of gold in this leathern purse," replied the old man.

" You may as well play with him," said the story-teller's

wife ; " and perhaps you'll have something to tell the king in the evening."

A smooth stone was placed between them, and upon it they cast their throws.

It was but a little while and the story-teller lost every penny of his money.

" Much good may it do you, friend," said he. " What better hap could I look for, fool that I am ! "

" Will you play again ? " asked the old man.

" Don't be talking, man : you have all my money."

" Haven't you chariot and horses and hounds ? "

" Well, what of them ! "

" I'll stake all the money I have against thine."

" Nonsense, man ! Do you think for all the money in Ireland, I'd run the risk of seeing my lady tramp home on foot ? "

" Maybe you'd win," said the bocough.

" Maybe I wouldn't," said the story-teller.

" Play with him, husband," said his wife. " I don't mind walking, if you do, love."

" I never refused you before," said the story-teller, " and I won't do so now."

Down he sat again, and in one throw lost houses, hounds, and chariot.

" Will you play again ? " asked the beggar.

" Are you making game of me, man ; what else have I to stake ? "

" I'll stake all my winnings against your wife," said the old man.

The story-teller turned away in silence, but his wife stopped him.

"Accept his offer," said she. "This is the third time, and who knows what luck you may have? You'll surely win now."

They played again, and the story-teller lost. No sooner had he done so, than to his sorrow and surprise, his wife went and sat down near the ugly old beggar.

"Is that the way you're leaving me?" said the story-teller.

"Sure I was won," said she. "You would not cheat the poor man, would you?"

"Have you any more to stake?" asked the old man.

"You know very well I have not," replied the story-teller.

"I'll stake the whole now, wife and all, against your own self," said the old man.

Again they played, and again the story-teller lost.

"Well! here I am, and what do you want with me?"

"I'll soon let you know," said the old man, and he took from his pocket a long cord and a wand.

"Now," said he to the story-teller, "what kind of animal would you rather be, a deer, a fox, or a hare? You have your choice now, but you may not have it later."

To make a long story short, the story-teller made his choice of a hare; the old man threw the cord round him, struck him with the wand, and lo! a long-eared, frisking hare was skipping and jumping on the green.

But it wasn't for long; who but his wife called the hounds, and set them on him. The hare fled, the dogs followed. Round the field ran a high wall, so that run as he might, he couldn't get out, and mightily diverted were beggar and lady to see him twist and double.

In vain did he take refuge with his wife, she kicked him back again to the hounds, until at length the beggar stopped the hounds, and with a stroke of the wand, panting and breathless, the story-teller stood before them again.

" And how did you like the sport ? " said the beggar.

" It might be sport to others," replied the story-teller looking at his wife, " for my part I could well put up with the loss of it."

" Would it be asking too much," he went on to the beggar, " to know who you are at all, or where you come from, or why you take a pleasure in plaguing a poor old man like me ? "

" Oh ! " replied the stranger, " I'm an odd kind of good-for-little fellow, one day poor, another day rich, but if you wish to know more about me or my habits, come with me and perhaps I may show you more than you would make out if you went alone."

" I'm not my own master to go or stay," said the story-teller, with a sigh.

The stranger put one hand into his wallet and drew out of it before their eyes a well-looking middle-aged man, to whom he spoke as follows :

" By all you heard and saw since I put you into my wallet, take charge of this lady and of the carriage and horses, and have them ready for me whenever I want them."

Scarcely had he said these words when all vanished, and the story-teller found himself at the Foxes' Ford, near the castle of Red Hugh O'Donnell.   He could see all but none could see him.

O'Donnell was in his hall, and heaviness of flesh and weariness of spirit were upon him.

"Go out," said he to his doorkeeper, "and see who or what may be coming."

The doorkeeper went, and what he saw was a lank, grey beggarman ; half his sword bared behind his haunch, his two

shoes full of cold road-a-wayish water sousing about him, the tips of his two ears out through his old hat, his two shoulders out through his scant tattered cloak, and in his hand a green wand of holly.

"Save you, O Donnell," said the lank grey beggarman.

"And you likewise," said O'Donnell. "Whence come you, and what is your craft?"

"I come from the outmost stream of earth,
From the glens where the white swans glide,
A night in Islay, a night in Man,
A night on the cold hillside."

"It's the great traveller you are," said O'Donnell. "Maybe you've learnt something on the road."

"I am a juggler," said the lank grey beggarman, "and for five pieces of silver you shall see a trick of mine."

"You shall have them," said O'Donnell, and the lank grey beggarman took three small straws and placed them in his hand.

"The middle one," said he, "I'll blow away; the other two I'll leave."

"Thou canst not do it," said one and all.

But the lank grey beggarman put a finger on either outside straw and, whiff, away he blew the middle one.

"'Tis a good trick," said O'Donnell; and he paid him his five pieces of silver.

"For half the money," said one of the chief's lads, "I'll do the same trick."

"Take him at his word, O'Donnell."

The lad put the three straws on his hand, and a finger on either outside straw and he blew; and what happened but that the fist was blown away with the straw.

"Thou art sore, and thou wilt be sorer," said O'Donnell.

"Six more pieces, O'Donnell, and I'll do another trick for thee," said the lank grey beggarman.

"Six shalt thou have."

"Seest thou my two ears! One I'll move but not t'other."

"'Tis easy to see them, they're big enough, but thou canst never move one ear and not the two together."

The lank grey beggarman put his hand to his ear, and he gave it a pull.

O'Donnell laughed and paid him the six pieces.

"Call that a trick," said the fistless lad, "any one can do that," and so saying, he put up his hand, pulled his ear, and what happened was that he pulled away ear and head.

"Sore thou art, and sorer thou'lt be," said O'Donnell.

"Well, O'Donnell," said the lank grey beggarman, "strange are the tricks I've shown thee, but I'll show thee a stranger one yet for the same money."

"Thou hast my word for it," said O'Donnell.

With that the lank grey beggarman took a bag from under his armpit, and from out the bag a ball of silk, and he unwound the ball and he flung it slantwise up into the clear blue heavens, and it became a ladder; then he took a hare and placed it upon the thread, and up it ran; again he took out a red-eared hound, and it swiftly ran up after the hare.

"Now," said the lank grey beggarman; "has any one a mind to run after the dog and on the course?"

"I will," said a lad of O'Donnell's.

"Up with you then," said the juggler; "but I warn you if you let my hare be killed I'll cut off your head when you come down."

The lad ran up the thread and all three soon disappeared. After looking up for a long time, the lank grey beggarman said: "I'm afraid the hound is eating the hare, and that our friend has fallen asleep."

Saying this he began to wind the thread, and down came the lad fast asleep ; and down came the red-eared hound and in his mouth the last morsel of the hare.

He struck the lad a stroke with the edge of his sword, and so cast his head off. As for the hound, if he used it no worse, he used it no better.

" It's little I'm pleased, and sore I'm angered," said O'Donnell, " that a hound and a lad should be killed at my court."

" Five pieces of silver twice over for each of them," said the juggler, " and their heads shall be on them as before."

" Thou shalt get that," said O'Donnell.

Five pieces, and again five were paid him, and lo ! the lad had his head and the hound his. And though they lived to the uttermost end of time, the hound would never touch a hare again, and the lad took good care to keep his eyes open.

Scarcely had the lank grey beggarman done this when he vanished from out their sight, and no one present could say if he had flown through the air or if the earth had swallowed him up.

> He moved as wave tumbling o'er wave
> As whirlwind following whirlwind,
> As a furious wintry blast,
> So swiftly, sprucely, cheerily,
> Right proudly,
> And no stop made
> Until he came
> To the court of Leinster's King,
> He gave a cheery light leap
> O'er top of turret,
> Of court and city
> Of Leinster's King.

Heavy was the flesh and weary the spirit of Leinster's

king. 'Twas the hour he was wont to hear a story, but send he might right and left, not a jot of tidings about the story-teller could he get.

"Go to the door," said he to his doorkeeper, "and see if a soul is in sight who may tell me something about my story-teller."

The doorkeeper went, and what he saw was a lank grey beggarman, half his sword bared behind his haunch, his two old shoes full of cold road-a-wayish water sousing about him, the tips of his two ears out through his old hat, his two shoulders out through his scant tattered cloak, and in his hand a three-stringed harp.

"What canst thou do?" said the doorkeeper.

"I can play," said the lank grey beggarman.

"Never fear," added he to the story-teller, "thou shalt see all, and not a man shall see thee."

When the king heard a harper was outside, he bade him in.

"It is I that have the best harpers in the five-fifths of Ireland," said he, and he signed them to play. They did so, and if they played, the lank grey beggarman listened.

"Heardst thou ever the like ?" said the king.

"Did you ever, O king, hear a cat purring over a bowl of broth, or the buzzing of beetles in the twilight, or a shrill tongued old woman scolding your head off ? "

"That I have often," said the king.

"More melodious to me," said the lank grey beggarman, "were the worst of these sounds than the sweetest harping of thy harpers."

When the harpers heard this, they drew their swords and rushed at him, but instead of striking him, their blows fell on each other, and soon not a man but was cracking his neighbour's skull and getting his own cracked in turn.

When the king saw this, he thought it hard the harpers weren't content with murdering their music, but must needs murder each other.

" Hang the fellow who began it all," said he ; " and if I can't have a story, let me have peace."

Up came the guards, seized the lank grey beggarman, marched him to the gallows and hanged him high and dry. Back they marched to the hall, and who should they see but the lank grey beggarman seated on a bench with his mouth to a flagon of ale.

" Never welcome you in," cried the captain of the guard, " didn't we hang you this minute, and what brings you here ? "

" Is it me myself, you mean ? "

" Who else ? " said the captain.

" May your hand turn into a pig's foot with you when you think of tying the rope ; why should you speak of hanging me ? "

Back they scurried to the gallows, and there hung the king's favourite brother.

Back they hurried to the king who had fallen fast asleep.

" Please your Majesty," said the captain, " we hanged that strolling vagabond, but here he is back again as well as ever."

" Hang him again," said the king, and off he went to sleep once more.

They did as they were told, but what happened was that

they found the king's chief harper hanging where the lank grey beggarman should have been.

The captain of the guard was sorely puzzled.

" Are you wishful to hang me a third time ? " said the lank grey beggarman.

" Go where you will," said the captain, " and as fast. as you please if you'll only go far enough. It's trouble enough you've given us already."

" Now you're reasonable," said the beggarman ; " and since you've given up trying to hang a stranger because he finds fault with your music, I don't mind telling you that if you go back to the gallows you'll find your friends sitting on the sward none the worse for what has happened."

As he said these words he vanished ; and the story-teller found himself on the spot where they first met, and where his wife still was with the carriage and horses.

" Now," said the lank grey beggarman, " I'll torment you no longer. There's your carriage and your horses, and your money and your wife ; do what you please with them."

" For my carriage and my horses and my hounds," said the story-teller, " I thank you ; but my wife and my money you may keep."

" No," said the other. " I want neither, and as for your wife, don't think ill of her for what she did, she couldn't help it."

" Not help it ! Not help kicking me into the mouth of my own hounds ! Not help casting me off for the sake of a beggarly old ——"

" I'm not as beggarly or as old as ye think. I am Angus of the Bruff ; many a good turn you've done me with the

King of Leinster. This morning my magic told me the difficulty you were in, and I made up my mind to get you out of it. As for your wife there, the power that changed your body changed her mind. Forget and forgive as man and wife should do, and now you have a story for the King of Leinster when he calls for one ; " and with that he disappeared.

It's true enough he now had a story fit for a king. From first to last he told all that had befallen him ; so long and loud laughed the king that he couldn't go to sleep at all. And he told the story-teller never to trouble for fresh stories, but every night as long as he lived he listened again and he laughed afresh at the tale of the lank grey beggarman.

The Sea-Maiden

HERE was once a poor old fisherman, and one year he was not getting much fish. On a day of days, while he was fishing, there rose a sea-maiden at the side of his boat, and she asked him, " Are you getting much fish ? " The old man answered and said, " Not I." " What reward would you give me for sending plenty of fish to you ? " " Ach ! " said the old man, " I have not much to spare." " Will you give me the first son you have ? " said she. " I would give ye that, were I to have a son," said he. " Then go home, and remember me when your son is twenty years of age, and you yourself will get plenty of fish after this." Everything happened as the sea-maiden said, and he himself got plenty of fish ; but when the end of the twenty years was nearing, the old man was growing more and more sorrowful and heavy hearted, while he counted each day as it came.

He had rest neither day nor night. The son asked his father one day, " Is any one troubling you ? " The old man said, "Some one is, but that's nought to do with you nor any one else." The lad said, "I *must* know what it is." His father told him at last how the matter was with him and the sea-maiden. "Let not that put you in any trouble," said the son; "I will not oppose you." "You shall not; you shall not go, my son, though I never get fish any more." "If you will not let me go with you, go to the smithy, and let the smith make me a great strong sword, and I will go seek my fortune."

His father went to the smithy, and the smith made a doughty sword for him. His father came home with the sword. The lad grasped it and gave it a shake or two, and it flew into a hundred splinters. He asked his father to go to the smithy and get him another sword in which there should be twice as much weight; and so his father did, and so likewise it happened to the next sword—it broke in two halves. Back went the old man to the smithy; and the smith made a great sword, its like he never made before. "There's thy sword for thee," said the smith, "and the fist must be good that plays this blade." The old man gave the sword to his son; he gave it a shake or two. "This will do," said he; "it's high time now to travel on my way."

On the next morning he put a saddle on a black horse that his father had, and he took the world for his pillow. When he went on a bit, he fell in with the carcass of a sheep beside the road. And there were a great black dog, a falcon, and an otter, and they were quarrelling over the spoil. So they asked him to divide it for them. He came down off the horse, and he divided the carcass amongst the three. Three shares to the dog, two shares to the otter, and a share to the falcon. "For this," said the dog, "if swiftness of foot or sharpness of tooth will give thee aid, mind me, and I will be at thy side." Said the otter, "If the swimming of foot on the ground of a pool will loose thee, mind me, and I will be at thy side." Said the falcon, "If hardship comes on thee, where swiftness of wing or crook of a claw will do good, mind me, and I will be at thy side."

On this he went onward till he reached a king's house, and he took service to be a herd, and his wages were to be according to the milk of the cattle. He went away with the cattle, and the grazing was but bare. In the evening when he took them home they had not much milk, the place was so bare, and his meat and drink was but spare that night.

On the next day he went on further with them ; and at last he came to a place exceedingly grassy, in a green glen, of which he never saw the like.

But about the time when he should drive the cattle homewards, who should he see coming but a great giant with his sword in his hand ? "Hi! Ho!! Hogarach!!!" says the giant. "Those cattle are mine ; they are on my land, and a dead man art thou." "I say not that," says the herd ; "there is no knowing, but that may be easier to say than to do."

He drew the great clean-sweeping sword, and he neared the giant. The herd drew back his sword, and the head was off the giant in a twinkling. He leaped on the black horse, and he went to look for the giant's house. In went the herd, and that's the place where there was money in plenty, and dresses of each kind in the wardrobe with gold and silver, and each thing finer than the other. At the mouth of night he took himself to the king's house, but he took not a thing from the giant's house. And when the cattle were milked this night there *was* milk. He got good feeding this night, meat and drink without stint, and the king was hugely pleased that he had caught such a herd. He went on for a time in this way, but at last the glen grew bare of grass, and the grazing was not so good.

So he thought he would go a little further forward in on the giant's land ; and he sees a great park of grass. He returned for the cattle, and he put them into the park.

They were but a short time grazing in the park when a great wild giant came full of rage and madness. " Hi ! Haw !! Hogaraich !!! " said the giant. " It is a drink of thy blood that will quench my thirst this night." " There is no knowing," said the herd, " but that's easier to say than to do." And at each other went the men. *There* was shaking of blades ! At length and at last it seemed as if the giant would get the victory over the herd. Then he called on the dog, and with one spring the black dog caught the giant by the neck, and swiftly the herd struck off his head.

He went home very tired this night, but it's a wonder if the king's cattle had not milk. The whole family was delighted that they had got such a herd.

Next day he betakes himself to the castle. When he reached the door, a little flattering carlin met him standing in the door. " All hail and good luck to thee, fisher's son ; 'tis 1 myself am pleased to see thee ; great is the honour for this kingdom, for thy like to be come into it—thy coming in is fame for this little bothy ; go in first ; honour to the gentles ; go on, and take breath."

" In before me, thou crone ; I like not flattery out of doors ; go in and let's hear thy speech." In went the crone, and when her back was to him he drew his sword and whips her head off; but the sword flew out of his hand. And swift the crone gripped her head with both hands, and puts it on her neck as it was before. The dog sprung on the crone, and she struck the generous dog with the club of magic ; and there he lay. But the herd struggled for a hold of the club of magic, and with one blow on the top of the head she was on earth in the twinkling of an eye. He went forward, up a little, and there was spoil! Gold and silver, and each thing more precious than another, in the crone's castle. He went back to the king's house, and then there was rejoicing.

He followed herding in this way for a time ; but one night after he came home, instead of getting " All hail " and " Good luck " from the dairymaid, all were at crying and woe.

He asked what cause of woe there was that night. The dairymaid said " There is a great beast with three heads in the loch, and it must get some one every year, and the lot had come this year on the king's daughter, and at midday to-morrow she is to meet the Laidly Beast at the upper end of the loch, but there is a great suitor yonder who is going to rescue her."

" What suitor is that ? " said the herd. " Oh, he is a great General of arms," said the dairymaid, " and when he kills the beast, he will marry the king's daughter, for the king has said that he who could save his daughter should get her to marry."

But on the morrow, when the time grew near, the king's daughter and this hero of arms went to give a meeting to the beast, and they reached the black rock, at the upper end of the loch. They were but a short time there when the beast stirred in the midst of the loch;

but when the General saw this terror of a beast with three heads, he took fright, and he slunk away, and he hid himself. And the king's daughter was under fear and under trembling, with no one at all to save her. Suddenly she sees a doughty handsome youth, riding a black horse, and coming where she was. He was marvellously arrayed and full armed, and his black dog moved after him. "There is gloom on your face, girl," said the youth; "what do you here ?"

"Oh! that's no matter," said the king's daughter. "It's not long I'll be here, at all events."

"I say not that," said he.

"A champion fled as likely as you, and not long since," said she.

"He is a champion who stands the war," said the youth. And to meet the beast he went with his sword and his dog. But there was a spluttering and a splashing between himself and the beast! The dog kept doing all he might, and the king's daughter was palsied by fear of the noise of the beast! One of them would now be under, and now above. But at last he cut one of the heads off it. It gave one roar, and the son of earth, echo of the rocks, called to its screech, and it drove the loch in spindrift from end to end, and in a twinkling it went out of sight.

"Good luck and victory follow you, lad!" said the king's daughter. "I am safe for one night, but the beast will come again and again, until the other two heads come off it." He caught the beast's head, and he drew a knot through it, and he told her to bring it with her there to-morrow. She gave him a gold ring, and went home with the head on her shoulder, and the herd betook himself to the cows. But she had not gone far when this great General saw her, and he said to her, "I will kill you if you do not say that 'twas I took the head off the beast." "Oh!" says she, "'tis I will say it; who else took the head off the beast but you!" They reached the king's house, and the head was on the General's shoulder. But here was rejoicing, that she should come home alive and whole, and this great captain with the beast's head full of blood in his hand. On the morrow they went away, and there was no question at all but that this hero would save the king's daughter.

They reached the same place, and they were not long there when the fearful Laidly Beast stirred in the midst of the loch, and the hero slunk away as he did on yesterday, but it was not long after this when the man of the black horse came, with another dress on. No matter; she knew that it was the very same lad. " It is I am pleased to see you," said she. " I am in hopes you will handle your great sword to-day as you did yesterday. Come up and take breath." But they were not long there when they saw the beast steaming in the midst of the loch.

At once he went to meet the beast, but *there* was Cloopersteich and Claperstich, spluttering, splashing, raving, and roaring on the beast ! They kept at it thus for a long time, and about the mouth of night he cut another head off the beast. He put it on the knot and gave it to her. She gave him one of her earrings, and he leaped on the black horse, and he betook himself to the herding. The king's daughter went home with the heads. The General met her, and took the heads from her, and he said to her, that she must tell that it was he who took the head off the beast this time also. " Who else took the head off the beast but you ? " said she. They reached the king's house with the heads. Then there was joy and gladness.

About the same time on the morrow, the two went away. The officer hid himself as he usually did. The king's daughter betook herself to the bank of the loch. The hero of the black horse came, and if roaring and raving were on the beast on the days that were passed, this day it was horrible. But no matter, he took the third head off the beast, and drew it through the knot, and gave it to her. She gave him her other earring, and then she went home with the heads. When they reached the king's house, all were full of smiles, and the General was to marry the king's daughter the next day. The wedding was going on,

and every one about the castle longing till the priest should come. But when the priest came, she would marry only the one who could take the heads off the knot without cutting it. "Who should take the heads off the knot but the man that put the heads on?" said the king.

The General tried them, but he could not loose them and at last there was no one about the house but had tried to take the heads off the knot, but they could not. The king asked if there were any one else about the house that

would try to take the heads off the knot. They said that
the herd had not tried them yet. Word went for the herd ;
and he was not long throwing them hither and thither.
" But stop a bit, my lad," said the king's daughter ; " the
man that took the heads off the beast, he has my ring and
my two earrings." The herd put his hand in his pocket,
and he threw them on the board. " Thou art my man,"
said the king's daughter. The king was not so pleased
when he saw that it was a herd who was to marry his
daughter, but he ordered that he should be put in a better
dress ; but his daughter spoke, and she said that he had a
dress as fine as any that ever was in his castle ; and thus
it happened. The herd put on the giant's golden dress,
and they married that same day.

They were now married, and everything went on well.
But one day, and it was the namesake of the day when his
father had promised him to the sea-maiden, they were
sauntering by the side of the loch, and lo and behold ! she
came and took him away to the loch without leave or asking. The king's daughter was now mournful, tearful, blind-
sorrowful for her married man ; she was always with her
eye on the loch. An old soothsayer met her, and she told
how it had befallen her married mate. Then he told her
the thing to do to save her mate, and that she did.

She took her harp to the sea-shore, and sat and played ;
and the sea-maiden came up to listen, for sea-maidens are
fonder of music than all other creatures. But when the
wife saw the sea-maiden she stopped. The sea-maiden
said, " Play on !" but the princess said, " No, not till I see
my man again." So the sea-maiden put up his head out of
the loch. Then the princess played again, and stopped till

the sea-maiden put him up to the waist. Then the princess
played and stopped again, and this time the sea-maiden put
him all out of the loch, and he called on the falcon and
became one and flew on shore. But the sea-maiden took
the princess, his wife.

Sorrowful was each one that was in the town on this night.
Her man was mournful, tearful, wandering down and up
about the banks of the loch, by day and night. The old
soothsayer met him. The soothsayer told him that there
was no way of killing the sea-maiden but the one way, and
this is it—" In the island that is in the midst of the loch
is the white-footed hind of the slenderest legs and the
swiftest step, and though she be caught, there will spring a
hoodie out of her, and though the hoodie should be caught,
there will spring a trout out of her, but there is an egg in
the mouth of the trout, and the soul of the sea-maiden is
in the egg, and if the egg breaks, she is dead."

Now, there was no way of getting to this island, for the
sea-maiden would sink each boat and raft that would go on
the loch. He thought he would try to leap the strait with
the black horse, and even so he did. The black horse
leaped the strait. He saw the hind, and he let the black
dog after her, but when he was on one side of the island,
the hind would be on the other side. " Oh ! would the
black dog of the carcass of flesh were here !" No sooner
spoke he the word than the grateful dog was at his side ;
and after the hind he went, and they were not long in
bringing her to earth. But he no sooner caught her than a
hoodie sprang out of her. " Would that the falcon grey, of
sharpest eye and swiftest wing, were here !" No sooner said
he this than the falcon was after the hoodie, and she was not

long putting her to earth ; and as the hoodie fell on the bank of the loch, out of her jumps the trout. " Oh! that thou wert by me now, oh otter!" No sooner said than the otter was at his side, and out on the loch she leaped, and brings the trout from the midst of the loch ; but no sooner was the otter on shore with the trout than the egg came from his mouth. He sprang and he put his foot on it. 'Twas then the sea-maiden appeared, and she said, " Break not the egg, and you shall get all you ask." " Deliver to me my wife!" In the wink of an eye she was by his side. When he got hold of her hand in both his hands, he let his foot down on the egg, and the sea-maiden died.

A Legend of Knockmany

HAT Irish man, woman, or child has not heard of our renowned Hibernian Hercules, the great and glorious Fin M'Coul? Not one, from Cape Clear to the Giant's Causeway, nor from that back again to Cape Clear. And, by-the-way, speaking of the Giant's Causeway brings me at once to the beginning of my story. Well, it so happened that Fin and his men were all working at the Causeway, in order to make a bridge across to Scotland; when Fin, who was very fond of his wife Oonagh, took it into his head that he would go home and see how the poor woman got on in his absence. So, accordingly, he pulled up a fir-tree, and, after lopping off the roots and branches, made a walking-stick of it, and set out on his way to Oonagh.

Oonagh, or rather Fin, lived at this time on the very tip-top of Knockmany Hill, which faces a cousin of its own called Cullamore, that rises up, half-hill, half-mountain, on the opposite side.

There was at that time another giant, named Cucullin— some say he was Irish, and some say he was Scotch—but whether Scotch or Irish, sorrow doubt of it but he was a targer. No other giant of the day could stand before him ; and such was his strength, that, when well vexed, he could give a stamp that shook the country about him. The fame and name of him went far and near ; and nothing in the shape of a man, it was said, had any chance with him in a fight. By one blow of his fists he flattened a thunderbolt and kept it in his pocket, in the shape of a pancake, to show to all his enemies, when they were about to fight him. Undoubtedly he had given every giant in Ireland a considerable beating, barring Fin M'Coul himself ; and he swore that he would never rest, night or day, winter or summer, till he would serve Fin with the same sauce, if he could catch him. However, the short and long of it was, with reverence be it spoken, that Fin heard Cucullin was coming to the Causeway to have a trial of strength with him ; and he was seized with a very warm and sudden fit of affection for his wife, poor woman, leading a very lonely, uncomfortable life of it in his absence. He accordingly pulled up the fir-tree, as I said before, and having snedded it into a walking-stick, set out on his travels to see his darling Oonagh on the top of Knockmany, by the way.

In truth, the people wondered very much why it was that Fin selected such a windy spot for his dwelling-house, and they even went so far as to tell him as much.

"What can you mane, Mr. M'Coul," said they, "by pitching your tent upon the top of Knockmany, where you never are without a breeze, day or night, winter or summer, and where you're often forced to take your nightcap without either going to bed or turning up your little finger ; ay, an' where, besides this, there's the sorrow's own want of water?"

"Why," said Fin, "ever since I was the height of a round tower, I was known to be fond of having a good prospect of my own; and where the dickens, neighbours, could I find a better spot for a good prospect than the top of Knockmany? As for water, I am sinking a pump, and, plase goodness, as soon as the Causeway's made, I intend to finish it."

Now, this was more of Fin's philosophy; for the real state of the case was, that he pitched upon the top of Knockmany in order that he might be able to see Cucullin coming towards the house. All we have to say is, that if he wanted a spot from which to keep a sharp look-out— and, between ourselves, he did want it grievously—barring Slieve Croob, or Slieve Donard, or its own cousin, Culla-more, he could not find a neater or more convenient situa-tion for it in the sweet and sagacious province of Ulster.

"God save all here!" said Fin, good-humouredly, on putting his honest face into his own door.

"Musha, Fin, avick, an' you're welcome home to your own Oonagh, you darlin' bully." Here followed a smack that is said to have made the waters of the lake at the bottom of the hill curl, as it were, with kindness and sympathy.

Fin spent two or three happy days with Oonagh, and felt himself very comfortable, considering the dread he had of Cucullin. This, however, grew upon him so much that his wife could not but perceive something lay on his mind which he kept altogether to himself. Let a woman alone, in the meantime, for ferreting or wheedling a secret

out of her good man, when she wishes. Fin was a proof
of this.

"It's this Cucullin," said he, "that's troubling me.
When the fellow gets angry, and begins to stamp, he'll
shake you a whole townland ; and it's well known that he
can stop a thunderbolt, for he always carries one about him
in the shape of a pancake, to show to any one that might
misdoubt it."

As he spoke, he clapped his thumb in his mouth, which
he always did when he wanted to prophesy, or to know
anything that happened in his absence ; and the wife asked
him what he did it for.

"He's coming," said Fin ; "I see him below Dun-
gannon."

"Thank goodness, dear! an' who is it, avick? Glory
be to God!"

"That baste, Cucullin," replied Fin ; "and how to
manage I don't know. If I run away, I am disgraced ; and
I know that sooner or later I must meet him, for my thumb
tells me so."

"When will he be here ?" said she.

"To-morrow, about two o'clock," replied Fin, with a
groan.

"Well, my bully, don't be cast down," said Oonagh;
" depend on me, and maybe I'll bring you better out of this
scrape than ever you could bring yourself, by your rule o'
thumb."

She then made a high smoke on the top of the hill, after
which she put her finger in her mouth, and gave three
whistles, and by that Cucullin knew he was invited to Culla-
more—for this was the way that the Irish long ago gave a

sign to all strangers and travellers, to let them know they were welcome to come and take share of whatever was going.

In the meantime, Fin was very melancholy, and did not know what to do, or how to act at all. Cucullin was an ugly customer to meet with ; and, the idea of the " cake " aforesaid flattened the very heart within him. What chance could he have, strong and brave though he was, with a man who could, when put in a passion, walk the country into earthquakes and knock thunderbolts into pancakes ? Fin knew not on what hand to turn him. Right or left— backward or forward—where to go he could form no guess whatsoever.

"Oonagh," said he, "can you do nothing for me ? Where's all your invention ? Am I to be skivered like a rabbit before your eyes, and to have my name disgraced for ever in the sight of all my tribe, and me the best man among them ? How am I to fight this man-mountain— this huge cross between an earthquake and a thunderbolt ? —with a pancake in his pocket that was once ———"

" Be easy, Fin," replied Oonagh ; "troth, I'm ashamed of you. Keep your toe in your pump, will you ? Talking of pancakes, maybe, we'll give him as good as any he brings with him—thunderbolt or otherwise. If I don't treat him to as smart feeding as he's got this many a day, never trust Oonagh again. Leave him to me, and do just as I bid you."

This relieved Fin very much ; for, after all, he had great confidence in his wife, knowing, as he did, that she had got him out of many a quandary before. Oonagh then drew the nine woollen threads of different colours, which she always did to find out the best way of succeeding in anything of importance she went about. She then platted them into three plats with three colours in each, putting one on her right arm, one round her heart, and the third round her right ankle, for then she knew that nothing could fail with her that she undertook.

Having everything now prepared, she sent round to the neighbours and borrowed one-and-twenty iron griddles, which she took and kneaded into the hearts of one-and-twenty cakes of bread, and these she baked on the fire in the usual way, setting them aside in the cupboard according as they were done. She then put down a large pot of new milk, which she made into curds and whey. Having done all this, she sat down quite contented, waiting for his arrival on the next day about two o'clock, that being the hour at which he was expected—for Fin knew as much by the sucking of his thumb. Now this was a curious property that Fin's thumb had. In this very thing, moreover, he was very much resembled by his great foe, Cucullin; for it was well known that the huge strength he possessed all lay in the middle finger of his right hand, and that, if he happened by any mischance to lose it, he was no more, for all his bulk, than a common man.

At length, the next day, Cucullin was seen coming across the valley, and Oonagh knew that it was time to commence operations. She immediately brought the cradle, and made Fin to lie down in it, and cover himself up with the clothes.

"You must pass for your own child," said she; "so just lie there snug, and say nothing, but be guided by me."

About two o'clock, as he had been expected, Cucullin came in. " God save all here ! " said he ; " is this where the great Fin M'Coul lives ? "

" Indeed it is, honest man," replied Oonagh ; " God save you kindly—won't you be sitting ? "

" Thank you, ma'am," says he, sitting down ; " you're Mrs. M'Coul, I suppose ? "

" I am," said she ; " and I have no reason, I hope, to be ashamed of my husband."

" No," said the other, " he has the name of being the strongest and bravest man in Ireland ; but for all that, there's a man not far from you that's very desirous of taking a shake with him.   Is he at home ? "

" Why, then, no," she replied ; " and if ever a man left his house in a fury, he did.   It appears that some one told him of a big basthoon of a giant called Cucullin being down at the Causeway to look for him, and so he set out there to try if he could catch him.   Troth, I hope, for the poor giant's sake, he won't meet with him, for if he does, Fin will make paste of him at once."

" Well," said the other, " I am Cucullin, and I have been seeking him these twelve months, but he always kept clear of me ; and I will never rest night or day till I lay my hands on him."

At this Oonagh set up a loud laugh, of great contempt, by-the-way, and looked at him as if he was only a mere handful of a man.

" Did you ever see Fin ? " said she, changing her manner all at once.

" How could I ? " said he ; " he always took care to keep his distance."

" I thought so," she replied ; " I judged as much ; and if you take my advice, you poor-looking creature, you'll pray night and day that you may never see him, for I tell you it will be a black day for you when you do. But, in the meantime, you perceive that the wind's on the door, and as Fin himself is from home, maybe you'd be civil enough to turn the house, for it's always what Fin does when he's here."

This was a startler even to Cucullin ; but he got up, however, and after pulling the middle finger of his right hand until it cracked three times, he went outside, and getting his arms about the house, turned it as she had wished. When Fin saw this, he felt the sweat of fear oozing out through every pore of his skin ; but Oonagh, depending upon her woman's wit, felt not a whit daunted.

" Arrah, then," said she, " as you are so civil, maybe you'd do another obliging turn for us, as Fin's not here to do it himself. You see, after this long stretch of dry weather we've had, we feel very badly off for want of water. Now, Fin says there's a fine spring-well somewhere under the rocks behind the hill here below, and it was his intention to pull them asunder ; but having heard of you, he left the place in such a fury, that he never thought of it. Now, if you try to find it, troth I'd feel it a kindness."

She then brought Cucullin down to see the place, which was then all one solid rock ; and, after looking at it for some time, he cracked his right middle finger nine times, and, stooping down, tore a cleft about four hundred feet deep, and a quarter of a mile in length, which has since been christened by the name of Lumford's Glen.

" You'll now come in," said she, " and eat a bit of such

humble fare as we can give you. Fin, even although he and you are enemies, would scorn not to treat you kindly in his own house ; and, indeed, if I didn't do it even in his absence, he would not be pleased with me."

She accordingly brought him in, and placing half-a-dozen of the cakes we spoke of before him, together with a can or two of butter, a side of boiled bacon, and a stack of cabbage, she desired him to help himself—for this, be it known, was long before the invention of potatoes. Cucullin put one of the cakes in his mouth to take a huge whack out of it, when he made a thundering noise, something between a growl and a yell. "Blood and fury!" he shouted ; "how is this? Here are two of my teeth out! What kind of bread this is you gave me."

"What's the matter?" said Oonagh coolly.

"Matter!" shouted the other again ; "why, here are the two best teeth in my head gone."

"Why," said she, "that's Fin's bread—the only bread he ever eats when at home ; but, indeed, I forgot to tell you that nobody can eat it but himself, and that child in the cradle there. I thought, however, that, as you were reported to be rather a stout little fellow of your size, you might be able to manage it, and I did not wish to affront a man that thinks himself able to fight Fin. Here's another cake—maybe it's not so hard as that."

Cucullin at the moment was not only hungry, but ravenous, so he accordingly made a fresh set at the second cake, and immediately another yell was heard twice as loud as the first. "Thunder and gibbets!" he roared, "take your bread out of this, or I will not have a tooth in my head ; there's another pair of them gone!"

" Well, honest man," replied Oonagh, " if you're not able
to eat the bread, say so quietly, and don't be wakening the
child in the cradle there.   There, now, he's awake upon
me."

Fin now gave a skirl that startled the giant, as coming
from such a youngster as he was supposed to be.

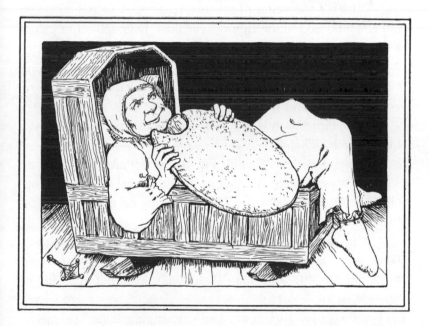

" Mother " said he, " I'm hungry—get me something to eat."
Oonagh went over, and putting into his hand a cake that
had no griddle in it, Fin, whose appetite in the meantime
had been sharpened by seeing eating going forward, soon
swallowed it. Cucullin was thunderstruck, and secretly
thanked his stars that he had the good fortune to miss
meeting Fin, for, as he said to himself, " I'd have no chance
with a man who could eat such bread as that, which even

his son that's but in his cradle can munch before my eyes."

"I'd like to take a glimpse at the lad in the cradle," said he to Oonagh ; "for I can tell you that the infant who can manage that nutriment is no joke to look at, or to feed of a scarce summer."

"With all the veins of my heart," replied Oonagh; "get up, acushla, and show this decent little man something that won't be unworthy of your father, Fin M'Coul."

Fin, who was dressed for the occasion as much like a boy as possible, got up, and bringing Cucullin out, "Are you strong?" said he.

"Thunder an' ounds!" exclaimed the other, "what a voice in so small a chap!"

"Are you strong?" said Fin again ; "are you able to squeeze water out of that white stone?" he asked, putting one into Cucullin's hand. The latter squeezed and squeezed the stone, but in vain.

"Ah, you're a poor creature!" said Fin. "You a giant! Give me the stone here, and when I'll show what Fin's little son can do, you may then judge of what my daddy himself is."

Fin then took the stone, and exchanging it for the curds, he squeezed the latter until the whey, as clear as water, oozed out in a little shower from his hand.

"I'll now go in," said he, "to my cradle; for I scorn to lose my time with any one that's not able to eat my daddy's bread, or squeeze water out of a stone. Bedad, you had better be off out of this before he comes back ; for if he catches you, it's in flummery he'd have you in two minutes."

Cucullin, seeing what he had seen, was of the same opinion himself ; his knees knocked together with the terror of Fin's return, and he accordingly hastened to bid Oonagh farewell, and to assure her, that from that day out, he never wished to hear of, much less to see, her husband. " I admit fairly that I'm not a match for him," said he, " strong as I am ; tell him I will avoid him as I would the plague, and that I will make myself scarce in this part of the country while I live."

Fin, in the meantime, had gone into the cradle, where he lay very quietly, his heart at his mouth with delight that Cucullin was about to take his departure, without discovering the tricks that had been played off on him.

" It's well for you," said Oonagh, " that he doesn't happen to be here, for it's nothing but hawk's meat he'd make of you."

" I know that," says Cucullin ; " divil a thing else he'd make of me ; but before I go, will you let me feel what kind of teeth Fin's lad has got that can eat griddle-bread like that ? "

" With all pleasure in life," said she ; " only, as they're far back in his head, you must put your finger a good way in."

Cucullin was surprised to find such a powerful set of grinders in one so young ; but he was still much more so on finding, when he took his hand from Fin's mouth, that he had left the very finger upon which his whole strength depended, behind him. He gave one loud groan, and fell down at once with terror and weakness. This was all Fin wanted, who now knew that his most powerful and bitterest enemy was at his mercy. He started out of the cradle, and in a few minutes the great Cucullin, that was for such a length of time the terror of him and all his followers, lay a corpse before him. Thus did Fin, through the wit and invention of Oonagh, his wife, succeed in overcoming his enemy by cunning, which he never could have done by force.

Fair, Brown, and Trembling

ING HUGH CÚRUCHA lived in Tir Conal, and he had three daughters, whose names were Fair, Brown, and Trembling.

Fair and Brown had new dresses, and went to church every Sunday. Trembling was kept at home to do the cooking and work. They would not let her go out of the house at all ; for she was more beautiful than the other two, and they were in dread she might marry before themselves.

They carried on in this way for seven years. At the end of seven years the son of the king of Emania fell in love with the eldest sister.

One Sunday morning, after the other two had gone to church, the old henwife came into the kitchen to Trembling, and said : "It's at church you ought to be this day, instead of working here at home."

"How could I go ?" said Trembling. "I have no clothes good enough to wear at church ; and if my sisters were to see me there, they'd kill me for going out of the house."

"I'll give you," said the henwife, "a finer dress than

either of them has ever seen.   And now tell me what dress will you have ? "

" I'll have," said Trembling, " a dress as white as snow, and green shoes for my feet."

Then the henwife put on the cloak of darkness, clipped a piece from the old clothes the young woman had on, and asked for the whitest robes in the world and the most beautiful that could be found, and a pair of green shoes.

That moment she had the robe and the shoes, and she brought them to Trembling, who put them on.   When Trembling was dressed and ready, the henwife said : " I have a honey-bird here to sit on your right shoulder, and a honey-finger to put on your left.   At the door stands a milk-white mare, with a golden saddle for you to sit on, and a golden bridle to hold in your hand."

Trembling sat on the golden saddle ; and when she was ready to start, the henwife said : " You must not go inside the door of the church, and the minute the people rise up at the end of Mass, do you make off, and ride home as fast as the mare will carry you."

When Trembling came to the door of the church there was no one inside who could get a glimpse of her but was striving to know who she was ; and when they saw her hurrying away at the end of Mass, they ran out to overtake her.   But no use in their running ; she was away before any man could come near her.   From the minute she left the church till she got home, she overtook the wind before her, and outstripped the wind behind.

She came down at the door, went in, and found the henwife had dinner ready.   She put off the white robes, and had on her old dress in a twinkling.

When the two sisters came home the henwife asked :
" Have you any news to-day from the church ? "

" We have great news," said they. " We saw a
wonderful grand lady at the church-door. The like of the
robes she had we have never seen on woman before. It's
little that was thought of our dresses beside what she had
on ; and there wasn't a man at the church, from the king
to the beggar, but was trying to look at her and know who
she was."

The sisters would give no peace till they had two dresses
like the robes of the strange lady ; but honey-birds and
honey-fingers were not to be found.

Next Sunday the two sisters went to church again, and
left the youngest at home to cook the dinner.

After they had gone, the henwife came in and asked :
" Will you go to church to-day ? "

" I would go," said Trembling, " if I could get the
going."

" What robe will you wear ? " asked the henwife.

" The finest black satin that can be found, and red shoes
for my feet."

" What colour do you want the mare to be ? "

" I want her to be so black and so glossy that I can see
myself in her body."

The henwife put on the cloak of darkness, and asked for
the robes and the mare. That moment she had them.
When Trembling was dressed, the henwife put the honey-
bird on her right shoulder and the honey-finger on her left.
The saddle on the mare was silver, and so was the bridle.

When Trembling sat in the saddle and was going away,
the henwife ordered her strictly not to go inside the door of

the church, but to rush away as soon as the people rose at the end of Mass, and hurry home on the mare before any man could stop her.

That Sunday the people were more astonished than ever, and gazed at her more than the first time ; and all they were thinking of was to know who she was. But they had no chance ; for the moment the people rose at the end of Mass she slipped from the church, was in the silver saddle, and home before a man could stop her or talk to her.

The henwife had the dinner ready. Trembling took off her satin robe, and had on her old clothes before her sisters got home.

" What news have you to-day ? " asked the henwife of the sisters when they came from the church.

" Oh, we saw the grand strange lady again ! And it's little that any man could think of our dresses after looking at the robes of satin that she had on ! And all at church, from high to low, had their mouths open, gazing at her, and no man was looking at us."

The two sisters gave neither rest nor peace till they got dresses as nearly like the strange lady's robes as they could find. Of course they were not so good ; for the like of those robes could not be found in Erin.

When the third Sunday came, Fair and Brown went to church dressed in black satin. They left Trembling at home to work in the kitchen, and told her to be sure and have dinner ready when they came back.

After they had gone and were out of sight, the henwife came to the kitchen and said : " Well, my dear, are you for church to-day ? "

" I would go if I had a new dress to wear."

"TREMBLING" AT THE CHURCH DOOR

" I'll get you any dress you ask for.   What dress would you like ? " asked the henwife.

" A dress red as a rose from the waist down, and white as snow from the waist up ; a cape of green on my shoulders ; and a hat on my head with a red, a white, and a green feather in it ; and shoes for my feet with the toes red, the middle white, and the backs and heels green."

The henwife put on the cloak of darkness, wished for all these things, and had them.   When Trembling was dressed, the henwife put the honey-bird on her right shoulder and the honey-finger on her left, and, placing the hat on her head, clipped a few hairs from one lock and a few from another with her scissors, and that moment the most beautiful golden hair was flowing down over the girl's shoulders.   Then the henwife asked what kind of a mare she would ride.   She said white, with blue and gold-coloured diamond-shaped spots all over her body, on her back a saddle of gold, and on her head a golden bridle.

The mare stood there before the door, and a bird sitting between her ears, which began to sing as soon as Trembling was in the saddle, and never stopped till she came home from the church.

The fame of the beautiful strange lady had gone out through the world, and all the princes and great men that were in it came to church that Sunday, each one hoping that it was himself would have her home with him after Mass.

The son of the king of Emania forgot all about the eldest sister, and remained outside the church, so as to catch the strange lady before she could hurry away.

The church was more crowded than ever before, and

there were three times as many outside. There was such
a throng before the church that Trembling could only come
inside the gate.

As soon as the people were rising at the end of Mass,
the lady slipped out through the gate, was in the golden
saddle in an instant, and sweeping away ahead of the wind.
But if she was, the prince of Emania was at her side, and,
seizing her by the foot, he ran with the mare for thirty
perches, and never let go of the beautiful lady till the shoe
was pulled from her foot, and he was left behind with it in
his hand. She came home as fast as the mare could carry
her, and was thinking all the time that the henwife would
kill her for losing the shoe.

Seeing her so vexed and so changed in the face, the old
woman asked : " What's the trouble that's on you now ? "

" Oh ! I've lost one of the shoes off my feet," said
Trembling.

" Don't mind that ; don't be vexed," said the henwife ;
" maybe it's the best thing that ever happened to you."

Then Trembling gave up all the things she had to the
henwife, put on her old clothes, and went to work in the
kitchen. When the sisters came home, the henwife asked :
" Have you any news from the church ? "

" We have indeed," said they, " for we saw the grandest
sight to-day. The strange lady came again, in grander
array than before. On herself and the horse she rode were
the finest colours of the world, and between the ears of the
horse was a bird which never stopped singing from the time
she came till she went away. The lady herself is the most
beautiful woman ever seen by man in Erin."

After Trembling had disappeared from the church, the

son of the king of Emania said to the other kings' sons :
" I will have that lady for my own."

They all said : " You didn't win her just by taking the
shoe off her foot ; you'll have to win her by the point of the
sword ; you'll have to fight for her with us before you can
call her your own."

" Well," said the son of the king of Emania, " when I
find the lady that shoe will fit, I'll fight for her, never fear,
before I leave her to any of you."

Then all the kings' sons were uneasy, and anxious to
know who was she that lost the shoe ; and they began to
travel all over Erin to know could they find her. The
prince of Emania and all the others went in a great company
together, and made the round of Erin ; they went everywhere,—north, south, east, and west. They visited every
place where a woman was to be found, and left not a house
in the kingdom they did not search, to know could they find
the woman the shoe would fit, not caring whether she was
rich or poor, of high or low degree.

The prince of Emania always kept the shoe ; and when
the young women saw it, they had great hopes, for it was
of proper size, neither large nor small, and it would beat
any man to know of what material it was made. One
thought it would fit her if she cut a little from her great
toe ; and another, with too short a foot, put something
in the tip of her stocking. But no use ; they only
spoiled their feet, and were curing them for months
afterwards.

The two sisters, Fair and Brown, heard that the princes
of the world were looking all over Erin for the woman that
could wear the shoe, and every day they were talking of

trying it on ; and one day Trembling spoke up and said :
" Maybe it's my foot that the shoe will fit."

" Oh, the breaking of the dog's foot on you!   Why say
so when you were at home every Sunday ? "

They were that way waiting, and scolding the younger
sister, till the princes were near the place.   The day they
were to come, the sisters put Trembling in a closet, and
locked the door on her.   When the company came to the
house, the prince of Emania gave the shoe to the sisters.
But though they tried and tried, it would fit neither of
them.

" Is there any other young woman in the house ? " asked
the prince.

" There is," said Trembling, speaking up in the closet ;
" I'm here."

" Oh ! we have her for nothing but to put out the ashes,"
said the sisters.

But the prince and the others wouldn't leave the house
till they had seen her ; so the two sisters had to open the
door.   When Trembling came out, the shoe was given to
her, and it fitted exactly.

The prince of Emania looked at her and said : " You
are the woman the shoe fits, and you are the woman I took
the shoe from."

Then Trembling spoke up, and said : " Do you stay here
till I return."

Then she went to the henwife's house.   The old woman
put on the cloak of darkness, got everything for her she
had the first Sunday at church, and put her on the white
mare in the same fashion.   Then Trembling rode along
the highway to the front of the house.   All who saw

her the first time said : " This is the lady we saw at church."

Then she went away a second time, and a second time came back on the black mare in the second dress which the henwife gave her. All who saw her the second Sunday said : " That is the lady we saw at church."

A third time she asked for a short absence, and soon came back on the third mare and in the third dress. All who saw her the third time said : " That is the lady we saw at church." Every man was satisfied, and knew that she was the woman.

Then all the princes and great men spoke up, and said to the son of the king of Emania : " You'll have to fight now for her before we let her go with you."

" I'm here before you, ready for combat," answered the prince.

Then the son of the king of Lochlin stepped forth. The struggle began, and a terrible struggle it was. They fought for nine hours ; and then the son of the king of Lochlin stopped, gave up his claim, and left the field. Next day the son of the king of Spain fought six hours, and yielded his claim. On the third day the son of the king of Nyerfói fought eight hours, and stopped. The fourth day the son of the king of Greece fought six hours, and stopped. On the fifth day no more strange princes wanted to fight ; and all the sons of kings in Erin said they would not fight with a man of their own land, that the strangers had had their chance, and, as no others came to claim the woman, she belonged of right to the son of the king of Emania.

The marriage-day was fixed, and the invitations were sent out. The wedding lasted for a year and a day. When the wedding was over, the king's son brought home the bride, and when the time came a son was born. The young woman sent for her eldest sister, Fair, to be with her and care for her. One day, when Trembling was well, and when her husband was away hunting, the two sisters went out to walk ; and when they came to the seaside, the eldest pushed the youngest sister in. A great whale came and swallowed her.

The eldest sister came home alone, and the husband asked, " Where is your sister ? "

" She has gone home to her father in Ballyshannon ; now that I am well, I don't need her."

" Well," said the husband, looking at her, " I'm in dread it's my wife that has gone."

" Oh ! no," said she ; " it's my sister Fair that's gone."

Since the sisters were very much alike, the prince was in doubt. That night he put his sword between them, and said : " If you are my wife, this sword will get warm ; if not, it will stay cold."

In the morning when he rose up, the sword was as cold as when he put it there.

It happened, when the two sisters were walking by the seashore, that a little cowboy was down by the water minding cattle, and saw Fair push Trembling into the sea ; and next day, when the tide came in, he saw the whale swim up and throw her out on the sand. When she was on the sand she said to the cowboy : " When you go home in the evening with the cows, tell the master that my sister Fair pushed me into the sea yesterday ; that a whale swallowed me, and then threw me out, but will come again and swallow me with the coming of the next tide ; then he'll go out with the tide, and come again with to-morrow's tide, and throw me again on the strand. The whale will cast me out three times. I'm under the enchantment of this whale, and cannot leave the beach or escape myself. Unless my husband saves me before I'm swallowed the fourth time, I shall be lost. He must come and shoot the whale with a silver bullet when he turns on the broad of his back. Under the breast-fin of the whale is a reddish-brown spot. My husband must hit him in that spot, for it is the only place in which he can be killed."

When the cowboy got home, the eldest sister gave him a draught of oblivion, and he did not tell.

Next day he went again to the sea. The whale came and cast Trembling on shore again. She asked the boy : " Did you tell the master what I told you to tell him ? "

" I did not," said he ; " I forgot."

" How did you forget ? " asked she.

" The woman of the house gave me a drink that made me forget."

" Well, don't forget telling him this night ; and if she gives you a drink, don't take it from her."

As soon as the cowboy came home, the eldest sister offered him a drink. He refused to take it till he had delivered his message and told all to the master. The third day the prince went down with his gun and a silver bullet in it. He was not long down when the whale came and threw Trembling upon the beach as the two days before. She had no power to speak to her husband till he had killed the whale. Then the whale went out, turned over once on the broad of his back, and showed the spot for a moment only. That moment the prince fired. He had but the one chance, and a short one at that ; but he took it, and hit the spot, and the whale, mad with pain, made the sea all around red with blood, and died.

That minute Trembling was able to speak, and went home with her husband, who sent word to her father what the eldest sister had done. The father came, and told him any death he chose to give her to give it. The prince told the father he would leave her life and death with himself. The father had her put out then on the sea in a barrel, with provisions in it for seven years.

In time Trembling had a second child, a daughter. The prince and she sent the cowboy to school, and trained him up as one of their own children, and said : " If the little girl that is born to us now lives, no other man in the world will get her but him."

The cowboy and the prince's daughter lived on till

they were married. The mother said to her husband : "You could not have saved me from the whale but for the little cowboy ; on that account I don't grudge him my daughter."

The son of the king of Emania and Trembling had fourteen children, and they lived happily till the two died of old age.

Jack and His Master

POOR woman had three sons. The eldest and second eldest were cunning clever fellows, but they called the youngest Jack the Fool, because they thought he was no better than a simpleton. The eldest got tired of staying at home, and said he'd go look for service. He stayed away a whole year, and then came back one day, dragging one foot after the other, and a poor wizened face on him, and he as cross as two sticks. When he was rested and got something to eat, he told them how he got service with the Gray Churl of the Townland of Mischance, and that the agreement was, whoever would first say he was sorry for his bargain, should get an inch wide of the skin of his back, from shoulder to hips, taken off. If it was the master, he should also pay double wages; if it was the servant, he should get no wages at all. "But the thief," says he, "gave me so little to eat, and kept me so hard at work, that flesh and blood couldn't stand it; and when he asked me once, when I was in a passion, if I was sorry for my bargain, I was mad enough to say I was, and here I am disabled for life."

Vexed enough were the poor mother and brothers ; and the second eldest said on the spot he'd go and take service with the Gray Churl, and punish him by all the annoyance he'd give him till he'd make him say he was sorry for his agreement. "Oh, won't I be glad to see the skin coming off the old villain's back!" said he. All they could say had no effect : he started off for the Townland of Mischance, and in a twelvemonth he was back just as miserable and helpless as his brother.

All the poor mother could say didn't prevent Jack the Fool from starting to see if he was able to regulate the Gray Churl. He agreed with him for a year for twenty pounds, and the terms were the same.

"Now, Jack," said the Gray Churl, "if you refuse to do anything you are able to do, you must lose a month's wages."

"I'm satisfied," said Jack ; "and if you stop me from doing a thing after telling me to do it, you are to give me an additional month's wages."

"I am satisfied," says the master.

"Or if you blame me for obeying your orders, you must give the same."

"I am satisfied," said the master again.

The first day that Jack served he was fed very poorly, and was worked to the saddleskirts. Next day he came in just before the dinner was sent up to the parlour. They were taking the goose off the spit, but well becomes Jack he whips a knife off the dresser, and cuts off one side of the breast, one leg and thigh, and one wing, and fell to. In came the master, and began to abuse him for his assurance. "Oh, you know, master, you're to feed me, and wherever the goose goes won't have to be filled again till supper. Are you sorry for our agreement?"

The master was going to cry out he was, but he bethought himself in time. " Oh no, not at all," said he.

" That's well," said Jack.

Next day Jack was to go clamp turf on the bog. They weren't sorry to have him away from the kitchen at dinner time. He didn't find his breakfast very heavy on his stomach ; so he said to the mistress, " I think, ma'am, it will be better for me to get my dinner now, and not lose time coming home from the bog."

" That's true, Jack," said she. So she brought out a good cake, and a print of butter, and a bottle of milk, thinking he'd take them away to the bog. But Jack kept his seat, and never drew rein till bread, butter, and milk went down the red lane.

" Now, mistress," said he, " I'll be earlier at my work to-morrow if I sleep comfortably on the sheltery side of a pile of dry peat on dry grass, and not be coming here and going back. So you may as well give me my supper, and be done with the day's trouble." She gave him that, thinking he'd take it to the bog ; but he fell to on the spot, and did not leave a scrap to tell tales on him ; and the mistress was a little astonished.

He called to speak to the master in the haggard, and said he, " What are servants asked to do in this country after aten their supper?"

" Nothing at all, but to go to bed."

" Oh, very well, sir." He went up on the stable-loft, stripped, and lay down, and some one that saw him told the master. He came up.

"Jack, you anointed scoundrel, what do you mean ? "

"To go to sleep, master. The mistress, God bless her, is after giving me my breakfast, dinner, and supper, and yourself told me that bed was the next thing. Do you blame me, sir ? "

"Yes, you rascal, I do."

"Hand me out one pound thirteen and fourpence, if you please, sir."

"One divel and thirteen imps, you tinker! what for ? "

"Oh, I see, you've forgot your bargain. Are you sorry for it ? "

"Oh, ya—no, I mean. I'll give you the money after your nap."

Next morning early, Jack asked how he'd be employed that day. "You are to be holding the plough in that fallow, outside the paddock." The master went over about nine o'clock to see what kind of a ploughman was Jack, and what did he see but the little boy driving the bastes, and the sock and coulter of the plough skimming along the sod, and Jack pulling ding-dong again' the horses.

"What are you doing, you contrary thief ? " said the master.

"An' ain't I strivin' to hold this divel of a plough, as you told me ; but that ounkrawn of a boy keeps whipping on the bastes in spite of all I say ; will you speak to him ? "

"No, but I'll speak to you. Didn't you know, you bosthoon, that when I said 'holding the plough,' I meant reddening the ground."

"Faith, an' if you did, I wish you had said so. Do you blame me for what I have done ? "

The master caught himself in time, but he was so stomached, he said nothing.

" Go on and redden the ground now, you knave, as other ploughmen do."

" An' are you sorry for our agreement ? "

" Oh, not at all, not at all ! "

Jack ploughed away like a good workman all the rest of the day.

In a day or two the master bade him go and mind the cows in a field that had half of it under young corn. " Be sure, particularly," said he, " to keep Browney from the wheat ; while she's out of mischief there's no fear of the rest."

About noon, he went to see how Jack was doing his duty, and what did he find but Jack asleep with his face to the sod, Browney grazing near a thorn-tree, one end of a long rope round her horns, and the other end round the tree, and the rest of the beasts all trampling and eating the green wheat. Down came the switch on Jack.

" Jack, you vagabone, do you see what the cows are at ? "

" And do you blame, master ? "

" To be sure, you lazy sluggard, I do ? "

" Hand me out one pound thirteen and fourpence, master. You said if I only kept Browney out of mischief, the rest would do no harm. There she is as harmless as a lamb. Are you sorry for hiring me, master ? "

" To be—that is, not at all. I'll give you your money when you go to dinner. Now, understand me ; don't let a cow go out of the field nor into the wheat the rest of the day."

" Never fear, master ! " and neither did he. But the

churl would rather than a great deal he had not hired him.

The next day three heifers were missing, and the master bade Jack go in search of them.

"Where will I look for them?" said Jack.

"Oh, every place likely and unlikely for them all to be in."

The churl was getting very exact in his words. When he was coming into the bawn at dinner-time, what work did he find Jack at but pulling armfuls of the thatch off the roof, and peeping into the holes he was making?

"What are you doing there, you rascal?"

"Sure, I'm looking for the heifers, poor things!"

"What would bring them there?"

"I don't think anything could bring them in it; but I looked first into the likely places, that is, the cow-houses, and the pastures, and the fields next 'em, and now I'm looking in the unlikeliest place I can think of. Maybe it's not pleasing to you it is."

"And to be sure it isn't pleasing to me, you aggravating goose-cap!"

"Please, sir, hand me one pound thirteen and four pence before you sit down to your dinner. I'm afraid it's sorrow that's on you for hiring me at all."

" May the div—oh no ; I'm not sorry. Will you begin, if you please, and put in the thatch again, just as if you were doing it for your mother's cabin ? "

" Oh, faith I will, sir, with a heart and a half ;" and by the time the farmer came out from his dinner, Jack had the roof better than it was before, for he made the boy give him new straw.

Says the master when he came out, " Go, Jack, and look for the heifers, and bring them home."

" And where will I look for 'em ? "

" Go and search for them as if they were your own." The heifers were all in the paddock before sunset.

Next morning, says the master, " Jack, the path across the bog to the pasture is very bad ; the sheep does be sinking in it every step ; go and make the sheep's feet a good path." About an hour after he came to the edge of the bog, and what did he find Jack at but sharpening a carving knife, and the sheep standing or grazing round.

" Is this the way you are mending the path, Jack ? " said he.

" Everything must have a beginning, master," said Jack, " and a thing well begun is half done. I am sharpening the knife, and I'll have the feet off every sheep in the flock while you'd be blessing yourself."

" Feet off my sheep, you anointed rogue ! and what would you be taking their feet off for ? "

" An' sure to mend the path as you told me. Says you, ' Jack, make a path with the foot of the sheep.' "

" Oh, you fool, I meant make good the path for the sheep's feet."

" It's a pity you didn't say so, master. Hand me out

one pound thirteen and fourpence if you don't like me to finish my job."

"Divel do you good with your one pound thirteen and fourpence!"

"It's better pray than curse, master. Maybe you're sorry for your bargain?"

"And to be sure I am——not yet, any way."

The next night the master was going to a wedding; and says he to Jack, before he set out : " I'll leave at midnight, and I wish you to come and be with me home, for fear I might be overtaken with the drink. If you're there before, you may throw a sheep's eye at me, and I'll be sure to see that they'll give you something for yourself."

About eleven o'clock, while the master was in great spirits, he felt something clammy hit him on the cheek. It fell beside his tumbler, and when he looked at it what was it but the eye of a sheep. Well, he couldn't imagine who threw it at him, or why it was thrown at him. After a little he got a blow on the other cheek, and still it was by another sheep's eye. Well, he was very vexed, but he thought better to say nothing. In two minutes more, when he was opening his mouth to take a sup, another sheep's eye was slapped into it. He sputtered it out, and cried, "Man o' the house, isn't it a great shame for you to have any one in the room that would do such a nasty thing?"

"Master," says Jack, "don't blame the honest man. Sure it's only myself that was throwin' them sheep's eyes at you, to remind you I was here, and that I wanted to drink the bride and bridegroom's health. You know yourself bade me."

"I know that you are a great rascal ; and where did you get the eyes ? "

"An' where would I get em' but in the heads of your own sheep ? Would you have me meddle with the bastes of any neighbour, who might put me in the Stone Jug for it ? "

"Sorrow on me that ever I had the bad luck to meet with you."

"You're all witness," said Jack, "that my master says he is sorry for having met with me. My time is up. Master, hand me over double wages, and come into the next room, and lay yourself out like a man that has some decency in him, till I take a strip of skin an inch broad from your shoulder to your hip."

Every one shouted out against that ; but, says Jack, "You didn't hinder him when he took the same strips from the backs of my two brothers, and sent them home in that state, and penniless, to their poor mother."

When the company heard the rights of the business, they were only too eager to see the job done. The master bawled and roared, but there was no help at hand. He was stripped to his hips, and laid on the floor in the next room, and Jack had the carving knife in his hand ready to begin..

"Now you cruel old villain," said he, giving the knife a couple of scrapes along the floor, "I'll make you an offer. Give me, along with my double wages, two hundred guineas to support my poor brothers, and I'll do without the strap."

"No ! " said he, " I'd let you skin me from head to foot first."

" Here goes then," said Jack with a grin, but the first little scar he gave, Churl roared out, " Stop your hand ; I'll give the money."

" Now, neighbours," said Jack, " you mustn't think worse of me than I deserve. I wouldn't have the heart to take an eye out of a rat itself ; I got half a dozen of them from the butcher, and only used three of them."

So all came again into the other room, and Jack was made sit down, and everybody drank his health, and he drank everybody's health at one offer. And six stout fellows saw himself and the master home, and waited in the parlour while he went up and brought down the two hundred guineas, and double wages for Jack himself. When he got home, he brought the summer along with him to the poor mother and the disabled brothers ; and he was no more Jack the Fool in the people's mouths, but " Skin Churl Jack."

Beth Gellert

PRINCE LLEWELYN had a favourite greyhound named Gellert that had been given to
him by his father-in-law, King John. He was
as gentle as a lamb at home but a lion in
the chase. One day Llewelyn went to the
chase and blew his horn in front of his castle. All his other
dogs came to the call but Gellert never answered it. So
he blew a louder blast on his horn and called Gellert by
name, but still the greyhound did not come. At last Prince
Llewelyn could wait no longer and went off to the hunt
without Gellert. He had little sport that day because
Gellert was not there, the swiftest and boldest of his hounds.

He turned back in a rage to his castle, and as he came
to the gate, who should he see but Gellert come bounding
out to meet him. But when the hound came near him, the
Prince was startled to see that his lips and fangs were
dripping with blood. Llewelyn started back and the greyhound crouched down at his feet as if surprised or afraid at
the way his master greeted him.

Now Prince Llewelyn had a little son a year old with
whom Gellert used to play, and a terrible thought crossed
the Prince's mind that made him rush towards the child's
nursery. And the nearer he came the more blood and dis-

order he found about the rooms. He rushed into it and found the child's cradle overturned and daubed with blood.

Prince Llewelyn grew more and more terrified, and sought for his little son everywhere. He could find him nowhere but only signs of some terrible conflict in which much blood had been shed. At last he felt sure the dog had destroyed his child, and shouting to Gellert, " Monster, thou hast devoured my child," he drew out his sword and plunged it in the greyhound's side, who fell with a deep yell and still gazing in his master's eyes.

As Gellert raised his dying yell, a little child's cry answered it from beneath the cradle, and there Llewelyn found his child unharmed and just awakened from sleep. But just beside him lay the body of a great gaunt wolf all torn to pieces and covered with blood. Too late, Llewelyn learned what had happened while he was away.   Gellert had stayed behind to guard the child and had fought and slain the wolf that had tried to destroy Llewelyn's heir.

In vain was all Llewelyn's grief ; he could not bring his faithful dog to life again.   So he buried him outside the castle walls within sight of the great mountain of Snowdon, where every passer-by might see his grave, and raised over it a great cairn of stones.   And to this day the place is called Beth Gellert, or the Grave of Gellert.

The Tale of Ivan

HERE were formerly a man and a woman living in the parish of Llanlavan, in the place which is called Hwrdh. And work became scarce, so the man said to his wife, "I will go search for work, and you may live here." So he took fair leave, and travelled far toward the East, and at last came to the house of a farmer and asked for work.

"What work can ye do?" said the farmer.

"I can do all kinds of work," said Ivan.

Then they agreed upon three pounds for the year's wages.

When the end of the year came his master showed him the three pounds. "See, Ivan," said he, "here's your wage; but if you will give it me back I'll give you a piece of advice instead."

"Give me my wage," said Ivan.

" No, I'll not," said the master; " I'll explain my advice."

" Tell it me, then," said Ivan.

Then said the master, " Never leave the old road for the sake of a new one."

After that they agreed for another year at the old wages, and at the end of it Ivan took instead a piece of advice, and this was it : " Never lodge where an old man is married to a young woman."

The same thing happened at the end of the third year, when the piece of advice was : " Honesty is the best policy."

But Ivan would not stay longer, but wanted to go back to his wife.

" Don't go to-day," said his master ; " my wife bakes to-morrow, and she shall make thee a cake to take home to thy good woman."

And when Ivan was going to leave, " Here," said his master, " here is a cake for thee to take home to thy wife, and, when ye are most joyous together, then break the cake, and not sooner."

So he took fair leave of them and travelled towards home, and at last he came to Wayn Her, and there he met three merchants from Tre Rhyn, of his own parish, coming home from Exeter Fair.   " Oho! Ivan," said they, " come with us ; glad are we to see you.   Where have you been so long ? "

" I have been in service," said Ivan, " and now I'm going home to my wife."

" Oh, come with us ! you'll be right welcome."

But when they took the new road Ivan kept to the old

one. And robbers fell upon them before they had gone far from Ivan as they were going by the fields of the houses in the meadow. They began to cry out, " Thieves ! " and Ivan shouted out " Thieves ! " too. And when the robbers heard Ivan's shout they ran away, and the merchants went by the new road and Ivan by the old one till they met again at Market-Jew.

" Oh, Ivan," said the merchants, " we are beholding to you ; but for you we would have been lost men. Come lodge with us at our cost, and welcome."

When they came to the place where they used to lodge, Ivan said, " I must see the host."

" The host," they cried ; " what do you want with the host ? Here is the hostess, and she's young and pretty. If you want to see the host you'll find him in the kitchen."

So he went into the kitchen to see the host ; he found him a weak old man turning the spit.

" Oh ! oh ! " quoth Ivan, " I'll not lodge here, but will go next door."

" Not yet," said the merchants, " sup with us, and welcome."

Now it happened that the hostess had plotted with a certain monk in Market-Jew to murder the old man in his bed that night while the rest were asleep, and they agreed to lay it on the lodgers.

So while Ivan was in bed next door, there was a hole in the pine-end of the house, and he saw a light through it. So he got up and looked, and heard the monk speaking. " I had better cover this hole," said he, " or people in the next house may see our deeds." So he stood with his back against it while the hostess killed the old man.

But meanwhile Ivan out with his knife, and putting it through the hole, cut a round piece off the monk's robe.

The very next morning the hostess raised the cry that her husband was murdered, and as there was neither man nor child in the house but the merchants, she declared they ought to be hanged for it.

So they were taken and carried to prison, till at last Ivan came to them. " Alas ! alas ! Ivan," cried they, " bad luck sticks to us ; our host was killed last night, and we shall be hanged for it."

" Ah, tell the justices," said Ivan, " to summon the real murderers."

" Who knows," they replied, " who committed the crime ? "

" Who committed the crime ! " said Ivan. " If I cannot prove who committed the crime, hang me in your stead."

So he told all he knew, and brought out the piece of cloth from the monk's robe, and with that the merchants were set at liberty, and the hostess and the monk were seized and hanged.

Then they came all together out of Market-Jew, and they said to him : " Come as far as Coed Carrn y Wylfa, the Wood of the Heap of Stones of Watching, in the parish of Burman. Then their two roads separated, and though the merchants wished Ivan to go with them, he would not go with them, but went straight home to his wife.

And when his wife saw him she said : " Home in the nick of time. Here's a purse of gold that I've found ; it has no name, but sure it belongs to the great lord yonder. I was just thinking what to do when you came."

Then Ivan thought of the third counsel, and he said: " Let us go and give it to the great lord."

So they went up to the castle, but the great lord was not in it, so they left the purse with the servant that minded the gate, and then they went home again and lived in quiet for a time.

But one day the great lord stopped at their house for a drink of water, and Ivan's wife said to him: " I hope your lordship found your lordship's purse quite safe with all its money in it."

" What purse is that you are talking about ? " said the lord.

" Sure, it's your lordship's purse that I left at the castle," said Ivan.

" Come with me and we will see into the matter," said the lord.

So Ivan and his wife went up to the castle, and there they pointed out the man to whom they had given the purse, and he had to give it up and was sent away from the castle. And the lord was so pleased with Ivan that he made him his servant in the stead of the thief.

" Honesty's the best policy ! " quoth Ivan, as he skipped about in his new quarters. " How joyful I am ! "

Then he thought of his old master's cake that he was to eat when he was most joyful, and when he broke it, lo and behold, inside it was his wages for the three years he had been with him.

Andrew Coffey

Y grandfather, Andrew Coffey, was known
to the whole barony as a quiet, decent
man. And if the whole barony knew
him, he knew the whole barony, every
inch, hill and dale, bog and pasture,
field and covert. Fancy his surprise one
evening, when he found himself in a part of the demesne
he couldn't recognise a bit. He and his good horse were
always stumbling up against some tree or stumbling down
into some bog-hole that by rights didn't ought to be there.
On the top of all this the rain came pelting down wherever there was a clearing, and the cold March wind tore
through the trees. Glad he was then when he saw a light
in the distance, and drawing near found a cabin, though
for the life of him he couldn't think how it came there.
However, in he walked, after tying up his horse, and right
welcome was the brushwood fire blazing on the hearth.
And there stood a chair right and tight, that seemed to say,
" Come, sit down in me." There wasn't a soul else in the
room. Well, he did sit, and got a little warm and cheered

after his drenching. But all the while he was wondering and wondering.

"Andrew Coffey! Andrew Coffey!"

Good heavens! who was calling him, and not a soul in sight? Look around as he might, indoors and out, he could find no creature with two legs or four, for his horse was gone.

"ANDREW COFFEY! ANDREW COFFEY! tell me a story."

It was louder this time, and it was nearer. And then what a thing to ask for! It was bad enough not to be let sit by the fire and dry oneself, without being bothered for a story.

"**Andrew Coffey! Andrew Coffey!** Tell me a story, or it'll be the worse for you."

My poor grandfather was so dumbfounded that he could only stand and stare.

"ANDREW COFFEY! ANDREW COFFEY! I told you it'd be the worse for you."

And with that, out there bounced, from a cupboard that Andrew Coffey had never noticed before, *a man*. And the man was in a towering rage. But it wasn't that. And he carried as fine a blackthorn as you'd wish to crack a man's head with. But it wasn't that either. But when my grandfather clapped eyes on him, he knew him for Patrick Rooney, and all the world knew *he'd* gone overboard, fishing one night long years before.

Andrew Coffey would neither stop nor stay, but he took to his heels and was out of the house as hard as he could. He ran and he ran taking little thought of what was before till at last he ran up against a big tree. And then he sat down to rest.

He hadn't sat for a moment when he heard voices. "It's heavy he is, the vagabond." "Steady now, we'll rest when we get under the big tree yonder." Now that happened to be the tree under which Andrew Coffey was sitting. At least he thought so, for seeing a branch handy he swung himself up by it and was soon snugly hidden away. Better see than be seen, thought he.

The rain had stopped and the wind fallen. The night was blacker than ever, but Andrew Coffey could see four men, and they were carrying between them a long box. Under the tree they came, set the box down, opened it, and who should they bring out but—Patrick Rooney. Never a word did he say, and he looked as pale as old snow.

Well, one gathered brushwood, and another took out tinder and flint, and soon they had a big fire roaring, and my grandfather could see Patrick plainly enough. If he had kept still before, he kept stiller now. Soon they had four poles up and a pole across, right over the fire, for all the world like a spit, and on to the pole they slung Patrick Rooney.

"He'll do well enough," said one ; "but who's to mind him whilst we're away, who'll turn the fire, who'll see that he doesn't burn ?"

With that Patrick opened his lips : "Andrew Coffey," said he.

"Andrew Coffey! Andrew Coffey! Andrew Coffey! Andrew Coffey!"

"I'm much obliged to you, gentlemen," said Andrew Coffey, "but indeed I know nothing about the business."

"You'd better come down, Andrew Coffey," said Patrick.

It was the second time he spoke, and Andrew Coffey decided he would come down. The four men went off and he was left all alone with Patrick.

Then he sat and he kept the fire even, and he kept the spit turning, and all the while Patrick looked at him.

Poor Andrew Coffey couldn't make it all out at all, at all, and he stared at Patrick and at the fire, and he thought of the little house in the wood, till he felt quite dazed.

"Ah, but it's burning me ye are!" says Patrick, very short and sharp.

"I'm sure I beg your pardon," said my grandfather "but might I ask you a question?"

"If you want a crooked answer," said Patrick; "turn away or it'll be the worse for you."

But my grandfather couldn't get it out of his head; hadn't everybody, far and near, said Patrick had fallen overboard. There was enough to think about, and my grandfather did think.

"**Andrew Coffey! Andrew Coffey! it's burning me ye are.**"

Sorry enough my grandfather was, and he vowed he wouldn't do so again.

"You'd better not," said Patrick, and he gave him a cock of his eye, and a grin of his teeth, that just sent a shiver down Andrew Coffey's back. Well it was odd, that here he should be in a thick wood he had never set eyes upon, turning Patrick Rooney upon a spit. You can't wonder at my grandfather thinking and thinking and not minding the fire.

"Andrew Coffey, Andrew Coffey, it's the death of you I'll be."

And with that what did my grandfather see, but Patrick unslinging himself from the spit and his eyes glared and his teeth glistened.

It was neither stop nor stay my grandfather made, but out he ran into the night of the wood.   It seemed to him

there wasn't a stone but was for his stumbling, not a branch but beat his face, not a bramble but tore his skin.   And wherever it was clear the rain pelted down and the cold March wind howled along.

Glad he was to see a light, and a minute after he was kneeling, dazed, drenched, and bedraggled by the hearth side.   The brushwood flamed, and the brushwood crackled, and soon my grandfather began to feel a little warm and dry and easy in his mind.

"Andrew Coffey! Andrew Coffey!"

It's hard for a man to jump when he has been through all my grandfather had, but jump he did.   And when he looked around, where should he find himself but in the very cabin he had first met Patrick in.

" Andrew Coffey, Andrew Coffey, tell me a story."

" Is it a story you want ?" said my grandfather as bold as may be, for he was just tired of being frightened. " Well if you can tell me the rights of this one, I'll be thankful."

And he told the tale of what had befallen him from first to last that night. The tale was long, and may be Andrew Coffey was weary. It's asleep he must have fallen, for when he awoke he lay on the hill-side under the open heavens, and his horse grazed at his side.

The Battle of the Birds

 WILL tell you a story about the wren. There was once a farmer who was seeking a servant, and the wren met him and said : " What are you seeking ? "

" I am seeking a servant," said the farmer to the wren.

" Will you take me ? " said the wren.

" You, you poor creature, what good would you do ? "

" Try me," said the wren.

So he engaged him, and the first work he set him to do was threshing in the barn. The wren threshed (what did he thresh with ? Why a flail to be sure), and he knocked off one grain. A mouse came out and she eats that.

" I'll trouble you not to do that again," said the wren.

He struck again, and he struck off two grains. Out came the mouse and she eats them. So they arranged a contest to see who was strongest, and the wren brings his twelve birds, and the mouse her tribe.

" You have your tribe with you," said the wren.

" As well as yourself," said the mouse, and she struck out her leg proudly.   But the wren broke it with his flail, and there was a pitched battle on a set day.

When every creature and bird was gathering to battle, the son of the king of Tethertown said that he would go to see the battle, and that he would bring sure word home to his father the king, who would be king of the creatures this year.   The battle was over before he arrived all but one fight, between a great black raven and a snake.   The snake was twined about the raven's neck, and the raven held the snake's throat in his beak, and it seemed as if the snake would get the victory over the raven.   When the king's son saw this he helped the raven, and with one blow takes the head off the snake.   When the raven had taken breath, and saw that the snake was dead, he said, " For thy kindness to me this day, I will give thee a sight. Come up now on the root of my two wings."   The king's son put his hands about the raven before his wings, and, before he stopped, he took him over nine Bens, and nine Glens, and nine Mountain Moors.

" Now," said the raven, " see you that house yonder ? Go now to it.   It is a sister of mine that makes her dwelling in it ; and I will go bail that you are welcome. And if she asks you, Were you at the battle of the birds ? say you were.   And if she asks, ' Did you see any one like me,' say you did, but be sure that you meet me to-morrow morning here, in this place."   The king's son got good and right good treatment that night.   Meat of each meat, drink of each drink, warm water to his feet, and a soft bed for his limbs.

On the next day the raven gave him the same sight over six Bens, and six Glens, and six Mountain Moors. They saw a bothy far off, but, though far off, they were soon there. He got good treatment this night, as before—plenty of meat and drink, and warm water to his feet, and a soft bed to his limbs—and on the next day it was the same thing, over three Bens and three Glens, and three Mountain Moors.

On the third morning, instead of seeing the raven as at the other times, who should meet him but the handsomest lad he ever saw, with gold rings in his hair, with a bundle in his hand. The king's son asked this lad if he had seen a big black raven.

Said the lad to him, " You will never see the raven again, for I am that raven. I was put under spells by a bad druid ; it was meeting you that loosed me, and for that you shall get this bundle. Now," said the lad, " you must turn back on the self-same steps, and lie a night in each house as before ; but you must not loose the bundle which I gave ye, till in the place where you would most wish to dwell."

The king's son turned his back to the lad, and his face to his father's house ; and he got lodging from the raven's sisters, just as he got it when going forward. When he was nearing his father's house he was going through a close wood. It seemed to him that the bundle was growing heavy, and he thought he would look what was in it.

When he loosed the bundle he was astonished. In a twinkling he sees the very grandest place he ever saw. A great castle, and an orchard about the castle, in which was every kind of fruit and herb. He stood full of wonder and regret for having loosed the bundle—for it was not in his power to put it back again—and he would have wished this pretty place to be in the pretty little green hollow that was opposite his father's house ; but he looked up and saw a great giant coming towards him.

" Bad's the place where you have built the house, king's son," says the giant.

" Yes, but it is not here I would wish it to be, though it happens to be here by mishap," says the king's son.

" What's the reward for putting it back in the bundle as it was before ? "

" What's the reward you would ask?" says the king's son.

" That you will give me the first son you have when he is seven years of age," says the giant.

" If I have a son you shall have him," said the king's son.

In a twinkling the giant put each garden, and orchard, and castle in the bundle as they were before.

" Now," says the giant, " take your own road, and I will take mine ; but mind your promise, and if you forget I will remember."

The king's son took to the road, and at the end of a few days he reached the place he was fondest of. He loosed the bundle, and the castle was just as it was before. And when he opened the castle door he sees the handsomest maiden he ever cast eye upon.

" Advance, king's son," said the pretty maid ; " every- thing is in order for you, if you will marry me this very day."

" It's I that am willing," said the king's son. And on the same day they married.

But at the end of a day and seven years, who should be seen coming to the castle but the giant. The king's son was reminded of his promise to the giant, and till now he had not told his promise to the queen.

"Leave the matter between me and the giant," says the queen.

"Turn out your son," says the giant; "mind your promise."

"You shall have him," says the king, "when his mother puts him in order for his journey."

The queen dressed up the cook's son, and she gave him to the giant by the hand. The giant went away with him; but he had not gone far when he put a rod in the hand of the little laddie. The giant asked him—

"If thy father had that rod what would he do with it?"

"If my father had that rod he would beat the dogs and the cats, so that they shouldn't be going near the king's meat," said the little laddie.

"Thou'rt the cook's son," said the giant. He catches him by the two small ankles and knocks him against the stone that was beside him. The giant turned back to the castle in rage and madness, and he said that if they did not send out the king's son to him, the highest stone of the castle would be the lowest.

Said the queen to the king, "We'll try it yet; the butler's son is of the same age as our son."

She dressed up the butler's son, and she gives him to the giant by the hand. The giant had not gone far when he put the rod in his hand.

"If thy father had that rod," says the giant, "what would he do with it?"

" He would beat the dogs and the cats when they would be coming near the king's bottles and glasses."

" Thou art the son of the butler," says the giant and dashed his brains out too. The giant returned in a very great rage and anger. The earth shook under the sole of his feet, and the castle shook and all that was in it.

" OUT HERE WITH THY SON," says the giant, " or in a twinkling the stone that is highest in the dwelling will be the lowest." So they had to give the king's son to the giant.

When they were gone a little bit from the earth, the giant showed him the rod that was in his hand and said: " What would thy father do with this rod if he had it ? "

The king's son said : " My father has a braver rod than that."

And the giant asked him, " Where is thy father when he has that brave rod ? "

And the king's son said: " He will be sitting in his kingly chair."

Then the giant understood that he had the right one.

The giant took him to his own house, and he reared him as his own son. On a day of days when the giant was from home, the lad heard the sweetest music he ever heard in a room at the top of the giant's house. At a glance he saw the finest face he had ever seen. She beckoned to him to come a bit nearer to her, and she said her name was Auburn Mary but she told him to go this time, but to be sure to be at the same place about that dead midnight.

And as he promised he did. The giant's daughter was at his side in a twinkling, and she said, " To-morrow you will get the choice of my two sisters to marry ; but say

that you will not take either, but me. My father wants me
to marry the son of the king of the Green City, but I don't
like him." On the morrow the giant took out his three
daughters, and he said :

" Now, son of the king of Tethertown, thou hast not lost
by living with me so long. Thou wilt get to wife one of
the two eldest of my daughters, and with her leave to go
home with her the day after the wedding."

" If you will give me this pretty little one," says the
king's son, " I will take you at your word."

The giant's wrath kindled, and he said : " Before thou
gett'st her thou must do the three things that I ask thee to
do."

" Say on," says the king's son.

The giant took him to the byre.

" Now," says the giant, " a hundred cattle are stabled
here, and it has not been cleansed for seven years. I am
going from home to-day, and if this byre is not cleaned
before night comes, so clean that a golden apple will run
from end to end of it, not only thou shalt not get my
daughter, but 'tis only a drink of thy fresh, goodly, beautiful blood that will quench my thirst this night."

He begins cleaning the byre, but he might just as well
to keep baling the great ocean. After midday when sweat
was blinding him, the giant's youngest daughter came
where he was, and she said to him :

" You are being punished, king's son."

" I am that," says the king's son.

" Come over," says Auburn Mary, " and lay down your
weariness."

" I will do that," says he, " there is but death awaiting

me, at any rate." He sat down near her. He was so tired that he fell asleep beside her. When he awoke, the giant's daughter was not to be seen, but the byre was so well cleaned that a golden apple would run from end to end of it and raise no stain. In comes the giant, and he said :

" Hast thou cleaned the byre, king's son ? "

" I have cleaned it," says he.

" Somebody cleaned it," says the giant.

" You did not clean it, at all events," said the king's son.

" Well, well !" says the giant, " since thou wert so active to-day, thou wilt get to this time to-morrow to thatch this byre with birds' down, from birds with no two feathers of one colour."

The king's son was on foot before the sun ; he caught up his bow and his quiver of arrows to kill the birds. He took to the moors, but if he did, the birds were not so easy to take. He was running after them till the sweat was blinding him. About mid-day who should come but Auburn Mary.

" You are exhausting yourself, king's son," says she.

" I am," said he.

" There fell but these two blackbirds, and both of one colour."

" Come over and lay down your weariness on this pretty hillock," says the giant's daughter.

" It's I am willing," said he.

He thought she would aid him this time, too, and he sat down near her, and he was not long there till he fell asleep.

When he awoke, Auburn Mary was gone. He thought

he would go back to the house, and he sees the byre thatched with feathers. When the giant came home, he said :

" Hast thou thatched the byre, king's son ? "

" I thatched it," says he.

" Somebody thatched it," says the giant.

" You did not thatch it," says the king's son.

" Yes, yes ! " says the giant. " Now," says the giant, " there is a fir tree beside that loch down there, and there is a magpie's nest in its top. The eggs thou wilt find in the nest. I must have them for my first meal. Not one must be burst or broken, and there are five in the nest."

Early in the morning the king's son went where the tree was, and that tree was not hard to hit upon. Its match was not in the whole wood. From the foot to the first branch was five hundred feet. The king's son was going all round the tree. She came who was always bringing help to him.

" You are losing the skin of your hands and feet."

" Ach ! I am," says he. " I am no sooner up than down."

" This is no time for stopping," says the giant's daughter. " Now you must kill me, strip the flesh from my bones, take all those bones apart, and use them as steps for climbing the tree. When you are climbing the tree, they will stick to the glass as if they had grown out of it ; but when you are coming down, and have put your foot on each one, they will drop into your hand when you touch them. Be sure and stand on each bone, leave none untouched ; if you do, it will stay behind. Put all my flesh into this clean cloth by the side of the spring at the

The Giant's Daughter

BIDS the BIRDS thatch her Father's Byre.

roots of the tree. When you come to the earth, arrange my bones together, put the flesh over them, sprinkle it with water from the spring, and I shall be alive before you. But don't forget a bone of me on the tree."

"How could I kill you," asked the king's son, "after what you have done for me?"

"If you won't obey, you and I are done for," said Auburn Mary. "You must climb the tree, or we are lost; and to climb the tree you must do as I say."

The king's son obeyed. He killed Auburn Mary, cut the flesh from her body, and unjointed the bones, as she had told him.

As he went up, the king's son put the bones of Auburn Mary's body against the side of the tree, using them as steps, till he came under the nest and stood on the last bone.

Then he took the eggs, and coming down, put his foot on every bone, then took it with him, till he came to the last bone, which was so near the ground that he failed to touch it with his foot.

He now placed all the bones of Auburn Mary in order again at the side of the spring, put the flesh on them, sprinkled it with water from the spring. She rose up before him, and said: "Didn't I tell you not to leave a bone of my body without stepping on it? Now I am lame for life! You left my little finger on the tree without touching it, and I have but nine fingers."

"Now," says she, "go home with the eggs quickly, and you will get me to marry to-night if you can know me. I and my two sisters will be arrayed in the same garments, and made like each other, but look at me when my father says, 'Go to thy wife, king's son;' and you will see a hand without a little finger."

He gave the eggs to the giant.

"Yes, yes!" says the giant, "be making ready for your marriage."

Then, indeed, there was a wedding, and it *was* a wedding! Giants and gentlemen, and the son of the king of the Green City was in the midst of them. They were married, and the dancing began, that was a dance! The giant's house was shaking from top to bottom.

But bed time came, and the giant said, "It is time for thee to go to rest, son of the king of Tethertown; choose thy bride to take with thee from amidst those."

She put out the hand off which the little finger was, and he caught her by the hand.

"Thou hast aimed well this time too; but there is no knowing but we may meet thee another way," said the giant.

But to rest they went. "Now," says she, "sleep not, or else you are a dead man. We must fly quick, quick, or for certain my father will kill you."

Out they went, and on the blue grey filly in the stable they mounted. "Stop a while," says she, "and I will play a trick to the old hero." She jumped in, and cut an apple into nine shares, and she put two shares at the head of the bed, and two shares at the foot of the bed, and two shares at the door of the kitchen, and two shares at the big door, and one outside the house.

The giant awoke and called, "Are you asleep?"

"Not yet," said the apple that was at the head of the bed.

At the end of a while he called again.

" Not yet," said the apple that was at the foot of the bed.

A while after this he called again : " Are your asleep ? "

" Not yet," said the apple at the kitchen door.

The giant called again.

The apple that was at the big door answered.

" You are now going far from me," says the giant.

" Not yet," says the apple that was outside the house.

" You are flying," says the giant. The giant jumped on his feet, and to the bed he went, but it was cold—empty.

" My own daughter's tricks are trying me," said the giant. " Here's after them," says he.

At the mouth of day, the giant's daughter said that her father's breath was burning her back.

" Put your hand, quick," said she, " in the ear of the grey filly, and whatever you find in it, throw it behind us."

" There is a twig of sloe tree," said he.

" Throw it behind us," said she.

No sooner did he that, than there were twenty miles of blackthorn wood, so thick that scarce a weasel could go through it.

The giant came headlong, and there he is fleecing his head and neck in the thorns.

" My own daughter's tricks are here as before," said the giant ; " but if I had my own big axe and wood knife here, I would not be long making a way through this."

He went home for the big axe and the wood knife, and sure he was not long on his journey, and he was the boy behind the big axe. He was not long making a way through the blackthorn.

"I will leave the axe and the wood knife here till I return," says he.

"If you leave 'em, leave 'em," said a hoodie that was in a tree, "we'll steal 'em, steal 'em."

"If you will do that," says the giant, "I must take them home." He returned home and left them at the house.

At the heat of day the giant's daughter felt her father's breath burning her back.

"Put your finger in the filly's ear, and throw behind whatever you find in it."

He got a splinter of grey stone, and in a twinkling there were twenty miles, by breadth and height, of great grey rock behind them.

The giant came full pelt, but past the rock he could not go.

"The tricks of my own daughter are the hardest things that ever met me," says the giant; "but if I had my lever and my mighty mattock, I would not be long in making my way through this rock also."

There was no help for it, but to turn the chase for them; and he was the boy to split the stones. He was not long in making a road through the rock.

"I will leave the tools here, and I will return no more."

"If you leave 'em, leave 'em," says the hoodie, "we will steal 'em, steal 'em."

"Do that if you will; there is no time to go back."

At the time of breaking the watch, the giant's daughter said that she felt her father's breath burning her back.

"Look in the filly's ear, king's son, or else we are lost."

He did so, and it was a bladder of water that was in her

ear this time.   He threw it behind him and there was a
fresh-water loch, twenty miles in length and breadth, behind
them.

The giant came on, but with the speed he had on him,
he was in the middle of the loch, and he went under, and
he rose no more.

On the next day the young companions were come in
sight of his father's house.   " Now," says she, " my father
is drowned, and he won't trouble us any more ; but before
we go further," says she, " go you to your father's house,
and tell that you have the likes of me ; but let neither man
nor creature kiss you, for if you do, you will not remember
that you have ever seen me."

Every one he met gave him welcome and luck, and he
charged his father and mother not to kiss him ; but as
mishap was to be, an old greyhound was indoors, and she
knew him, and jumped up to his mouth, and after that he
did not remember the giant's daughter.

She was sitting at the well's side as he left her, but
the king's son was not coming.   In the mouth of night she
climbed up into a tree of oak that was beside the well, and
she lay in the fork of that tree all night.   A shoemaker
had a house near the well, and about mid-day on the
morrow, the shoemaker asked his wife to go for a drink for
him out of the well.   When the shoemaker's wife reached
the well, and when she saw the shadow of her that was in
the tree, thinking it was her own shadow—and she never
thought till now that she was so handsome—she gave a
cast to the dish that was in her hand, and it was broken on
the ground, and she took herself to the house without
vessel or water.

"Where is the water, wife?" said the shoemaker.

"You shambling, contemptible old carle, without grace, I have stayed too long your water and wood thrall."

"I think, wife, that you have turned crazy. Go you, daughter, quickly, and fetch a drink for your father."

His daughter went, and in the same way so it happened to her. She never thought till now that she was so lovable, and she took herself home.

"Up with the drink," said her father.

"You home-spun shoe carle, do you think I am fit to be your thrall?"

The poor shoemaker thought that they had taken a turn in their understandings, and he went himself to the well. He saw the shadow of the maiden in the well, and he looked up to the tree, and he sees the finest woman he ever saw.

"Your seat is wavering, but your face is fair," said the shoemaker. "Come down, for there is need of you for a short while at my house."

The shoemaker understood that this was the shadow that had driven his people mad. The shoemaker took her to his house, and he said that he had but a poor bothy, but that she should get a share of all that was in it.

One day, the shoemaker had shoes ready, for on that very day the king's son was to be married. The shoemaker was going to the castle with the shoes of the young people, and the girl said to the shoemaker, "I would like to get a sight of the king's son before he marries."

"Come with me," says the shoemaker, "I am well acquainted with the servants at the castle, and you shall get a sight of the king's son and all the company."

And when the gentles saw the pretty woman that was here they took her to the wedding-room, and they filled for her a glass of wine. When she was going to drink what is in it, a flame went up out of the glass, and a golden pigeon and a silver pigeon sprang out of it. They were flying about when three grains of barley fell on the floor. The silver pigeon sprung, and ate that up.

Said the golden pigeon to him, " If you remembered when I cleared the byre, you would not eat that without giving me a share."

Again there fell three other grains of barley, and the silver pigeon sprung, and ate that up as before.

" If you remembered when I thatched the byre, you would not eat that without giving me my share," says the golden pigeon.

Three other grains fall, and the silver pigeon sprung, and ate that up.

" If you remembered when I harried the magpie's nest, you would not eat that without giving me my share," says the golden pigeon ; " I lost my little finger bringing it down, and I want it still."

The king's son minded, and he knew who it was that was before him.

" Well," said the king's son to the guests at the feast, "when I was a little younger than I am now, I lost the key of a casket that I had. I had a new key made, but after it was brought to me I found the old one. Now, I'll leave it to any one here to tell me what I am to do. Which of the keys should I keep ? "

" My advice to you," said one of the guests, " is to keep

the old key, for it fits the lock better and you're more used to it."

Then the king's son stood up and said: " I thank you for a wise advice and an honest word. This is my bride the daughter of the giant who saved my life at the risk of her own. I'll have her and no other woman."

So the king's son married Auburn Mary and the wedding lasted long and all were happy. But all I got was butter on a live coal, porridge in a basket, and they sent me for water to the stream, and the paper shoes came to an end.

Brewery of Eggshells

N Treneglwys there is a certain shepherd's cot known by the name of Twt y Cymrws because of the strange strife that occurred there. There once lived there a man and his wife, and they had twins whom the woman nursed tenderly. One day she was called away to the house of a neighbour at some distance. She did not much like going and leaving her little ones

all alone in a solitary house, especially as she had heard
tell of the good folk haunting the neighbourhood.

Well, she went and came back as soon as she could, but
on her way back she was frightened to see some old elves
of the blue petticoat crossing her path though it was midday.
She rushed home, but found her two little ones in the cradle
and everything seemed as it was before.

But after a time the good people began to suspect
that something was wrong, for the twins didn't grow
at all.

The man said : " They're not ours."

The woman said : " Whose else should they be ? "

And so arose the great strife so that the neighbours
named the cottage after it.   It made the woman very sad,
so one evening she made up her mind to go and see the
Wise Man of Llanidloes, for he knew everything and would
advise her what to do.

So she went to Llanidloes and told the case to the Wise
Man.   Now there was soon to be a harvest of rye and oats,
so the Wise Man said to her, " When you are getting
dinner for the reapers, clear out the shell of a hen's egg and
boil some potage in it, and then take it to the door as if you
meant it as a dinner for the reapers.   Then listen if the
twins say anything.   If you hear them speaking of things
beyond the understanding of children, go back and take
them up and throw them into the waters of Lake Elvyn.
But if you don't hear anything remarkable, do them no
injury."

So when the day of the reap came the woman did all
that the Wise Man ordered, and put the eggshell on the fire
and took it off and carried it to the door, and there she stood

and listened.   Then she heard one of the children say to
the other :

> Acorn before oak I knew,
> An egg before a hen,
> But I never heard of an eggshell brew
> A dinner for harvest men.

So she went back into the house, seized the children and
threw them into the Llyn, and the goblins in their blue
trousers came and saved their dwarfs and the mother
had her own children back and so the great strife
ended.

The Lad with the Goat-skin

ONG ago, a poor widow woman lived down near the iron forge, by Enniscorth, and she was so poor she had no clothes to put on her son ; so she used to fix him in the ash-hole, near the fire, and pile the warm ashes about him ; and according as he grew up, she sunk the pit deeper. At last, by hook or by crook, she got a goat-skin, and fastened it round his waist, and he felt quite grand, and took a walk down the street. So says she to him next morning, " Tom, you thief, you never done any good yet, and you six foot high, and past nineteen ;—take that rope and bring me a faggot from the wood."

" Never say't twice, mother," says Tom—" here goes."

When he had it gathered and tied, what should come up but a big giant, nine foot high, and made a lick of a club at him. Well become Tom, he jumped a-one side, and picked up a ram-pike ; and the first crack he gave the big fellow, he made him kiss the clod.

" If you have e'er a prayer," says Tom, " now's the time to say it, before I make fragments of you."

" I have no prayers," says the giant ; "but if you spare

my life I'll give you that club ; and as long as you keep
from sin, you'll win every battle you ever fight with it."

Tom made no bones about letting him off ; and as soon
as he got the club in his hands, he sat down on the bresna,
and gave it a tap with the kippeen, and says, " Faggot, I
had great trouble gathering you, and run the risk of my life
for you, the least you can do is to carry me home." And
sure enough, the wind o' the word was all it wanted. It
went off through the wood, groaning and crackling, till it
came to the widow's door.

Well, when the sticks were all burned, Tom was sent off
again to pick more ; and this time he had to fight with a
giant that had two heads on him. Tom had a little more
trouble with him—that's all ; and the prayers he said, was
to give Tom a fife, that nobody could help dancing when he
was playing it. Begonies, he made the big faggot dance
home, with himself sitting on it. The next giant was a
beautiful boy with three heads on him. He had neither
prayers nor catechism no more nor the others ; and so he
gave Tom a bottle of green ointment, that wouldn't let you
be burned, nor scalded, nor wounded. " And now," says
he, " there's no more of us. You may come and gather
sticks here till little Lunacy Day in Harvest, without giant
or fairy-man to disturb you."

Well, now, Tom was prouder nor ten paycocks, and used
to take a walk down street in the heel of the evening ; but
some o' the little boys had no more manners than if they
were Dublin jackeens, and put out their tongues at Tom's
club and Tom's goat-skin. He didn't like that at all, and
it would be mean to give one of them a clout. At last,
what should come through the town but a kind of a bell-

man, only it's a big bugle he had, and a huntsman's cap on his head, and a kind of a painted shirt. So this—he wasn't a bellman, and I don't know what to call him— bugle-man, maybe, proclaimed that the King of Dublin's daughter was so melancholy that she didn't give a laugh for seven years, and that hei father would grant her in marriage to whoever could make her laugh three times.

"That's the very thing for me to try," says Tom; and so, without burning any more daylight, he kissed his mother, curled his club at the little boys, and off he set along the yalla highroad to the town of Dublin.

At last Tom came to one of the city gates, and the guards laughed and cursed at him instead of letting him in. Tom stood it all for a little time, but at last one of them— out of fun, as he said—drove his bayonet half an inch or so into his side. Tom done nothing but take the fellow by the scruff o' the neck and the waistband of his corduroys, and fling him into the canal. Some run to pull the fellow out, and others to let manners into the vulgarian with their swords and daggers; but a tap from his club sent them headlong into the moat or down on the stones, and they were soon begging him to stay his hands.

So at last one of them was glad enough to show Tom the way to the palace-yard; and there was the king, and the queen, and the princess, in a gallery, looking at all sorts of wrestling, and sword-playing, and long-dances, and mumming, all to please the princess; but not a smile came over her handsome face.

Well, they all stopped when they seen the young giant, with his boy's face, and long black hair, and his short curly beard—for his poor mother couldn't afford to buy razors—

and his great strong arms, and bare legs, and no covering but the goat-skin that reached from his waist to his knees. But an envious wizened bit of a fellow, with a red head, that wished to be married to the princess, and didn't like how she opened her eyes at Tom, came forward, and asked his business very snappishly.

"My business," says Tom, says he, "is to make the beautiful princess, God bless her, laugh three times."

"Do you see all them merry fellows and skilful swords-men," says the other, "that could eat you up with a grain of salt, and not a mother's soul of 'em ever got a laugh from her these seven years?"

So the fellows gathered round Tom, and the bad man aggravated him till he told them he didn't care a pinch o' snuff for the whole bilin' of 'em; let 'em come on, six at a time, and try what they could do.

The king, who was too far off to hear what they were saying, asked what did the stranger want.

"He wants," says the red-headed fellow, "to make hares of your best men."

"Oh!" says the king, "if that's the way, let one of 'em turn out and try his mettle."

So one stood forward, with sword and pot-lid, and made a cut at Tom. He struck the fellow's elbow with the club, and up over their heads flew the sword, and down went the owner of it on the gravel from a thump he got on the helmet. Another took his place, and another, and another, and then half a dozen at once, and Tom sent swords, helmets, shields, and bodies, rolling over and over, and themselves bawling out that they were kilt, and disabled, and damaged, and rubbing their poor elbows and hips, and limping away. Tom contrived not to kill any one; and the princess was so amused, that she let a great sweet laugh out of her that was heard over all the yard.

"King of Dublin," says Tom," "I've quarter your daughter."

And the king didn't know whether he was glad or sorry, and all the blood in the princess's heart run into her cheeks.

So there was no more fighting that day, and Tom was invited to dine with the royal family. Next day, Redhead told Tom of a wolf, the size of a yearling heifer, that used to be serenading about the walls, and eating people and cattle; and said what a pleasure it would give the king to have it killed.

"With all my heart," says Tom; "send a jackeen to show me where he lives, and we'll see how he behaves to a stranger."

The princess was not well pleased, for Tom looked a different person with fine clothes and a nice green birredh over his long curly hair; and besides, he'd got one laugh out of her. However, the king gave his consent; and in an hour and a half the horrible wolf was walking into the palace-yard, and Tom a step or two behind, with his club on his shoulder, just as a shepherd would be walking after a pet lamb.

The king and queen and princess were safe up in their gallery, but the officers and people of the court that wor padrowling about the great bawn, when they saw the big baste coming in, gave themselves up, and began to make for doors and gates; and the wolf licked his chops, as if he was saying, "Wouldn't I enjoy a breakfast off a couple of yez!"

The king shouted out, "O Tom with the Goat-skin, take away that terrible wolf, and you must have all my daughter."

But Tom didn't mind him a bit.   He pulled out his flute and began to play like vengeance ; and dickens a man or

boy in the yard but began shovelling away heel and toe, and the wolf himself was obliged to get on his hind legs and dance "Tatther Jack Walsh," along with the rest.   A good deal of the people got inside, and shut the doors, the way the hairy fellow wouldn't pin them ; but Tom kept playing, and the outsiders kept dancing and shouting, and the wolf kept dancing and roaring with the pain his legs were giving him ; and all the time he had his eyes on Red-head, who was shut out along with the rest.   Wherever Redhead went, the wolf followed, and kept one eye on him and the other on Tom, to see if he would give him leave to eat him.   But Tom shook his head, and never stopped the tune, and Redhead never stopped dancing and bawling, and the wolf dancing and roaring, one leg up and the other down, and he ready to drop out of his standing from fair tiresomeness.

When the princess seen that there was no fear of any one being kilt, she was so divarted by the stew that Red-head was in, that she gave another great laugh ; and well become Tom, out he cried, " King of Dublin, I have two halves of your daughter."

" Oh, halves or alls," says the king, " put away that divel of a wolf, and we'll see about it."

So Tom put his flute in his pocket, and says he to the baste that was sittin' on his currabingo ready to faint, " Walk off to your mountain, my fine fellow, and live like a respectable baste ; and if ever I find you come within seven miles of any town, I'll ——"

He said no more, but spit in his fist, and gave a flourish of his club.   It was all the poor divel of a wolf wanted : he put his tail between his legs, and took to his pumps without looking at man or mortal, and neither sun, moon, or stars ever saw him in sight of Dublin again.

At dinner every one laughed but the foxy fellow ; and sure enough he was laying out how he'd settle poor Tom next day.

" Well, to be sure ! " says he, " King of Dublin, you are in luck.   There's the Danes moidhering us to no end.

Deuce run to Lusk wid 'em ! and if any one can save us
from 'em, it is this gentleman with the goat-skin.   There is
a flail hangin' on the collar-
beam in hell, and neither Dane
nor devil can stand before it."

"So," says Tom to the king,
"will you let me have the other
half of the princess if I bring you the
flail ? "

"No, no," says the princess ; "I'd rather
never be your wife than see you in that danger."

But Redhead whispered and nudged Tom
about how shabby it would look to reneague the
adventure.   So he asked which way he was to go,
and Redhead directed him.

Well, he travelled and travelled, till he came in
sight of the walls of hell ; and, bedad, before he knocked
at the gates, he rubbed himself over with the greenish
ointment.   When he knocked, a hundred little imps popped
their heads out through the bars, and axed him what he
wanted.

"I want to speak to the big divel of all," says Tom :
"open the gate."

It wasn't long till the gate was thrune open, and the
Ould Boy received Tom with bows and scrapes, and axed
his business.

"My business isn't much," says Tom.   "I only came
for the loan of that flail that I see hanging on the collar-
beam, for the King of Dublin to give a thrashing to the
Danes."

"Well," says the other, "the Danes is much better

customers to me ; but since you walked so far I won't refuse.   Hand that flail," says he to a young imp ; and he winked the far-off eye at the same time.   So, while some were barring the gates, the young devil climbed up, and took down the flail that had the handstaff and booltheen both made out of red-hot iron.   The little vagabond was grinning to think how it would burn the hands o' Tom, but the dickens a burn it made on him, no more nor if it was a good oak sapling.

"Thankee," says Tom.   "Now would you open the gate for a body, and I'll give you no more trouble."

"Oh, tramp!" says Ould Nick ; "is that the way ?   It is easier getting inside them gates than getting out again. Take that tool from him, and give him a dose of the oil of stirrup."

So one fellow put out his claws to seize on the flail, but Tom gave him such a welt of it on the side of the head that he broke off one of his horns, and made him roar like a devil as he was.   Well, they rushed at Tom, but he gave them, little and big, such a thrashing as they didn't forget for a while.   At last says the ould thief of all, rubbing his elbow, "Let the fool out ; and woe to whoever lets him in again, great or small."

So out marched Tom, and away with him, without minding the shouting and cursing they kept up at him from the tops of the walls ; and when he got home to the big bawn of the palace, there never was such running and racing as to see himself and the flail.   When he had his story told, he laid down the flail on the stone steps, and bid no one for their lives to touch it.   If the king, and queen, and princess, made much of him before, they made

ten times more of him now ; but Redhead, the mean scruff-
hound, stole over, and thought to catch hold of the flail to
make an end of him. His fingers hardly touched it, when
he let a roar out of him as if heaven and earth were coming
together, and kept flinging his arms about and dancing, that
it was pitiful to look at him. Tom run at him as soon as
he could rise, caught his hands in his own two, and rubbed
them this way and that, and the burning pain left them
before you could reckon one. Well the poor fellow,
between the pain that was only just gone, and the comfort
he was in, had the comicalest face that you ever see, it was
such a mixtherum-gatherum of laughing and crying.
Everybody burst out a laughing—the princess could not
stop no more than the rest ; and then says Tom, " Now,
ma'am, if there were fifty halves of you, I hope you'll give
me them all."

Well, the princess looked at her father, and by my word,
she came over to Tom, and put her two delicate hands into
his two rough ones, and I wish it was myself was in his
shoes that day !

Tom would not bring the flail into the palace. You may
be sure no other body went near it ; and when the early
risers were passing next morning, they found two long
clefts in the stone, where it was after burning itself an
opening downwards, nobody could tell how far. But a
messenger came in at noon, and said that the Danes were
so frightened when they heard of the flail coming into
Dublin, that they got into their ships, and sailed away.

Well, I suppose, before they were married, Tom got
some man, like Pat Mara of Tomenine, to learn him the
" principles of politeness," fluxions, gunnery and fortifi-

cation, decimal fractions, practice, and the rule of three direct, the way he'd be able to keep up a conversation with the royal family. Whether he ever lost his time learning them sciences, I'm not sure, but it's as sure as fate that his mother never more saw any want till the end of her days.

MAN ᴏʀ WOMAN
BOY ᴏʀ GIRL
THAT READS WHAT
FOLLOWS
3 TIMES
SHALL FALL ASLEEP
AN HUNDRED YEARS

JOHN D. BATTEN DREW THIS : AUG 29ᵗʰ 1891   GOOD-NIGHT.

Notes and References

IT may be as well to give the reader some account of the enormous extent of the Celtic folk-tales in existence. I reckon these to extend to 2000, though only about 250 are in print The former number exceeds that known in France, Italy, Germany, and Russia, where collection has been most active, and is only exceeded by the MS. collection of Finnish folk-tales at Helsingfors, said to exceed 12,000. As will be seen. this superiority of the Celts is due to the phenomenal and patriotic activity of one man, the late J. F. Campbell, of Islay, whose *Popular Tales* and MS. collections (partly described by Mr. Alfred Nutt in *Folk-Lore*, i. 369–83) contain references to no less than 1281 tales (many of them, of course, variants and scraps). Celtic folk-tales, while more numerous, are also the oldest of the tales of modern European races ; some of them—*e g*, "Connla." in the present selection, occurring in the oldest Irish vellums. They include (1) fairy tales properly so-called—*i.e.*, tales or anecdotes *about* fairies, hobgoblins, &c., told as natural occurrences ; (2) hero-tales, stories of adventure told of national or mythical heroes ; (3) folk-tales proper, describing marvellous adventures of otherwise unknown heroes, in which there is a defined plot and supernatural characters (speaking animals, giants, dwarfs, &c.) ; and finally (4) drolls, comic anecdotes of feats of stupidity or cunning.

The collection of Celtic folk-tales began in IRELAND as early as 1825, with T. Crofton Croker's *Fairy Legends and Traditions of the South of Ireland*. This contained some 38 anecdotes of the first class mentioned above, anecdotes showing the belief of the Irish peasantry in the existence of fairies, gnomes, goblins, and the like. The Grimms did Croker the honour of translating part of his book, under the title of *Irische Elfenmärchen*. Among the novelists and tale-writers of the schools of Miss Edgeworth and Lever folk-tales were occasionally utilised, as by Carleton in his *Traits and Stories*, by S. Lover in his *Legends and Stories*, and by G. Griffin in his *Tales of a Jury-Room*. These all tell their tales in the manner of the stage Irishman. Chapbooks, *Royal Fairy Tales* and *Hibernian Tales*, also contained genuine folk-tales, and attracted Thackeray's attention in his *Irish Sketch-Book*. The Irish Grimm, however, was Patrick Kennedy, a Dublin bookseller, who believed in fairies, and in five years (1866–71) printed about 100 folk- and hero-tales and drolls (classes 2, 3, and 4 above) in his *Legendary Fictions of the Irish Celts*, 1866, *Fireside Stories of Ireland*, 1870, and *Bardic Stories of Ireland*, 1871 ; all three are now unfortunately out of print. He tells his stories neatly and with spirit, and retains much that is *volkstümlich* in his diction. He derived his materials from the English-speaking peasantry of county Wexford, who changed from Gaelic to English while story-telling was in full vigour, and therefore carried over the stories with the change of language. Lady Wylde has told many folk-tales very effectively in her *Ancient Legends of Ireland*, 1887. More recently two collectors have published stories gathered from peasants of the West and North who can only speak Gaelic. These are by an American gentleman named Curtin, *Myths and Folk-Tales of Ireland*, 1890 ; while Dr. Douglas Hyde has published in *Beside the Fireside*, 1891, spirited English versions of some of the stories he had published in the original Irish in his *Leabhar Sgeulaighteachta*, Dublin, 1889. Miss Maclintoch has a large MS. collection, part of which has appeared in various periodicals ; and Messrs. Larminie and D. Fitzgerald are known to have much story material in their possession.

But beside these more modern collections there exist in old and middle Irish a large number of hero-tales (class 2) which formed the staple of the old *ollamhs* or bards. Of these tales of "cattle-liftings, elopements, battles, voyages, courtships, caves, lakes, feasts, sieges, and eruptions," a bard of even the fourth class had to know seven fifties, presumably one for each day of the year. Sir William Temple knew of a north-country gentleman of Ireland who was sent to sleep every evening with a fresh tale from his bard. The *Book of Leinster*, an Irish vellum of the twelfth century, contains a list of 189 of these hero-tales, many of which are extant to this day ; E. O'Curry gives the list in the Appendix to his *MS. Materials of Irish History*.

Another list of about 70 is given in the preface to the third volume of the Ossianic Society's publications. Dr. Joyce published a few of the more celebrated of these in *Old Celtic Romances;* others appeared in *Atlantis* (see notes on "Deirdre"), others in Kennedy's *Bardic Stories,* mentioned above.

Turning to SCOTLAND, we must put aside Chambers' *Popular Rhymes of Scotland,* 1842, which contains for the most part folk-tales common with those of England rather than those peculiar to the Gaelic-speaking Scots. The first name here in time as in importance is that of J. F. Campbell, of Islay. His four volumes, *Popular Tales of the West Highlands* (Edinburgh, 1860-2, recently republished by the Islay Association), contain some 120 folk- and hero-tales, told with strict adherence to the language of the narrators, which is given with a literal, a rather too literal, English version. This careful accuracy has given an un-English air to his versions, and has prevented them attaining their due popularity. What Campbell has published represents only a tithe of what he collected. At the end of the fourth volume he gives a list of 791 tales, &c., collected by him or his assistants in the two years 1859–61 ; and in his MS. collections at Edinburgh are two other lists containing 400 more tales. Only a portion of these are in the Advocates' Library ; the rest, if extant, must be in private hands, though they are distinctly of national importance and interest.

Campbell's influence has been effective of recent years in Scotland. The *Celtic Magazine* (vols. xii. and xiii.), while under the editorship of Mr. MacBain, contained several folk- and hero-tales in Gaelic, and and so did the *Scotch Celtic Review.* These were from the collections of Messrs. Campbell of Tiree, Carmichael, and K. Mackenzie. Recently Lord Archibald Campbell has shown laudable interest in the preservation of Gaelic folk- and hero-tales. Under his auspices a whole series of handsome volumes, under the general title of *Waifs and Strays of Celtic Tradition,* has been recently published, four volumes having already appeared, each accompanied by notes by Mr. Alfred Nutt, which form the most important aid to the study of Celtic Folk-Tales since Campbell himself. Those to the second volume in particular (Tales collected by Rev. D. MacInnes) fill 100 pages, with condensed information on all aspects of the subject dealt with in the light of the most recent research in the European folk-tales as well as on Celtic literature. Thanks to Mr. Nutt, Scotland is just now to the fore in the collection and study of the British Folk-Tale.

WALES makes a poor show beside Ireland and Scotland. Sikes'
British Goblins, and the tales collected by Prof. Rhys in *Y Cymrodor*,
vols. ii.–vi., are mainly of our first-class fairy anecdotes. Borrow, in
his *Wild Wales*, refers to a collection of fables in a journal called
The Greal, while the *Cambrian Quarterly Magazine* for 1830 and
1831 contained a few fairy anecdotes, including a curious version of
the " Brewery of Eggshells " from the Welsh. In the older literature,
the *Iolo MS.*, published by the Welsh MS. Society, has a few fables
and apologues, and the charming *Mabinogion*, translated by Lady
Guest, has tales that can trace back to the twelfth century and are
on the border-line between folk-tales and hero-tales.

CORNWALL and MAN are even worse than Wales. Hunt's *Drolls
from the West of England* has nothing distinctively Celtic, and it is
only by a chance Lhuyd chose a folk-tal as his specimen of Cornish
in his *Archæologia Britannica*, 1709 (see *Tale of Ivan*). The
Manx folk-tales published, including the most recent by Mr. Moore,
in his *Folk-Lore of the Isle of Man*, 1891, are mainly fairy anecdotes
and legends.

From this survey of the field of Celtic folk-tales it is clear that
Ireland and Scotland provide the lion's share. The interesting thing
to notice is the remarkable similarity of Scotch and Irish folk-tales.
The continuity of language and culture between these two divisions
of Gaeldom has clearly brought about this identity of their folk-tales.
As will be seen from the following notes, the tales found in Scotland
can almost invariably be paralleled by those found in Ireland, and
vice versâ. This result is a striking confirmation of the general
truth that the folk-lores of different countries resemble one another
in proportion to their contiguity and to the continuity of language and
culture between them.

Another point of interest in these Celtic folk-tales is the light they
throw upon the relation of hero-tales and folk-tales (classes 2 and 3
above). Tales told of Finn or Cuchulain, and therefore coming under
the definition of hero-tales, are found elsewhere told of anonymous or
unknown heroes. The question is, were the folk-tales the earliest,
and were they localised and applied to the heroes, or were the heroic
sagas generalised and applied to an unknown τίς? All the evidence,
in my opinion, inclines to the former view, which, as applied to Celtic
folk-tales, is of very great literary importance ; for it is becoming
more and more recognised, thanks chiefly to the admirable work of
Mr. Alfred Nutt, in his *Studies on the Holy Grail*, that the outburst of

European Romance in the twelfth century was due, in large measure, to an infusion of Celtic hero-tales into the literature of the Romance-speaking nations. Now the remarkable thing is, how these hero-tales have lingered on in oral tradition even to the present day. (See a marked case in " Deirdre.") We may, therefore, hope to see considerable light thrown on the most characteristic spiritual product of the Middle Ages, the literature of Romance and the spirit of chivalry, from the Celtic folk-tales of the present day. Mr. Alfred Nutt has already shown this to be true of a special section of Romance literature, that connected with the Holy Grail, and it seems probable that further study will extend the field of application of this new method of research.

The Celtic folk-tale again has interest in retaining many traits of primitive conditions among the early inhabitants of these isles which are preserved by no other record. Take, for instance, the calm assumption of polygamy in "Gold Tree and Silver Tree." That represents a state of feeling that is decidedly pre-Christian. The belief in an external soul "Life Index," recently monographed by Mr. Frazer in his " Golden Bough," also finds expression in a couple of the Tales (see notes on "Sea-Maiden" and "Fair, Brown, and Trembling "), and so with many other primitive ideas.

Care, however, has to be taken in using folk-tales as evidence for primitive practice among the nations where they are found. For the tales may have come from another race—that is, for example, probably the case with "Gold Tree and Silver Tree" (see Notes). Celtic tales are of peculiar interest in this connection, as they afford one of the best fields for studying the problem of diffusion, the most pressing of the problems of the folk-tales just at present, at least in my opinion. The Celts are at the furthermost end of Europe. Tales that travelled to them could go no further and must therefore be the last links in the chain.

For all these reasons, then, Celtic folk-tales are of high scientific interest to the folk-lorist, while they yield to none in imaginative and literary qualities. In any other country of Europe some national means of recording them would have long ago been adopted. M. Luzel, e.g., was commissioned by the French Minister of Public Instruction to collect and report on the Breton folk-tales. England, here as elsewhere without any organised means of scientific research in the historical and philological sciences, has to depend on the enthusiasm of a few private individuals for work of national importance. Every Celt of these islands or in the Gaeldom beyond the sea, a..d every Celt-lover among the English-speaking nations, should regard it as one of the duties of the race to put its traditions on record in the few years that now remain before they will cease for ever to be living in the hearts and memories of the humbler members of the race.

In the following Notes I have done as in my *English Fairy Tales*, and given first, the *sources* whence I drew the tales, then *parallels* at length for the British Isles, with bibliographical references for parallels abroad, and finally, *remarks* where the tales seemed to need them. In these I have not wearied or worried the reader with conventional tall talk about the Celtic genius and its manifestations in the folk-tale ; on that topic one can only repeat Matthew Arnold when at his best, in his *Celtic Literature.* Nor have I attempted to deal with the more general aspects of the study of the Celtic folk-tale. For these I must refer to Mr. Nutt's series of papers in *The Celtic Magazine*, vol. xii., or, still better, to the masterly introductions he is contributing to the series of *Waifs and Strays of Celtic Tradition*, and to Dr. Hyde's *Beside the Fireside.* In my remarks I have mainly confined myself to discussing the origin and diffusion of the various tales, so far as anything definite could be learnt or conjectured on that subject.

Before proceeding to the Notes, I may "put in," as the lawyers say, a few summaries of the results reached in them. Of the twenty-six tales, twelve (i., ii., v., viii., ix., x., xi., xv., xvi., xvii., xix., xxiv.) have Gaelic originals ; three (vii., xiii., xxv.) are from the Welsh ; one (xxii.) from the now extinct Cornish ; one an adaptation of an English poem founded on a Welsh tradition (xxi., " Gellert ") ; and the remaining nine are what may be termed Anglo-Irish. Regarding their diffusion among the Celts, twelve are both Irish and Scotch (iv., v., vi., ix., x., xiv.–xvii., xix., xx., xxiv) ; one (xxv.) is common to Irish and Welsh ; and one (xxii.) to Irish and Cornish ; seven are found only among the Celts in Ireland (i.–iii., xii., xviii., xxii., xxvi) ; two (viii., xi.) among the Scotch ; and three (vii., xiii., xxi.) among the Welsh. Finally, so far as we can ascertain their origin, four (v., xvi., xxi., xxii.) are from the East ; five (vi., x., xiv., xx., xxv.) are European drolls ; three of the romantic tales seem to have been imported (vii., ix., xix.) ; while three others are possibly Celtic exportations to the Continent (xv., xvii., xxiv.) though the last may have previously come thence ; the remaining eleven are, as far as known, original to Celtic lands. Somewhat the same result would come out, I believe, as the analysis of any representative collection of folk-tales of any European district.

Notes and References 243

I. CONNLA AND THE FAIRY MAIDEN.

Source.—From the old Irish "Echtra Condla chaim maic Cuind Chetchathaig" of the *Leabhar na h-Uidhre* (" Book of the Dun Cow"), which must have been written before 1106, when its scribe Maelmori (" Servant of Mary ") was murdered. The original is given by Windisch in his *Irish Grammar*, p. 120, also in the *Trans. Kilkenny Archæol. Soc.* for 1874. A fragment occurs in a Rawlinson MS., described by Dr. W. Stokes, *Tripartite Life*, p. xxxvi. I have used the translation of Prof. Zimmer in his *Keltische Beitrage*, ii. (*Zeits. f. deutsches Altertum*, Bd. xxxiii. 262-4). Dr. Joyce has a somewhat florid version in his *Old Celtic Romances*, from which I have borrowed a touch or two. I have neither extenuated nor added aught but the last sentence of the Fairy Maiden's last speech. Part of the original is in metrical form, so that the whole is of the *cante-fable* species which I believe to be the original form of the folk-tale (*Cf. Eng. Fairy Tales*, notes, p. 240, and *infra*, p. 257).

Parallels.—Prof. Zimmer's paper contains three other accounts of the *terra repromissionis* in the Irish sagas, one of them being the similar adventure of Cormac the nephew of Connla, or Condla Ruad as he should be called. The fairy apple of gold occurs in Cormac Mac Art's visit to the Brug of Manannan (Nutt's *Holy Grail*, 193).

Remarks.—Conn the hundred-fighter had the head-kingship of Ireland 123-157 A.D., according to the *Annals of the Four Masters*, i. 105. On the day of his birth the five great roads from Tara to all parts of Ireland were completed : one of them from Dublin is still used. Connaught is said to have been named after him, but this is scarcely consonant with Joyce's identification with Ptolemy's *Nagnatai* (*Irish Local Names*, i. 75). But there can be little doubt of Conn's existence as a powerful ruler in Ireland in the second century. The historic existence of Connla seems also to be authenticated by the reference to him as Conly, the eldest son of Conn, in the Annals of Clonmacnoise. As Conn was succeeded by his third son, Art Enear, Connla was either slain or disappeared during his father's lifetime. Under these circumstances it is not unlikely that our legend grew up within the century after Conn—*i.e.*, during the latter half of the second century.

As regards the present form of it, Prof. Zimmer (*l.c.* 261-2) places it in the seventh century. It has clearly been touched up by a Christian hand who introduced the reference to the day of judgment and to the waning power of the Druids. But nothing turns upon this interpolation, so that it is likely that even the present form of the legend is pre-Christian—*i.e.* for Ireland, prePatrician, before the fifth century. The tale of Connla is thus the earliest fairy tale of modern Europe. Besides this interest it contains an early account of one of the most characteristic Celtic conceptions, that of the earthly Paradise, the Isle of Youth, *Tir-na n-Og.* This has impressed itself on the European imagination ; in the Arthuriad it is represented by the Vale of Avalon, and as represented in the various Celtic visions of the future life, it forms one of the main sources of Dante's *Divina Commedia.* It is possible too, I think, that the Homeric Hesperides and the Fortunate Isles of the ancients had a Celtic origin (as is well known, the early place-names of Europe are predominantly Celtic). I have found, I believe, a reference to the conception in one of the earliest passages in the classics dealing with the Druids. Lucan, in his *Pharsalia* (i. 450–8), addresses them in these high terms of reverence :

> Et vos barbaricos ritus, moremque sinistrum,
> Sacrorum, Druidæ, positis repetistis ab armis,
> Solis nôsse Deos et cœli numera vobis
> Aut solis nescire datum ; nemora alta remotis
> Incolitis lucis. Vobis auctoribus umbræ,
> Non tacitas Erebi sedes, Ditisque profundi,
> Pallida regna p. tunt : *regit idem spiritus artus*
> *Orbe alio :* longæ, canitis si cognita, vitæ
> Mors media est.

The passage certainly seems to me to imply a different conception from the ordinary classical views of the life after death, the dark and dismal plains of Erebus peopled with ghosts ; and the passage I have italicised would chime in well with the conception of a continuance of youth (*idem spiritus*) in Tir-na n-Og (*orbe alio*).

One of the most pathetic, beautiful, and typical scenes in Irish legend is the return of Ossian from Tir-na n-Og, and his interview with St. Patrick. The old faith and the new, the old order of things and that which replaced it, meet in two of the most characteristic products of the Irish imagination (for the Patrick of legend is as much a legendary figure as Oisin himself). Ossian had gone away to Tir-na n-Og with the fairy Niamh under very much the same circumstances as Condla Ruad ; time flies in the land of eternal youth, and when Ossian returns, after a year as he thinks, more than three centuries had passed, and St. Patrick had just succeeded in introducing the new faith. The contrast of Past and Present has never been more vividly or beautifully represented.

II. GULEESH.

Source.—From Dr. Douglas Hyde's *Beside the Fire*, 104-28, where it is a translation from the same author's *Leabhar Sgeulaighteachta.* Dr Hyde got it from one Shamus O'Hart, a gamekeeper of French-park. One is curious to know how far the very beautiful landscapes in the story are due to Dr. Hyde, who confesses to have only taken notes. I have omitted a journey to Rome, paralleled, as Mr. Nutt has pointed out, by the similar one of Michael Scott (*Waifs and Strays*, i. 46), and not bearing on the main lines of the story. I have also dropped a part of Guleesh's name: In the original he is "Guleesh na guss dhu," Guleesh of the black feet, because he never washed them; nothing turns on this in the present form of the story, but one cannot but suspect it was of importance in the original form.

Parallels.—Dr. Hyde refers to two short stories, "Midnight Ride" (to Rome) and "Stolen Bride," in Lady Wilde's *Ancient Legends.* But the closest parallel is given by Miss Maclintock's Donegal tale of "Jamie Freel and the Young Lady," reprinted in Mr. Yeats' *Irish Folk and Fairy Tales*, 52-9. In the *Hibernian Tales*, "Mann o' Malaghan and the Fairies," as reported by Thackeray in the *Irish Sketch-Book*, c. xvi., begins like "Guleesh."

III. FIELD OF BOLIAUNS.

Source.—T. Crofton Croker's *Fairy Legends of the South of Ireland*, ed. Wright, pp. 135-9. In the original the gnome is a Cluricaune, but as a friend of Mr. Batten's has recently heard the tale told of a Lepracaun, I have adopted the better known title.

Remarks.—*Lepracaun* is from the Irish *leith bhrogan*, the one-shoemaker (*cf.* brogue), according to Dr. Hyde. He is generally seen (and to this day, too) working at a single shoe, *cf.* Croker's story "Little Shoe," *l.c.* pp. 142-4. According to a writer in the *Revue Celtique*, i. 256, the true etymology is *luchor pan*, "little man" Dr. Joyce also gives the same etymology in *Irish Names and Places*, i. 183, where he mentions several places named after them.

IV. HORNED WOMEN.

Source.—Lady Wilde's *Ancient Legends*, the first story.

Parallels.—A similar version was given by Mr. D. Fitzgerald in the *Revue Celtique*, iv. 181, but without the significant and impressive horns. He refers to *Cornhill* for February 1877, and to Campbell's "Sauntraigh" No. xxii. *Pop. Tales*, ii. 52-4, in which a "woman of peace" (a fairy) borrows a woman's kettle and returns it with flesh in it, but at last the woman refuses, and is persecuted by the fairy. I fail to see much analogy. A much closer one is in Campbell, ii. p. 63, where fairies are got rid of by shouting "Dunveilg is on fire." The familiar "lady-bird, lady-bird, fly away home, your house is on fire and your children at home," will occur to English minds. Another version in Kennedy's *Legendary Fictions*, p. 164, "Black Stairs on Fire."

Remarks.—Slievenamon is a famous fairy palace in Tipperary according to Dr. Joyce, *l.c.* i. 178. It was the hill on which Finn stood when he gave himself as the prize to the Irish maiden who should run up it quickest. Grainne won him with dire consequences, as all the world knows or ought to know (Kennedy, *Legend Fict.*, 222, "How Fion selected a Wife").

V. CONAL YELLOWCLAW.

Source.—Campbell, *Pop. Tales of West Highlands*, No. v. pp. 105-8, "Conall Cra Bhuidhe." I have softened the third episode, which is somewhat too ghastly in the original. I have translated "Cra Bhuide" Yellowclaw on the strength of Campbell's etymology, *l.c.* p. 158.

Parallels.—Campbell's vi. and vii. are two variants showing how widespread the story is in Gaelic Scotland. It occurs in Ireland where it has been printed in the chapbook, *Hibernian Tales*, as the "Black Thief and the Knight of the Glen," the Black Thief being Conall, and the knight corresponding to the King of Lochlan (it is given in Mr. Lang's *Red Fairy Book*). Here it attracted the notice of Thackeray, who gives a good abstract of it in his *Irish Sketch-Book*, ch. xvi. He thinks it "worthy of the Arabian Nights, as wild and odd as an Eastern tale." "That fantastical way of bearing testimony to the previous tale by producing an old woman who says the tale is not only true, but who was the very old woman who lived in the giant's castle is almost" (why "almost," Mr. Thackeray ?) "a stroke of genius." The incident of the giant's breath occurs in the story of Koisha Kayn, MacInnes' *Tales*,

i. 241, as well as the Polyphemus one, *ibid.* 265. One-eyed giants are frequent in Celtic folk-tales (*e.g.*, in *The Pursuit of Diarmaid* and in the *Mabinogi* of Owen).

Remarks.—Thackeray's reference to the "Arabian Nights" is especially apt, as the tale of Conall is a framework story like *The* 1001 *Nights*, the three stories told by Conall being framed, as it were, in a fourth which is nominally the real story. This method employed by the Indian story-tellers and from them adopted by Boccaccio and thence into all European literatures (Chaucer, Queen Margaret, &c.), is generally thought to be peculiar to the East, and to be ultimately derived from the Jatakas or Birth Stories of the Buddha who tells his adventures in former incarnations. Here we find it in Celtdom, and it occurs also in "The Story-teller at Fault" in this collection, and the story of *Koisha Kayn* in MacInnes' *Argyllshire Tales*, a variant of which collected but not published by Campbell has no less than nineteen tales enclosed in a framework. The question is whether the method was adopted independently in Ireland, or was due to foreign influences. Confining ourselves to "Conal Yellowclaw," it seems not unlikely that the whole story is an importation. For the second episode is clearly the story of Polyphemus from the Odyssey which was known in Ireland perhaps as early as the tenth century (see Prof. K. Meyer's edition of *Merugud Uilix maic Leirtis*, Pref. p. xii). It also crept into the voyages of Sindbad in the *Arabian Nights*. And as told in the Highlands it bears comparison even with the Homeric version. As Mr. Nutt remarks (*Celt. Mag.* xii.) the address of the giant to the buck is as effective as that of Polyphemus to his ram. The narrator, James Wilson, was a blind man who would naturally feel the pathos of the address; "it comes from the heart of the narrator;" says Campbell (*l.c.*, 148), "it is the ornament which his mind hangs on the frame of the story."

VI. HUDDEN AND DUDDEN.

Source.—From oral tradition, by the late D. W. Logie, taken down by Mr. Alfred Nutt.

Parallels.—Lover has a tale, "Little Fairly," obviously derived from this folk-tale; and there is another very similar, "Darby Darly." Another version of our tale is given under the title "Donald and his Neighbours," in the chapbook *Hibernian Tales*, whence it was reprinted by Thackeray in his *Irish Sketch-Book*, c. xvi. This has the incident of the "accidental matricide," on which see Prof. R. Köhler on Gonzenbach *Sicil. Mährchen*, ii. 224. No less than four tales of Campbell are of this type (*Pop. Tales*, ii. 218–31). M. Cosquin, in his "Contes populaires de Lorraine," the storehouse of "storiology," has elaborate excursuses in this class of tales attached to his Nos. x. and xx. Mr. Clouston discusses it also in his *Pop. Tales*, ii. 229–88. Both these writers are inclined to trace the chief incidents to India. It is to be observed that one of the earliest popular drolls in Europe, *Unibos*, a Latin poem of the eleventh, and perhaps the tenth, century, has the main outlines of the story, the fraudulent sale of worthless objects and the escape from the sack trick. The same story occurs in Straparola, the European earliest collection of folk-tales in the sixteenth century. On the other hand, the gold sticking to the scales is familiar to us in *Ali Baba*. (*Cf.* Cosquin, *l.c.*, i. 225–6, 229).

Remarks.—It is indeed curious to find, as M. Cosquin points out a cunning fellow tied in a sack getting out by crying, "I won't marry the princess," in countries so far apart as Ireland, Sicily (Gonzenbach, No. 71), Afghanistan (Thorburn, *Bannu*, p. 184), and Jamaica (*Folk-Lore Record*, iii. 53). It is indeed impossible to think these are disconnected, and for drolls of this kind a good case has been made out for the borrowing hypotheses by M. Cosquin and Mr. Clouston. Who borrowed from whom is another and more difficult question which has to be judged on its merits in each individual case.

This is a type of Celtic folk-tales which are European in spread, have analogies with the East, and can only be said to be Celtic by adoption and by colouring. They form a distinct section of the tales told by the Celts, and must be represented in any characteristic selection. Other examples are xi., xv., xx., and perhaps xxii.

VII. SHEPHERD OF MYDDVAI.

Source.—Preface to the edition of "The Physicians of Myddvai"; their prescription-book, from the Red Book of Hergest, published by the Welsh MS. Society in 1861. The legend is not given in the Red Book, but from oral tradition by Mr. W. Rees, p. xxi. As this is the first of the Welsh tales in this book it may be as well to give the reader such guidance as I can afford him on the intricacies of Welsh pronunciation, especially with regard to the mysterious *w*'s and *y*'s of Welsh orthography. For *w* substitute double *o*, as in "*fool*," and for *y*, the short *u* in b*u*t, and as near approach to Cymric speech will be reached as is possible for the outlander. It may be added that double *d* equals *th*, and double *l* is something like *Fl*, as Shakespeare knew in calling his Welsh soldier Fluellen (Llewelyn). Thus "Meddygon Myddvai" would be *Anglicè* "Methugon Muthvai."

Parallels.—Other versions of the legend of the Van Pool are given in *Cambro-Briton*, ii. 315 ; W. Sikes, *British Goblins*, p. 40. Mr. E. Sidney Hartland has discussed these and others in a set of papers contributed to the first volume of *The Archæological Review* (now incorporated into *Folk-Lore*), the substance of which is now given in his *Science of Fairy Tales*, 274-332. (See also the references given in *Revue Celtique*, iv., 187 and 268). Mr. Hartland gives there an ecumenical collection of parallels to the several incidents that go to make up our story—(1) The bride-capture of the Swan-Maiden, (2) the recognition of the bride, (3) the taboo against causeless blows, (4) doomed to be broken, and (5) disappearance of the Swan-Maiden, with (6) her return as Guardian Spirit to her descendants. In each case Mr. Hartland gives what he considers to be the most primitive form of the incident. With reference to our present tale, he comes to the conclusion, if I understand him aright, that the lake-maiden was once regarded as a local divinity. The physicians of Myddvai were historic personages, renowned for their medical skill for some six centuries, till the race died out with John Jones, *fl.* 1743. To explain their skill and uncanny knowledge of herbs, the folk traced them to a supernatural ancestress, who taught them their craft in a place still called Pant-y-Meddygon ("Doctors' Dingle"). Their medical knowledge did not require any such remarkable origin, as Mr. Hartland has shown in a paper "On Welsh Folk-Medicine," contributed to *Y Cymmrodor*, vol. xii. On the other hand, the Swan-Maiden type of story is widespread through the Old World. Mr. Morris' "Land East of the Moon and West of the Sun," in *The Earthly Paradise*, is taken from the Norse version. Parallels are accumulated by the Grimms, ii. 432 ; Köhler on Gonzenbach, ii. 20 ; or Blade, 149 ; Stokes' *Indian Fairy Tales*, 243, 276 ; and Messrs. Jones and Koopf, *Magyar Folk-Tales*, 362-5. It remains to be proved that one of these versions did not travel to Wales, and become there localised. We shall see other instances of such localisation or specialisation of general legends.

VIII. THE SPRIGHTLY TAILOR.

Source.—*Notes and Queries* for December 21, 1861, to which it was communicated by "Cuthbert Bede," the author of *Verdant Green,* who collected it in Cantyre.

Parallels.—Miss Dempster gives the same story in her Sutherland Collection, No. vii. (referred to by Campbell in his Gaelic list, at end of vol. iv.) ; Mrs. John Faed, I am informed by a friend, knows the Gaelic version, as told by her nurse in her youth. Chambers' "Strange Visitor," *Pop. Rhymes of Scotland*, 64, of which I gave an Anglicised version in my *English Fairy Tales*, No. xxxii., is clearly a variant.

Remarks.—The Macdonald of Saddell Castle was a very great man indeed. Once, when dining with the Lord-Lieutenant, an apology was made to him for placing him so far away from the head of the table. "Where the Macdonald sits," was the proud response, "there is the head of the table."

IX. DEIRDRE.

Source.—*Celtic Magazine*, xiii. pp. 69, *seq.* I have abridged somewhat, made the sons of Fergus all faithful instead of two traitors, and omitted an incident in the house of the wild men called here "strangers." The original Gaelic was given in the *Transactions of the Inverness Gaelic Society* for 1887, p. 241, *seq.*, by Mr. Carmichael. I have inserted Deirdre's "Lament" from the *Book of Leinster*.

Parallels.—This is one of the three most sorrowful Tales of Erin, (the other two, *Children of Lir* and *Children of Tureen*, are given in Dr. Joyce's *Old Celtic Romances*), and is a specimen of the old heroic sagas of elopement, a list of which is given in the *Book of Leinster*. The "outcast child" is a frequent episode in folk and hero-tales : an instance occurs in my *English Fairy Tales*, No. xxxv., and Prof. Köhler gives many others in *Archiv. f. Slav. Philologie*, i. 288. Mr. Nutt adds tenth century Celtic parallels in *Folk-Lore*, vol. ii. The wooing of hero by heroine is a characteristic Celtic touch. See "Connla" here, and other examples given by Mr. Nutt in his notes to MacInnes' *Tales*. The trees growing from the lovers' graves occurs in the English ballad of *Lord Lovel* and has been studied in *Mélusine*.

Remarks.—The "Story of Deirdre" is a remarkable instance of the tenacity of oral tradition among the Celts. It has been preserved in no less than five versions (or six, including Macpherson's "Darthula") ranging from the twelfth to the nineteenth century. The earliest is in the twelfth century, *Book of Leinster*, to be dated about 1140 (edited in facsimile under the auspices of the Royal Irish Academy, i. 147, *seq.*). Then comes a fifteenth century version, edited and translated by Dr. Stokes in Windisch's *Irische Texte* II., ii. 109, *seq.*, "Death of the Sons of Uisnech." Keating in his *History of Ireland* gave another version in the seventeenth century. The Dublin Gaelic Society published an eighteenth century version in their *Transactions* for 1808. And lastly we have the version before us, collected only a few years ago, yet agreeing in all essential details with the version of the *Book of Leinster*. Such a record is unique in the history of oral tradition, outside Ireland, where, however, it is quite a customary experience in the study of the Finn-saga. It is now recognised that Macpherson had, or could have had, ample material for his *rechauffé* of the Finn or "Fingal" saga. His "Darthula" is a similar cobbling of our present story. I leave to Celtic specialists the task of settling the exact relations of these various texts. I content myself with pointing out the fact that in these latter days of a seemingly prosaic century in these British Isles there has been collected from the lips of the folk a heroic story like this of "Deirdre," full of romantic incidents, told with tender feeling and considerable literary skill. No other country in Europe, except perhaps Russia, could provide a parallel to this living on of Romance among the common folk. Surely it is a bounden duty of those who are in the position to put on record any such utterances of the folk-imagination of the Celts before it is too late.

X. MUNACHAR AND MANACHAR.

Source.—I have combined the Irish version given by Dr. Hyde in his *Leabhar Sgeul.*, and translated by him for Mr. Yeats' *Irish Folk and Fairy Tales*, and the Scotch version given in Gaelic and English by Campbell, No. viii.

Parallels.—Two English versions are given in my *Eng. Fairy Tales*, No. iv., "The Old Woman and her Pig," and xxxiv., "The Cat and the Mouse," where see notes for other variants in these isles. M. Cosquin, in his notes to No. xxxiv., of his *Contes de Lorraine*, t. ii. pp. 35-41, has drawn attention to an astonishing number of parallels scattered through all Europe and the East (*cf.*, too, Crane, *Ital. Pop. Tales*, notes, 372-5). One of the earliest allusions to the jingle is in *Don Quixote*, pt. i, c. xvi. : "Y asi como suele decirse *el gato al rato, el rato á la cuerda, la cuerda al palo*, daba el arriero á Sancho, Sancho á la moza, la moza á él, el ventero á la moza." As I have pointed out, it is used to this day by Bengali women at the end of each folk-tale they recite (L. B. Day, *Folk-Tales of Bengal*, Pref.).

Remarks.—Two ingenious suggestions have been made as to the origin of this curious jingle, both connecting it with religious ceremonies: (1) Something very similar occurs in Chaldaic at the end of the Jewish *Hagada*, or domestic ritual for the Passover night. It has, however, been shown that this does not occur in early MSS. or editions, and was only added at the end to amuse the children after the service, and was therefore only a translation or adaptation of a current German form of the jingle; (2) M. Basset, in the *Revue des Traditions populaires*, 1890, t. v. p. 549, has suggested that it is a survival of the old Greek custom at the sacrifice of the Bouphonia for the priest to contend that *he* had not slain the sacred beast, the axe declares that the handle did it, the handle transfers the guilt further, and so on. This is ingenious, but fails to give any reasonable account of the diffusion of the jingle in countries which have had no historic connection with classical Greece.

XI. GOLD TREE AND SILVER TREE.

Source.—*Celtic Magazine*, xiii. 213-8, Gaelic and English from Mr. Kenneth Macleod.

Parallels.—Mr. Macleod heard another version in which "Gold Tree" (anonymous in this variant) is bewitched to kill her father's horse, dog, and cock. Abroad it is the Grimm's *Schneewitchen* (No. 53), for the Continental variants of which see Köhler on Gonzenbach, *Sicil. Märchen*, Nos. 2-4, Grimm's notes on 53, and Crane, *Ital. Pop. Tales*, 331. No other version is known in the British Isles.

Remarks.—It is unlikely, I should say impossible, that this tale, with the incident of the dormant heroine, should have arisen independently in the Highlands: it is most likely an importation from abroad. Yet in it occurs a most "primitive" incident, the bigamous household of the hero: this is glossed over in Mr. Macleod's other variant. On the "survival" method of investigation this would possibly be used as evidence for polygamy in the Highlands. Yet if, as is probable, the story came from abroad, this trait may have come with it, and only implies polygamy in the original home of the tale.

XII. KING O'TOOLE AND HIS GOOSE.

Source.—S. Lover's *Stories and Legends of the Irish Peasantry.*

Remarks.—This is really a moral apologue on the benefits of keeping your word. Yet it is told with such humour and vigour, that the moral glides insensibly into the heart.

XIII. THE WOOING OF OLWEN.

Source.—The *Mabinogi* of Kulhwych and Olwen from the translation of Lady Guest, abridged.

Parallels.—Prof. Rhys, *Hibbert Lectures*, p. 486, considers that our tale is paralleled by Cuchulain's "Wooing of Emer," a translation of which by Prof. K. Meyer appeared in the *Archæological Review*, vol. i. I fail to see much analogy. On the other hand in his *Arthurian Legend*, p. 41, he rightly compares the tasks set by Yspythadon to those set to Jason. They are indeed of the familiar type of the Bride Wager (on which see Grimm-Hunt, i. 399). The incident of the three animals, old, older, and oldest, has a remarkable resemblance to the *Tettira Jataka* (ed. Fausböll, No. 37, transl. Rhys Davids, i. p. 310 *seq.*) in which the partridge, monkey, and elephant dispute as to their relative age, and the partridge turns out to have voided the seed of the Banyan-tree under which they were sheltered, whereas the elephant only knew it when a mere bush, and the monkey had nibbled the topmost shoots. This apologue got to England at the end of the twelfth century as the sixty-ninth fable, "Wolf, Fox, and Dove," of a rhymed prose collection of "Fox Fables" (*Mishle Shu'alim*), of an Oxford Jew, Berachyah Nakdan, known in the Records as "Benedict le Puncteur" (see my *Fables of Æsop*, i. p. 170). Similar incidents occur in "Jack and his Snuff-box" in my *English Fairy Tales*, and in Dr. Hyde's "Well of D'Yerree-in-Dowan." The skilled companions of Kulhwych are common in European folk-tales (*Cf.* Cosquin, i. 123-5), and especially among the Celts (see Mr. Nutt's note in MacInnes' *Tales*, 445-8), among whom they occur very early, but not so early as Lynceus and the other skilled comrades of the Argonauts.

Remarks.—The hunting of the boar Trwyth can be traced back in Welsh tradition at least as early as the ninth century. For it is referred to in the following passage of Nennius' *Historia Britonum* ed. Stevenson, p: 60, "Est aliud miraculum in regione quæ dicitur Buelt [Builth, co. Brecon] Est ibi cumulus lapidum et unus lapis super-positus super congestum cum vestigia canis in eo. Quando venatus est porcum Troynt [*var. lec.* Troit] impressit Cabal, qui erat canis Arthuri militis, vestigium in lapide et Arthur postea congregavit congestum lapidum sub lapide in quo erat vestigium canis sui et vocatur Carn Cabal." Curiously enough there is still a mountain called Carn Cabal in the district of Builth, south of Rhayader Gwy in Breconshire. Still more curiously a friend of Lady Guest's found on this a cairn with a stone two feet long by one foot wide in which there was an indentation 4 in. × 3 in. × 2 in. which could easily have been mistaken for a paw-print of a dog, as may be seen from the engraving given of it (Mabinogion, ed. 1874, p. 269).

The stone and the legend are thus at least one thousand years old. "There stands the stone to tell if I lie." According to Prof. Rhys (*Hibbert Lect.* 486–97) the whole story is a mythological one, Kulhwych's mother being the dawn, the clover blossoms that grow under Olwen's feet being comparable to the roses that sprung up where Aphrodite had trod, and Yspyddadon being the incarnation of the sacred hawthorn. Mabon, again (*l.c.* pp. 21, 28–9), is the Apollo Maponus discovered in Latin inscriptions at Ainstable in Cumberland and elsewhere (Hübner, *Corp. Insc. Lat. Brit.* Nos. 218, 332, 1345). Granting all this, there

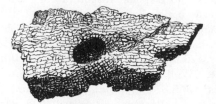

is nothing to show any mythological significance in the tale, though there may have been in the names of the *dramatis personæ*. I observe from the proceedings of the recent Eisteddfod that the bardic name of Mr. W. Abraham, M.P., is 'Mabon.' It scarcely follows that Mr. Abraham is in receipt of divine honours nowadays.

XIV. JACK AND HIS COMRADES.

Source.—Kennedy's *Legendary Fictions of the Irish Celts*.

Parallels.—This is the fullest and most dramatic version I know of the Grimm's "Town Musicians of Bremen" (No. 27). I have given an English (American) version in my *English Fairy Tales*, No. 5, in the notes to which would be found references to other versions known in the British Isles (*e.g.*, Campbell, No. 11) and abroad. *Cf.* remarks on No. vi.

XV. SHEE AN GANNON AND GRUAGACH GAIRE.

Source.—Curtin, *Myths and Folk-Lore of Ireland*, p. 114 *seq.* I have shortened the earlier part of the tale, and introduced into the

latter a few touches from Campbell's story of "Fionn's Enchantment," in *Revue Celtique*, t. i., 193 *seq*.

Parallels.—The early part is similar to the beginning of " The Sea-
Maiden " (No. xvii., which see). The latter part is practically the
same as the story of " Fionn's Enchantment," just referred to. It also
occurs in MacInnes' *Tales*, No. iii., "The King of Albainn" (see
Mr. Nutt's notes, 454). The head-crowned spikes are Celtic, *cf.* Mr.
Nutt's notes (MacInnes' *Tales*, 453).

Remarks.—Here again we meet the question whether the folk-tale
precedes the hero-tale about Finn or was derived from it, and again
the probability seems that our story has the priority as a folk-tale,
and was afterwards applied to the national hero, Finn. This is confirmed by the fact that a thirteenth century French romance, *Conte du
Graal*, has much the same incidents, and was probably derived from
a similar folk-tale of the Celts. Indeed, Mr. Nutt is inclined to think
that the original form of our story (which contains a mysterious
healing vessel) is the germ out of which the legend of the Holy Grail
was evolved (see his *Studies in the Holy Grail*, p. 202 *seq*.).

XVI. THE STORY-TELLER AT FAULT.

Source.—Griffin's *Tales from a Jury-Room*, combined with Campbell, No. xvii. *c*, " The Slim Swarthy Champion."

Parallels.—Campbell gives another variant, *l.c.* i. 318. Dr. Hyde
has an Irish version of Campbell's tale written down in 1762, from
which he gives the incident of the air-ladder (which I have had to
euphemise in my version) in his *Beside the Fireside*, p. 191, and other
passages in his Preface. The most remarkable parallel to this incident,
however, is afforded by the feats of Indian jugglers reported briefly by
Marco Polo, and illustrated with his usual wealth of learning by the
late Sir Henry Yule, in his edition, vol. i. p. 308 *seq*. The accompanying illustration (reduced from Yule) will tell its own tale : it is
taken from the Dutch account of the travels of an English sailor,
E. Melton, *Zeldzaame Reizen*, 1702, p. 468. It tells the tale in five acts,
all included in one sketch. Another instance quoted by Yule is
still more parallel, so to speak. The twenty-third trick performed
by some conjurors before the Emperor Jahangueir (*Memoirs*, p. 102)
is thus described : " They produced a chain of 50 cubits in length,
and in my presence threw one end of it towards the sky, where
it remained as if fastened to something in the air. A dog was then
brought forward, and being placed at the lower end of the chain, im-

mediately ran up, and, reaching the other end, immediately disappeared in the air. In the same manner a hog, a panther, a lion, and
a tiger were successively sent up the chain." It has been suggested
that the conjurors hypnotise the spectators, and make them believe
they see these things. This is practically the suggestion of a wise
Mohammedan, who is quoted by Yule as saying, " *Wallah!* 'tis my
opinion there has been neither going up nor coming down ; 'tis all
hocus-pocus," hocus-pocus being presumably the Mohammedan term
for hypnotism.

Remarks.—Dr. Hyde (*l.c.* Pref. xxix.) thinks our tale cannot be
older than 1362, because of a reference to one O'Connor Sligo which
occurs in all its variants ; it is, however, omitted in our somewhat
abridged version. Mr. Nutt (*ap.* Campbell, *The Fians,* Introd. xix.)
thinks that this does not prevent a still earlier version having existed.
I should have thought that the existence of so distinctly Eastern a
trick in the tale, and the fact that it is a framework story (another
Eastern characteristic), would imply that it is a rather late importation, with local allusions superadded (*cf.* notes on " Conal Yellowclaw," No. v.).

The passages in verse from pp. 137, 139, and the description of the

Beggarman, pp. 136, 140, are instances of a curious characteristic of Gaelic folk-tales called " runs." Collections of conventional epithets are used over and over again to describe the same incident, the beaching of a boat, sea-faring, travelling and the like, and are inserted in different tales. These " runs " are often similar in both the Irish and the Scotch form of the same tale or of the same incident. The vo umes of *Waifs and Strays* contain numerous examples of these " runs," which have been indexed in each volume. These " runs " are another confirmation of my view that the original form of the folk-tale was that of the *Cante-fable* (see note on "Connla" and on "Childe Rowland" in *English Fairy Tales*).

XVII. SEA-MAIDEN.

Source.—Campbell, *Pop. Tales*, No. 4. I have omitted the births of the animal comrades and transposed the carlin to the middle of the tale. Mr. Batten has considerably idealised the Sea-Maiden in his frontispiece. When she restores the husband to the wife in one of the variants, she brings him out of her mouth ! " So the sea-maiden put up his head (*Who do you mean ? Out of her mouth to be sure. She had swallowed him*)."

Parallels.—The early part of the story occurs in No. xv., " Shee an Gannon," and the last part in No. xix., " Fair, Brown, and Trembling " (both from Curtin), Campbell's No. 1. " The Young King " is much like it ; also MacInnes' No. iv., " Herding of Cruachan " and No. viii., " Lod the Farmer's Son." The third of Mr. Britten's Irish folk-tales in the *Folk-Lore Journal* is a Sea-Maiden story. The story is obviously a favourite one among the Celts. Yet its main incidents occur with frequency in Continental folk-tales. Prof. Köhler has collected a number in his notes on Campbell's Tales in *Orient und Occident*, Bnd. ii. 115-8. The trial of the sword occurs in the saga of Sigurd, yet it is also frequent in Celtic saga and folk-tales (see Mr. Nutt's note, MacInnes' *Tales*, 473, and add. Curtin, 320). The hideous carlin and her three giant sons is also common form in Celtic. The external soul of the Sea-Maiden carried about in an egg, in a trout, in a hoodie, in a hind, is a remarkable instance of a peculiarly savage conception which has been studied by Major Temple, *Wide-awake Stories*, 404-5 ; by Mr. E. Clodd, in the " Philosophy of Punchkin," in *Folk-Lore Journal*, vol. ii., and by Mr. Frazer in his *Golden Bough*, vol. ii.

Remarks.—As both Prof. Rhys (*Hibbert Lect.*, 464) and Mr. Nutt (MacInnes' *Tales*, 477) have pointed out, practically the same story (that of Perseus and Andromeda) is told of the Ultonian hero, Cuchulain, in the *Wooing of Emer*, a tale which occurs in the Book of Leinster, a MS. of the twelfth century, and was probably copied from one of the eighth. Unfortunately it is not complete, and the Sea-Maiden incident is only to be found in a British Museum MS. of about 1300. In this Cuchulain finds that the daughter of Ruad is to be given as a tribute to the Fomori, who, according to Prof. Rhys, *Folk-Lore*, ii. 293, have something of the night*mare* about their etymology. Cuchulain fights *three* of them successively, has his wounds bound up by a strip of the maiden's garment, and then departs. Thereafter many boasted of having slain the Fomori, but the maiden believed them not till at last by a stratagem she recognises Cuchulain. I may add to this that in Mr. Curtin's *Myths*, 330, the threefold trial of the sword is told of Cuchulain. This would seem to trace our story back to the seventh or eighth century and certainly to the thirteenth. If so, it is likely enough that it spread from Ireland through Europe with the Irish missions (for the wide extent of which see map in Mrs. Bryant's *Celtic Ireland*). The very letters that have spread through all Europe except Russia, are to be traced to the script of these Irish monks : why not certain folk-tales ? There is a further question whether the story was originally told of Cuchulain as a hero-tale and then became departicularised as a folk-tale, or was the process *vice versâ*. Certainly in the form in which it appears in the *Tochmarc Emer* it is not complete, so that here, as elsewhere, we seem to have an instance of a folk-tale applied to a well-known heroic name, and becoming a hero-tale or saga.

XVIII. LEGEND OF KNOCKMANY.

Source.—W. Carleton, *Traits and Stories of the Irish Peasantry.*

Parallels.—Kennedy's "Fion MacCuil and the Scotch Giant," *Legend. Fict.*, 203–5.

Remarks.—Though the venerable names of Finn and Cucullin (Cuchulain) are attached to the heroes of this story, this is probably only to give an extrinsic interest to it. The two heroes could not have come together in any early form of their sagas, since Cuchulain's reputed date is of the first, Finn's of the third century A.D. (*cf.* however, MacDougall's *Tales*, notes, 272). Besides, the grotesque form of the legend is enough to remove it from the region of the hero-tale· On the other hand, there is a distinct reference to Finn's wisdom-tooth, which presaged the future to him (on this see *Revue Celtique*, v. 201, Joyce, *Old Celt. Rom.*, 434–5, and MacDougall, *l.c.* 274).

Cucullin's power-finger is another instance of the life-index or external soul, on which see remarks on Sea-Maiden. Mr. Nutt informs me that parodies of the Irish sagas occur as early as the sixteenth century, and the present tale may be regarded as a specimen.

XIX. FAIR, BROWN, AND TREMBLING.

Source.—Curtin, *Myths, &c., of Ireland*, 78 *seq.*

Parallels.—The latter half resembles the second part of the Sea-Maiden (No. xvii.), which see. The earlier portion is a Cinderella tale (on which see the late Mr. Ralston's article in *Nineteenth Century*, Nov. 1879, and Mr. Lang's treatm nt in his Perrault). Miss Roal'e Cox is about to publish for the Folk-Lore Society a whole volume of variants of the Cinderella group of stories, which are remarkably well represented In these isles, nearly a dozen different versions being known in England, Ireland, and Scotland.

XX. JACK AND HIS MASTER.

Source.—Kennedy, *Fireside Stories of Ireland*, 74–80, " Shan an Omadhan and his Master."

Parallels.—It occurs also in Campbell, No. xlv., " Mac a Rusgaich." It is a European droll, the wide occurrence of which—" the loss of temper bet" I should call it—is bibliographised by M. Cosquin, *l.c.* ii. 50 (*cf.* notes on No. vi.).

XXI. BETH GELLERT.

Source.—I have paraphrased the well-known poem of Hon. W. R. Spencer, " Beth Gêlert, or the Grave of the Greyhound," first printed privately as a broadsheet in 1800 when it was composed (" August 11, 1800, Dolymalynllyn " is the colophon). It was published in Spencer's *Poems*, 1811, pp. 78–86. These dates, it will be seen, are of importance. Spencer states in a note : " The story of this ballad is traditionary in a village at the foot of Snowdon where Llewellyn the Great had a house. The Greyhound named Gêlert was given him by his father-in-law, King John, in the year 1205, and the place to this day is called Beth-Gêlert, or the grave of Gêlert." As a matter of fact, no trace of the tradition in connection with Bedd Gellert can be found before Spen er's time. It is not mentioned in Leland's *Itinerary*, ed. Hearne, v. p. 37 (" Beth Kellarth "), in Pennant's *Tour* (1770), ii. 176, or in Bingley's

Tour in Wales (1800). Borrow in his *Wild Wales*, p. 146, gives the legend, but does not profess to derive it from local tradition.

Parallels.—The only parallel in Celtdom is that noticed by Croker in his third volume, the legend of Partholan who killed his wife's greyhound from jealousy : this is found sculptured in stone at Ap Brune, co. Limerick. As is well known, and has been elaborately discussed by Mr. Baring-Gould (*Curious Myths of the Middle Ages*, p. 134 *seq.*), and Mr. W. A. Clouston (*Popular Tales and Fictions*, ii 166, *seq.*), the story of the man who rashly slew the dog (ichneumon, weasel, &c.) that had saved his babe from death, is one of those which have spread from East to West. It is indeed, as Mr. Clouston points out, still current in India, the land of its birth. There is little doubt that it is originally Buddhistic : the late Prof. S. Beal gave the earliest known version from the Chinese translation of the *Vinaya Pitaka* in the *Academy* of Nov. 4, 1882. The conception of an animal sacrificing itself for the sake of others is peculiarly Buddhistic ; the "hare in the moon" is an apotheosis of such a piece of self-sacrifice on the part of Buddha (*Sasa Jataka*). There are two forms that have reached the West, the first being that of an animal saving men at the cost of its own life. I pointed out an early instance of this, quoted by a Rabbi of the second century, in my *Fables of Æsop*, i. 105. This concludes with a strangely close parallel to Gellert ; "They raised a cairn over his grave, and the place is still called The Dog's Grave." The *Culex* attributed to Virgil seems to be another variant of this. The second form of the legend is always told as a moral apologue against precipitate action, and originally occurred in *The Fables of Bidpai* in its hundred and one forms, all founded on Buddhistic originals (*cf.* Benfey, *Pantschatantra*, Einleitung, § 201).* Thence, according to Benfey, it was inserted in the *Book of Sindibad*, another collection of Oriental Apologues framed on what may be called the Mrs. Potiphar formula. This came to Europe with the Crusades, and is known in its Western versions as the *Seven Sages of Rome*. The Gellert story occurs in all the Oriental and Occidental versions ; *e.g.*, it is the First Master's story in Wynkyn de Worde's (ed. G. L. Gomme, for the Villon Society.) From the *Seven Sages* it was taken into the particular branch of the *Gesta Romanorum* current in England and known as the English *Gesta*,

---

* It occurs in the same chapter as the story of La Perrette, which has been traced, after Benfey, by Prof. M. Müller in his "Migration of Fables" (*Sel. Essays*, i. 500-74) ; exactly the same history applies to Gellert.

where it occurs as c. xxxii., "Story of Folliculus." We have thus traced it to England whence it passed to Wales, where I have discovered it as the second apologue of "The Fables of Cattwg the Wise," in the Iolo MS. published by the Welsh MS. Society, p. 561, "The man who killed his Greyhound." (These Fables, Mr. Nutt informs me, are a pseudonymous production probably of the sixteenth century.) This concludes the literary route of the Legend of Gellert from India to Wales : Buddhistic *Vinaya Pitaka—Fables of Bidpai ;—* Oriental *Sindibad ;—*Occidental *Seven Sages of Rome ;—*" English " (Latin), *Gesta Romanorum ;—*Welsh, *Fables of Cattwg.*

Remarks.—We have still to connect the legend with Llewelyn and with Bedd Gelert. But first it may be desirable to point out why it is necessary to assume that the legend is a legend and not a fact. The saving of an infant's life by a dog, and the mistaken slaughter of the dog, are not such an improbable combination as to make it impossible that the same event occurred in many places. But what is impossible, in my opinion, is that such an event should have independently been used in different places as the typical instance of, and warning against, rash action. That the Gellert legend, before it was localised, was used as a moral apologue in Wales is shown by the fact that it occurs among the Fables of Cattwg, which are all of that character. It was also utilised as a proverb : " *Yr wy'n edivaru cymmaint a'r Gŵr a laddodd ei Vilgi* (" I repent as much as the man who slew his greyhound"). The fable indeed, from this point of view, seems greatly to have attracted the Welsh mind, perhaps as of especial value to a proverbially impetuous temperament. Croker (*Fairy Legends of Ireland,* vol. iii. p. 165) points out several places where the legend seems to have been localised in place-names—two places, called "Gwal y Vilast" (" Greyhound's Couch "), in Carmarthen and Glamorganshire; "Llech y Asp" ("Dog's Stone"), in Cardigan, and another place named in Welsh "Spring of the Greyhound's Stone." Mr. Baring-Gould mentions that the legend is told of an ordinary tombstone, with a knight and a greyhound, in Abergavenny Church ; while the Fable of Cattwg is told of a man in Abergarwan. So widespread and well known was the legend that it was in Richard III.'s time adopted as the national crest. In the Warwick Roll, at the Herald's Office, after giving separate crests for England, Scotland, and Ireland, that for Wales is given as figured in the margin, and blazoned " on a coronet in a cradle or, a greyhound argent for Walys" (see

J. R. Planché, *Twelve Designs for the Costume of Shakespeare's Richard III.*, 1830, frontispiece). If this Roll is authentic, the popularity of the legend is thrown back into the fifteenth century. It still remains to explain how and when this general legend of rash action was localised and specialised at Bedd Gelert: I believe I have discovered this. There certainly was a local legend about a dog named Gelert at that place ; E. Jones, in the first edition of his *Musical Relicks of the Welsh Bards*, 1784, p. 40, gives the following *englyn* or epigram :

> Claddwyd Cylart celfydd (ymlyniad)
> Ymlaneau Efionydd
> Parod giuio i'w gynydd
> Parai'r dydd yr heliai Hŷdd ;

which he Englishes thus:

> The remains of famed Cylart, so faithful and good,
> The bounds of the cantred conceal ;
> Whenever the doe or the stag he pursued
> His master was sure of a meal.

No reference was made in the first edition to the Gellert legend, but in the second edition of 1794, p. 75, a note was added telling the legend, "There is a general tradition in North Wales that a wolf had entered the house of Prince Llewellyn. Soon after the Prince returned home, and, going into the nursery, he met his dog *Kill-hart*, all bloody and wagging his tail at him ; Prince Llewellyn, on entering the room found the cradle where his child lay overturned, and the floor flowing with blood ; imagining that the greyhound had killed the child, he immediately drew his sword and stabbed it ; then, turning up the cradle, found under it the child alive, and the wolf dead. This so grieved the Prince, that he erected a tomb over his faithful dog's grave ; where afterwards the parish church was built and goes by that name—*Bedd Cilhart*, or the grave of Kill-hart, in *Carnarvonshire*. From this incident is elicited a very common Welsh proverb [that given above which occurs also in 'The Fables of Cattwg ;' it will be observed that it is quite indefinite.]" "Prince Llewellyn ab Jorwerth married Joan, [natural] daughter of King John, by *Agatha*, daughter of Robert Ferrers, Earl of Derby ; and the dog was a present to the prince from his father-in-law about the year 1205." It was clearly from this note that the Hon. Mr. Spencer got his account ; oral tradition does not indulge in dates *Anno Domini*. The application of the general legend of "the man who slew his greyhound" to the dog Cylart, was due to the learning of E. Jones, author of the *Musical Relicks*. I am convinced of this, for by a lucky chance I am enabled to give the real legend about Cylart, which is thus given in Carlisle's *Topographical Dictionary of Wales*, s.v., "Bedd Celert," published in 1811, the date of publication of Mr. Spencer's *Poems*. "Its name, according to tradition, implies *The Grave of Celert*, a Greyhound which belonged to Llywelyn, the last Prince of Wales: and a large Rock is still pointed out as the monument of this celebrated Dog, being on the spot where it was found dead, together with the stag which it had pursued from Carnarvon," which is thirteen miles distant. The cairn was thus a monument of a "record" run of a greyhound: the *englyn* quoted by Jones is suitable enough for this, while quite inadequate to record the later legendary exploits of Gelert. Jones found an *englyn* devoted to *an* exploit of a dog named Cylart, and chose to interpret it in his second edition, 1794, as *the* exploit of a greyhound with which all the world (in Wales) were acquainted. Mr. Spencer took the legend from Jones (the reference to the date 1205 proves that), enshrined it in his somewhat *banal* verses, which were lucky enough to be copied into several reading-books, and thus became known to all English-speaking folk.

It remains only to explain why Jones connected the legend with Llewelyn. Llewelyn had local connection with Bedd Gellert, which was the seat of an Augustinian abbey, one of the oldest in Wales. An inspeximus of Edward I. given in Dugdale, *Monast. Angl.*, ed. pr. ii. 100a, quotes as the earliest charter of the abbey "Cartam Lewelini magni." The name of the abbey was "Beth Kellarth"; the name is thus given by Leland, *l.c.*, and as late as 1794 an engraving at the British Museum is entitled "Beth Kelert," while Carlisle gives it as "Beth Celert." The place was thus named after the abbey, not after the cairn or rock. This is confirmed by the fact of which Prof. Rhys had informed me, that the collocation of letters *rt* is un-Welsh. Under these circumstances it is not impossible, I think, that the earlier legend of the marvellous run of "Cylart" from Carnarvon was due to the etymologising fancy of some English-speaking Welshman who interpreted the name as Killhart, so that the simpler legend would be only a folk-etymology.

But whether Kellarth, Kelert, Cylart, Gêlert or Gellert ever existed and run a hart from Carnarvon to Bedd Gellert or no, there can be little doubt after the preceding that he was not the original hero of the

fable of "the man that slew his greyhound," which came to Wales from
Buddhistic India through channels which are perfectly traceable. It
was Edward Jones who first raised him to that proud position, and
William Spencer who securely installed him there, probably for all
time. The legend is now firmly established at Bedd Gellert. There
is said to be an ancient air, "Bedd Gelert," "as sung by the Ancient
Britons"; it is given in a pamphlet published at Carnarvon in the
"fifties," entitled *Gellert's Grave; or, Llewellyn's Rashness: a Ballad*,
by the Hon. W. R. Spencer, to which is added that ancient Welsh air,
"*Bedd Gelert*," *as sung by the Ancient Britons*. The air is from
R. Roberts' "Collection of Welsh Airs," but what connection it has
with the legend I have been unable to ascertain. This is probably
another case of adapting one tradition to another. It is almost
impossible to distinguish palœozoic and cainozoic strata in oral
tradition. According to Murray's *Guide to N. Wales*, p. 125, the only
authority for the cairn now shown is that of the landlord of the Goat
Inn, "who felt compelled by the cravings of tourists to invent a
grave." Some old men at Bedd Gellert, Prof. Rhys informs me, are
ready to testify that they saw the cairn laid. They might almost have
been present at the birth of the legend, which, if my affiliation of it
is correct, is not yet quite 100 years old.

XXII. STORY OF IVAN.

Source.—Lluyd, *Archæologia Britannia*, 1707, the first comparative
Celtic grammar and the finest piece of work in comparative philology
hitherto done in England, contains this tale as a specimen of Cornish
then still spoken in Cornwall. I have used the English version contained in *Blackwood's Magazine* as long ago as May 1818. I have
taken the third counsel from the Irish version, as the original is not
suited *virginibus puerisque*, though harmless enough in itself.

Parallels.—Lover has a tale, *The Three Advices*. It occurs also in
modern Cornwall *ap.* Hunt, *Drolls of West of England*, 344, "The
Tinner of Chyamor." Borrow, *Wild Wales*, 41, has a reference which
seems to imply that the story had crystallised into a Welsh proverb.
Curiously enough, it forms the chief episode of the so-called "Irish
Odyssey" ("*Merugud Uilix maicc Leirtis*"—"Wandering of Ulysses
M'Laertes"). It was derived, in all probability, from the *Gesta
Romanorum*, c. 103, where two of the three pieces of advice are
"Avoid a byeway," "Beware of a house where the housewife is younger
than her husband." It is likely enough that this chapter, like others of

the *Gesta*, came from the East, for it is found in some versions of "The Forty Viziers," and in the *Turkish Tales* (see Oesterley's parallels and *Gesta*, ed. Swan and Hooper, note 9).

XXIII. ANDREW COFFEY.

Source.—From the late D. W. Logie, written down by Mr. Alfred Nutt.

Parallels.—Dr. Hyde's "Teig O'Kane and the Corpse," and Kennedy's "Cauth Morrisy," *Legend. Fict.*, 158, are practically the same.

Remarks.—No collection of Celtic Folk-Tales would be representative that did not contain some specimen of the gruesome. The most effective ghoul story in existence is Lover's "Brown Man."

XXIV. BATTLE OF BIRDS.

Source.—Campbell (*Pop. Tales, W. Highlands*, No. ii.), with touches from the seventh variant and others, including the casket and key finish, from Curtin's "Son of the King of Erin" (*Myths, &c.*, 32 *seq.*). I have also added a specimen of the humorous end pieces added by Gaelic story-tellers ; on these tags see an interesting note in MacDougall's *Tales*, note on p. 112. I have found some difficulty in dealing with Campbell's excessive use of the second person singular, "If thou thouest him some two or three times, 'tis well," but beyond that it is wearisome. Practically, I have reserved *thou* for the speech of giants, who may be supposed to be somewhat old-fashioned. I fear, however, I have not been quite consistent, though the *you's* addressed to the apple-pips are grammatically correct as applied to the pair of lovers.

Parallels.—Besides the eight versions given or abstracted by Campbell and Mr. Curtin's, there is Carleton's "Three Tasks," Dr. Hyde's "Son of Branduf" (MS.) ; there is the First Tale of MacInnes (where see Mr. Nutt's elaborate notes, 431–43), two in the *Celtic Magazine*, vol. xii., "Grey Norris from Warland" (*Folk-Lore Journ.* i. 316), and Mr. Lang's Morayshire Tale, "Nicht Nought Nothing" (see *Eng. Fairy Tales*, No. vii.), no less than sixteen variants found among the Celts. It must have occurred early among them. Mr. Nutt found the feather-thatch incident in the *Agallamh na Senoraib* ("Discourse of Elders"), which is at least as old as the fifteenth century. Yet the story is to be found throughout the Indo-European world, as is shown by Prof. Köhler's elaborate list of parallels attached to

Mr. Lang's variant in *Revue Celtique*, iii. 374 ; and Mr. Lang, in his *Custom and Myth* ("A far travelled Tale"), has given a number of parallels from savage sources. And strangest of all, the story is practically the same as the classical myth of Jason and Medea.

Remarks.—Mr. Nutt, in his discussion of the tale (MacInnes, *Tales* 441), makes the interesting suggestion that the obstacles to pursuit, the forest, the mountain, and the river, exactly represent the boundary of the old Teutonic Hades, so that the story was originally one of the Descent to Hell. Altogether it seems likely that it is one of the oldest folk-tales in existence, and belonged to the story-store of the original Aryans, whoever they were, was passed by them with their language on to the Hellenes and perhaps to the Indians, was developed in its modern form in Scandinavia (where its best representative "The Master Maid" of Asbjörnsen is still found), was passed by them to the Celts and possibly was transmitted by these latter to other parts of Europe, perhaps by early Irish monks (see notes on "Sea-Maiden"). The spread in the Buddhistic world, and thence to the South Seas and Madagascar, would be secondary from India. I hope to have another occasion for dealing with this most interesting of all folk-tales in the detail it deserves.

XXV. BREWERY OF EGGSHELLS.

Source.—From the *Cambrian Quarterly Magazine*, 1830, vol. ii. p. 86 ; it is stated to be literally translated from the Welsh.

Parallels.—Another variant from Glamorganshire is given in *Y Cymmrodor*, vi. 209. Croker has the story under the title I have given the Welsh one in his *Fairy Legends*, 41. Mr. Hartland, in his *Science of Fairy Tales*, 113-6, gives the European parallels.

XXVI. LAD WITH THE GOAT SKIN.

Source.—Kennedy, *Legendary Fictions*, pp. 23-31. The Adventures of " Gilla na Chreck an Gour'."

Parallels.—"The Lad with the Skin Coverings" is a popular Celtic figure, *cf.* MacDougall's Third Tale, MacInnes' Second, and a reference in Campbell, iii. 147. According to Mr. Nutt (*Holy Grail*, 134), he is the original of Parzival. But the adventures in these tales are not the "cure by laughing" incident which forms the centre of our tale, and is Indo-European in extent (*cf.* references in *English Fairy Tales*, notes to No. xxvii.). " The smith who made hell too hot for him is Sisyphus," says Mr. Lang (Introd. to Grimm, p. xiii.) ; in Ireland he is Billy Dawson (Carleton, *Three Wishes*). In the Finn-Saga, Conan harries hell, as readers of *Waverley* may remember " ' Claw for claw, and devil take the shortest nails,' as Conan said to the Devil " (*cf.* Campbell, *The Fians*, 73, and notes, 283). Red-haired men in Ireland and elsewhere are always rogues (see Mr. Nutt's references, MacInnes' *Tales*, 477 ; to which add the case in "Lough Neagh," Yeats, *Irish Folk-Tales*, p. 210).

THE END.

A CATALOGUE OF SELECTED DOVER BOOKS
IN ALL FIELDS OF INTEREST

A CATALOGUE OF SELECTED DOVER BOOKS
IN ALL FIELDS OF INTEREST

AMERICA'S OLD MASTERS, James T. Flexner. Four men emerged unexpectedly from provincial 18th century America to leadership in European art: Benjamin West, J. S. Copley, C. R. Peale, Gilbert Stuart. Brilliant coverage of lives and contributions. Revised, 1967 edition. 69 plates. 365pp. of text.

21806-6 Paperbound $3.00

FIRST FLOWERS OF OUR WILDERNESS: AMERICAN PAINTING, THE COLONIAL PERIOD, James T. Flexner. Painters, and regional painting traditions from earliest Colonial times up to the emergence of Copley, West and Peale Sr., Foster, Gustavus Hesselius, Feke, John Smibert and many anonymous painters in the primitive manner. Engaging presentation, with 162 illustrations. xxii + 368pp.

22180-6 Paperbound $3.50

THE LIGHT OF DISTANT SKIES: AMERICAN PAINTING, 1760-1835, James T. Flexner. The great generation of early American painters goes to Europe to learn and to teach: West, Copley, Gilbert Stuart and others. Allston, Trumbull, Morse; also contemporary American painters—primitives, derivatives, academics—who remained in America. 102 illustrations. xiii + 306pp.

22179-2 Paperbound $3.50

A HISTORY OF THE RISE AND PROGRESS OF THE ARTS OF DESIGN IN THE UNITED STATES, William Dunlap. Much the richest mine of information on early American painters, sculptors, architects, engravers, miniaturists, etc. The only source of information for scores of artists, the major primary source for many others. Unabridged reprint of rare original 1834 edition, with new introduction by James T. Flexner, and 394 new illustrations. Edited by Rita Weiss. 6⅝ x 9⅝.

21695-0, 21696-9, 21697-7 Three volumes, Paperbound $15.00

EPOCHS OF CHINESE AND JAPANESE ART, Ernest F. Fenollosa. From primitive Chinese art to the 20th century, thorough history, explanation of every important art period and form, including Japanese woodcuts; main stress on China and Japan, but Tibet, Korea also included. Still unexcelled for its detailed, rich coverage of cultural background, aesthetic elements, diffusion studies, particularly of the historical period. 2nd, 1913 edition. 242 illustrations. lii + 439pp. of text.

20364-6, 20365-4 Two volumes, Paperbound $6.00

THE GENTLE ART OF MAKING ENEMIES, James A. M. Whistler. Greatest wit of his day deflates Oscar Wilde, Ruskin, Swinburne; strikes back at inane critics, exhibitions, art journalism; aesthetics of impressionist revolution in most striking form. Highly readable classic by great painter. Reproduction of edition designed by Whistler. Introduction by Alfred Werner. xxxvi + 334pp.

21875-9 Paperbound $3.00

VISUAL ILLUSIONS: THEIR CAUSES, CHARACTERISTICS, AND APPLICATIONS, Matthew Luckiesh. Thorough description and discussion of optical illusion, geometric and perspective, particularly; size and shape distortions, illusions of color, of motion; natural illusions; use of illusion in art and magic, industry, etc. Most useful today with op art, also for classical art. Scores of effects illustrated. Introduction by William H. Ittleson. 100 illustrations. xxi + 252pp.

21530-X Paperbound $2.00

A HANDBOOK OF ANATOMY FOR ART STUDENTS, Arthur Thomson. Thorough, virtually exhaustive coverage of skeletal structure, musculature, etc. Full text, supplemented by anatomical diagrams and drawings and by photographs of undraped figures. Unique in its comparison of male and female forms, pointing out differences of contour, texture, form. 211 figures, 40 drawings, 86 photographs. xx + 459pp. 5⅜ x 8⅜.

21163-0 Paperbound $3.50

150 MASTERPIECES OF DRAWING, Selected by Anthony Toney. Full page reproductions of drawings from the early 16th to the end of the 18th century, all beautifully reproduced: Rembrandt, Michelangelo, Dürer, Fragonard, Urs, Graf, Wouwerman, many others. First-rate browsing book, model book for artists. xviii + 150pp. 8⅜ x 11¼.

21032-4 Paperbound $2.50

THE LATER WORK OF AUBREY BEARDSLEY, Aubrey Beardsley. Exotic, erotic, ironic masterpieces in full maturity: Comedy Ballet, Venus and Tannhauser, Pierrot, Lysistrata, Rape of the Lock, Savoy material, Ali Baba, Volpone, etc. This material revolutionized the art world, and is still powerful, fresh, brilliant. With *The Early Work*, all Beardsley's finest work. 174 plates, 2 in color. xiv + 176pp. 8⅛ x 11.

21817-1 Paperbound $3.75

DRAWINGS OF REMBRANDT, Rembrandt van Rijn. Complete reproduction of fabulously rare edition by Lippmann and Hofstede de Groot, completely reedited, updated, improved by Prof. Seymour Slive, Fogg Museum. Portraits, Biblical sketches, landscapes, Oriental types, nudes, episodes from classical mythology—All Rembrandt's fertile genius. Also selection of drawings by his pupils and followers. "Stunning volumes," *Saturday Review*. 550 illustrations. lxxviii + 552pp. 9⅛ x 12¼.

21485-0, 21486-9 Two volumes, Paperbound $10.00

THE DISASTERS OF WAR, Francisco Goya. One of the masterpieces of Western civilization—83 etchings that record Goya's shattering, bitter reaction to the Napoleonic war that swept through Spain after the insurrection of 1808 and to war in general. Reprint of the first edition, with three additional plates from Boston's Museum of Fine Arts. All plates facsimile size. Introduction by Philip Hofer, Fogg Museum. v + 97pp. 9⅜ x 8¼.

21872-4 Paperbound $2.50

GRAPHIC WORKS OF ODILON REDON. Largest collection of Redon's graphic works ever assembled: 172 lithographs, 28 etchings and engravings, 9 drawings. These include some of his most famous works. All the plates from *Odilon Redon: oeuvre graphique complet*, plus additional plates. New introduction and caption translations by Alfred Werner. 209 illustrations. xxvii + 209pp. 9⅛ x 12¼.

21966-8 Paperbound $4.50

DESIGN BY ACCIDENT; A BOOK OF "ACCIDENTAL EFFECTS" FOR ARTISTS AND DESIGNERS, James F. O'Brien. Create your own unique, striking, imaginative effects by "controlled accident" interaction of materials: paints and lacquers, oil and water based paints, splatter, crackling materials, shatter, similar items. Everything you do will be different; first book on this limitless art, so useful to both fine artist and commercial artist. Full instructions. 192 plates showing "accidents," 8 in color. viii + 215pp. 8⅜ x 11¼.   21942-9 Paperbound $3.75

THE BOOK OF SIGNS, Rudolf Koch. Famed German type designer draws 493 beautiful symbols: religious, mystical, alchemical, imperial, property marks, runes, etc. Remarkable fusion of traditional and modern. Good for suggestions of timelessness, smartness, modernity. Text. vi + 104pp. 6⅛ x 9¼.
                    20162-7 Paperbound $1.50

HISTORY OF INDIAN AND INDONESIAN ART, Ananda K. Coomaraswamy. An unabridged republication of one of the finest books by a great scholar in Eastern art. Rich in descriptive material, history, social backgrounds; Sunga reliefs, Rajput paintings, Gupta temples, Burmese frescoes, textiles, jewelry, sculpture, etc. 400 photos. viii + 423pp. 6⅜ x 9¾.   21436-2 Paperbound $5.00

PRIMITIVE ART, Franz Boas. America's foremost anthropologist surveys textiles, ceramics, woodcarving, basketry, metalwork, etc.; patterns, technology, creation of symbols, style origins. All areas of world, but very full on Northwest Coast Indians. More than 350 illustrations of baskets, boxes, totem poles, weapons, etc. 378 pp.
                    20025-6 Paperbound $3.00

THE GENTLEMAN AND CABINET MAKER'S DIRECTOR, Thomas Chippendale. Full reprint (third edition, 1762) of most influential furniture book of all time, by master cabinetmaker. 200 plates, illustrating chairs, sofas, mirrors, tables, cabinets, plus 24 photographs of surviving pieces. Biographical introduction by N. Bienenstock. vi + 249pp. 9⅞ x 12¾.   21601-2 Paperbound $5.00

AMERICAN ANTIQUE FURNITURE, Edgar G. Miller, Jr. The basic coverage of all American furniture before 1840. Individual chapters cover type of furniture—clocks, tables, sideboards, etc.—chronologically, with inexhaustible wealth of data. More than 2100 photographs, all identified, commented on. Essential to all early American collectors. Introduction by H. E. Keyes. vi + 1106pp. 7⅞ x 10¾.
                    21599-7, 21600-4 Two volumes, Paperbound $11.00

PENNSYLVANIA DUTCH AMERICAN FOLK ART, Henry J. Kauffman. 279 photos, 28 drawings of tulipware, Fraktur script, painted tinware, toys, flowered furniture, quilts, samplers, hex signs, house interiors, etc. Full descriptive text. Excellent for tourist, rewarding for designer, collector. Map. 146pp. 7⅞ x 10¾.
                    21205-X Paperbound $3.00

EARLY NEW ENGLAND GRAVESTONE RUBBINGS, Edmund V. Gillon, Jr. 43 photographs, 226 carefully reproduced rubbings show heavily symbolic, sometimes macabre early gravestones, up to early 19th century. Remarkable early American primitive art, occasionally strikingly beautiful; always powerful. Text. xxvi + 207pp. 8⅜ x 11¼.   21380-3 Paperbound $4.00

THE ARCHITECTURE OF COUNTRY HOUSES, Andrew J. Downing. Together with Vaux's *Villas and Cottages* this is the basic book for Hudson River Gothic architecture of the middle Victorian period. Full, sound discussions of general aspects of housing, architecture, style, decoration, furnishing, together with scores of detailed house plans, illustrations of specific buildings, accompanied by full text. Perhaps the most influential single American architectural book. 1850 edition. Introduction by J. Stewart Johnson. 321 figures, 34 architectural designs. xvi + 560pp.
22003-6 Paperbound $5.00

LOST EXAMPLES OF COLONIAL ARCHITECTURE, John Mead Howells. Full-page photographs of buildings that have disappeared or been so altered as to be denatured, including many designed by major early American architects. 245 plates. xvii + 248pp. 7⅞ x 10¾.
21143-6 Paperbound $3.50

DOMESTIC ARCHITECTURE OF THE AMERICAN COLONIES AND OF THE EARLY REPUBLIC, Fiske Kimball. Foremost architect and restorer of Williamsburg and Monticello covers nearly 200 homes between 1620-1825. Architectural details, construction, style features, special fixtures, floor plans, etc. Generally considered finest work in its area. 219 illustrations of houses, doorways, windows, capital mantels, xx + 314pp. 7⅞ x 10¾.
21743-4 Paperbound $4.00

EARLY AMERICAN ROOMS: 1650-1858, edited by Russell Hawes Kettell. Tour of 12 rooms, each representative of a different era in American history and each furnished, decorated, designed and occupied in the style of the era. 72 plans and elevations, 8-page color section, etc., show fabrics, wall papers, arrangements, etc. Full descriptive text. xvii + 200pp. of text. 8⅜ x 11¼.
21633-0 Paperbound $5.00

THE FITZWILLIAM VIRGINAL BOOK, edited by J. Fuller Maitland and W. B. Squire. Full modern printing of famous early 17th-century ms. volume of 300 works by Morley, Byrd, Bull, Gibbons, etc. For piano or other modern keyboard instrument; easy to read format. xxxvi + 938pp. 8⅜ x 11.
21068-5, 21069-3 Two volumes, Paperbound $12.00

KEYBOARD MUSIC, Johann Sebastian Bach. Bach Gesellschaft edition. A rich selection of Bach's masterpieces for the harpsichord: the six English Suites, six French Suites, the six Partitas (Clavierübung part I), the Goldberg Variations (Clavierübung part IV), the fifteen Two-Part Inventions and the fifteen Three-Part Sinfonias. Clearly reproduced on large sheets with ample margins; eminently playable. vi + 312pp. 8⅛ x 11.
22360-4 Paperbound $5.00

THE MUSIC OF BACH: AN INTRODUCTION, Charles Sanford Terry. A fine, nontechnical introduction to Bach's music, both instrumental and vocal. Covers organ music, chamber music, passion music, other types. Analyzes themes, developments, innovations. x + 114pp.
21075-8 Paperbound $1.95

BEETHOVEN AND HIS NINE SYMPHONIES, Sir George Grove. Noted British musicologist provides best history, analysis, commentary on symphonies. Very thorough, rigorously accurate; necessary to both advanced student and amateur music lover. 436 musical passages. vii + 407 pp.
20334-4 Paperbound $4.00

THE RED FAIRY BOOK, Andrew Lang. Lang's color fairy books have long been children's favorites. This volume includes Rapunzel, Jack and the Bean-stalk and 35 other stories, familiar and unfamiliar. 4 plates, 93 illustrations x + 367pp.
21673-X Paperbound $2.50

THE BLUE FAIRY BOOK, Andrew Lang. Lang's tales come from all countries and all times. Here are 37 tales from Grimm, the Arabian Nights, Greek Mythology, and other fascinating sources. 8 plates, 130 illustrations. xi + 390pp.
21437-0 Paperbound $2.75

HOUSEHOLD STORIES BY THE BROTHERS GRIMM. Classic English-language edition of the well-known tales — Rumpelstiltskin, Snow White, Hansel and Gretel, The Twelve Brothers, Faithful John, Rapunzel, Tom Thumb (52 stories in all). Translated into simple, straightforward English by Lucy Crane. Ornamented with headpieces, vignettes, elaborate decorative initials and a dozen full-page illustrations by Walter Crane. x + 269pp.
21080-4 Paperbound $2.00

THE MERRY ADVENTURES OF ROBIN HOOD, Howard Pyle. The finest modern versions of the traditional ballads and tales about the great English outlaw. Howard Pyle's complete prose version, with every word, every illustration of the first edition. Do not confuse this facsimile of the original (1883) with modern editions that change text or illustrations. 23 plates plus many page decorations. xxii + 296pp.
22043-5 Paperbound $2.75

THE STORY OF KING ARTHUR AND HIS KNIGHTS, Howard Pyle. The finest children's version of the life of King Arthur; brilliantly retold by Pyle, with 48 of his most imaginative illustrations. xviii + 313pp. 6⅛ x 9¼.
21445-1 Paperbound $2.50

THE WONDERFUL WIZARD OF OZ, L. Frank Baum. America's finest children's book in facsimile of first edition with all Denslow illustrations in full color. The edition a child should have. Introduction by Martin Gardner. 23 color plates, scores of drawings. iv + 267pp.
20691-2 Paperbound $3.50

THE MARVELOUS LAND OF OZ, L. Frank Baum. The second Oz book, every bit as imaginative as the Wizard. The hero is a boy named Tip, but the Scarecrow and the Tin Woodman are back, as is the Oz magic. 16 color plates, 120 drawings by John R. Neill. 287pp.
20692-0 Paperbound $2.50

THE MAGICAL MONARCH OF MO, L. Frank Baum. Remarkable adventures in a land even stranger than Oz. The best of Baum's books not in the Oz series. 15 color plates and dozens of drawings by Frank Verbeck. xviii + 237pp.
21892-9 Paperbound $2.25

THE BAD CHILD'S BOOK OF BEASTS, MORE BEASTS FOR WORSE CHILDREN, A MORAL ALPHABET, Hilaire Belloc. Three complete humor classics in one volume. Be kind to the frog, and do not call him names . . . and 28 other whimsical animals. Familiar favorites and some not so well known. Illustrated by Basil Blackwell. 156pp.
(USO) 20749-8 Paperbound $1.50

TWO LITTLE SAVAGES; BEING THE ADVENTURES OF TWO BOYS WHO LIVED AS INDIANS AND WHAT THEY LEARNED, Ernest Thompson Seton. Great classic of nature and boyhood provides a vast range of woodlore in most palatable form, a genuinely entertaining story. Two farm boys build a teepee in woods and live in it for a month, working out Indian solutions to living problems, star lore, birds and animals, plants, etc. 293 illustrations. vii + 286pp.

20985-7 Paperbound $2.50

PETER PIPER'S PRACTICAL PRINCIPLES OF PLAIN & PERFECT PRONUNCIATION. Alliterative jingles and tongue-twisters of surprising charm, that made their first appearance in America about 1830. Republished in full with the spirited woodcut illustrations from this earliest American edition. 32pp. 4½ x 6⅜.

22560-7 Paperbound $1.00

SCIENCE EXPERIMENTS AND AMUSEMENTS FOR CHILDREN, Charles Vivian. 73 easy experiments, requiring only materials found at home or easily available, such as candles, coins, steel wool, etc.; illustrate basic phenomena like vacuum, simple chemical reaction, etc. All safe. Modern, well-planned. Formerly *Science Games for Children.* 102 photos, numerous drawings. 96pp. 6⅛ x 9¼.

21856-2 Paperbound $1.25

AN INTRODUCTION TO CHESS MOVES AND TACTICS SIMPLY EXPLAINED, Leonard Barden. Informal intermediate introduction, quite strong in explaining reasons for moves. Covers basic material, tactics, important openings, traps, positional play in middle game, end game. Attempts to isolate patterns and recurrent configurations. Formerly *Chess.* 58 figures. 102pp. (USO) 21210-6 Paperbound $1.25

LASKER'S MANUAL OF CHESS, Dr. Emanuel Lasker. Lasker was not only one of the five great World Champions, he was also one of the ablest expositors, theorists, and analysts. In many ways, his Manual, permeated with his philosophy of battle, filled with keen insights, is one of the greatest works ever written on chess. Filled with analyzed games by the great players. A single-volume library that will profit almost any chess player, beginner or master. 308 diagrams. xli x 349pp.

20640-8 Paperbound $2.75

THE MASTER BOOK OF MATHEMATICAL RECREATIONS, Fred Schuh. In opinion of many the finest work ever prepared on mathematical puzzles, stunts, recreations; exhaustively thorough explanations of mathematics involved, analysis of effects, citation of puzzles and games. Mathematics involved is elementary. Translated by F. Göbel. 194 figures. xxiv + 430pp.

22134-2 Paperbound $4.00

MATHEMATICS, MAGIC AND MYSTERY, Martin Gardner. Puzzle editor for Scientific American explains mathematics behind various mystifying tricks: card tricks, stage "mind reading," coin and match tricks, counting out games, geometric dissections, etc. Probability sets, theory of numbers clearly explained. Also provides more than 400 tricks, guaranteed to work, that you can do. 135 illustrations. xii + 176pp.

20335-2 Paperbound $2.00

"ESSENTIAL GRAMMAR" SERIES

All you really need to know about modern, colloquial grammar. Many educational shortcuts help you learn faster, understand better. Detailed cognate lists teach you to recognize similarities between English and foreign words and roots—make learning vocabulary easy and interesting. Excellent for independent study or as a supplement to record courses.

ESSENTIAL FRENCH GRAMMAR, Seymour Resnick. 2500-item cognate list. 159pp.
(EBE) 20419-7 Paperbound $1.50

ESSENTIAL GERMAN GRAMMAR, Guy Stern and Everett F. Bleiler. Unusual shortcuts on noun declension, word order, compound verbs. 124pp.
(EBE) 20422-7 Paperbound $1.25

ESSENTIAL ITALIAN GRAMMAR, Olga Ragusa. 111pp.
(EBE) 20779-X Paperbound $1.25

ESSENTIAL JAPANESE GRAMMAR, Everett F. Bleiler. In Romaji transcription; no characters needed. Japanese grammar is regular and simple. 156pp.
21027-8 Paperbound $1.50

ESSENTIAL PORTUGUESE GRAMMAR, Alexander da R. Prista. vi + 114pp.
21650-0 Paperbound $1.35

ESSENTIAL SPANISH GRAMMAR, Seymour Resnick. 2500 word cognate list. 115pp.
(EBE) 20780-3 Paperbound $1.25

ESSENTIAL ENGLISH GRAMMAR, Philip Gucker. Combines best features of modern, functional and traditional approaches. For refresher, class use, home study. x + 177pp.
21649-7 Paperbound $1.75

A PHRASE AND SENTENCE DICTIONARY OF SPOKEN SPANISH. Prepared for U. S. War Department by U. S. linguists. As above, unit is idiom, phrase or sentence rather than word. English-Spanish and Spanish-English sections contain modern equivalents of over 18,000 sentences. Introduction and appendix as above. iv + 513pp.
20495-2 Paperbound $3.50

A PHRASE AND SENTENCE DICTIONARY OF SPOKEN RUSSIAN. Dictionary prepared for U. S. War Department by U. S. linguists. Basic unit is not the word, but the idiom, phrase or sentence. English-Russian and Russian-English sections contain modern equivalents for over 30,000 phrases. Grammatical introduction covers phonetics, writing, syntax. Appendix of word lists for food, numbers, geographical names, etc. vi + 573 pp. 6⅛ x 9¼.
20496-0 Paperbound $5.50

CONVERSATIONAL CHINESE FOR BEGINNERS, Morris Swadesh. Phonetic system, beginner's course in Pai Hua Mandarin Chinese covering most important, most useful speech patterns. Emphasis on modern colloquial usage. Formerly *Chinese in Your Pocket*. xvi + 158pp.
21123-1 Paperbound $1.75

How to Know the Wild Flowers, Mrs. William Starr Dana. This is the classical book of American wildflowers (of the Eastern and Central United States), used by hundreds of thousands. Covers over 500 species, arranged in extremely easy to use color and season groups. Full descriptions, much plant lore. This Dover edition is the fullest ever compiled, with tables of nomenclature changes. 174 full-page plates by M. Satterlee. xii + 418pp. 20332-8 Paperbound $3.00

Our Plant Friends and Foes, William Atherton DuPuy. History, economic importance, essential botanical information and peculiarities of 25 common forms of plant life are provided in this book in an entertaining and charming style. Covers food plants (potatoes, apples, beans, wheat, almonds, bananas, etc.), flowers (lily, tulip, etc.), trees (pine, oak, elm, etc.), weeds, poisonous mushrooms and vines, gourds, citrus fruits, cotton, the cactus family, and much more. 108 illustrations. xiv + 290pp. 22272-1 Paperbound $2.50

How to Know the Ferns, Frances T. Parsons. Classic survey of Eastern and Central ferns, arranged according to clear, simple identification key. Excellent introduction to greatly neglected nature area. 57 illustrations and 42 plates. xvi + 215pp. 20740-4 Paperbound $2.00

Manual of the Trees of North America, Charles S. Sargent. America's foremost dendrologist provides the definitive coverage of North American trees and tree-like shrubs. 717 species fully described and illustrated: exact distribution, down to township; full botanical description; economic importance; description of subspecies and races; habitat, growth data; similar material. Necessary to every serious student of tree-life. Nomenclature revised to present. Over 100 locating keys. 783 illustrations. lii + 934pp. 20277-1, 20278-X Two volumes, Paperbound $7.00

Our Northern Shrubs, Harriet L. Keeler. Fine non-technical reference work identifying more than 225 important shrubs of Eastern and Central United States and Canada. Full text covering botanical description, habitat, plant lore, is paralleled with 205 full-page photographs of flowering or fruiting plants. Nomenclature revised by Edward G. Voss. One of few works concerned with shrubs. 205 plates, 35 drawings. xxviii + 521pp. 21989-5 Paperbound $3.75

The Mushroom Handbook, Louis C. C. Krieger. Still the best popular handbook: full descriptions of 259 species, cross references to another 200. Extremely thorough text enables you to identify, know all about any mushroom you are likely to meet in eastern and central U. S. A.: habitat, luminescence, poisonous qualities, use, folklore, etc. 32 color plates show over 50 mushrooms, also 126 other illustrations. Finding keys. vii + 560pp. 21861-9 Paperbound $4.50

Handbook of Birds of Eastern North America, Frank M. Chapman. Still much the best single-volume guide to the birds of Eastern and Central United States. Very full coverage of 675 species, with descriptions, life habits, distribution, similar data. All descriptions keyed to two-page color chart. With this single volume the average birdwatcher needs no other books. 1931 revised edition. 195 illustrations. xxxvi + 581pp. 21489-3 Paperbound $5.00

AMERICAN FOOD AND GAME FISHES, David S. Jordan and Barton W. Evermann. Definitive source of information, detailed and accurate enough to enable the sportsman and nature lover to identify conclusively some 1,000 species and sub-species of North American fish, sought for food or sport. Coverage of range, physiology, habits, life history, food value. Best methods of capture, interest to the angler, advice on bait, fly-fishing, etc. 338 drawings and photographs. 1 + 574pp. 6⅝ x 9⅜.

22196-2 Paperbound $5.00

THE FROG BOOK, Mary C. Dickerson. Complete with extensive finding keys, over 300 photographs, and an introduction to the general biology of frogs and toads, this is the classic non-technical study of Northeastern and Central species. 58 species; 290 photographs and 16 color plates. xvii + 253pp.

21973-9 Paperbound $4.00

THE MOTH BOOK: A GUIDE TO THE MOTHS OF NORTH AMERICA, William J. Holland. Classical study, eagerly sought after and used for the past 60 years. Clear identification manual to more than 2,000 different moths, largest manual in existence. General information about moths, capturing, mounting, classifying, etc., followed by species by species descriptions. 263 illustrations plus 48 color plates show almost every species, full size. 1968 edition, preface, nomenclature changes by A. E. Brower. xxiv + 479pp. of text. 6½ x 9¼.

21948-8 Paperbound $6.00

THE SEA-BEACH AT EBB-TIDE, Augusta Foote Arnold. Interested amateur can identify hundreds of marine plants and animals on coasts of North America; marine algae; seaweeds; squids; hermit crabs; horse shoe crabs; shrimps; corals; sea anemones; etc. Species descriptions cover: structure; food; reproductive cycle; size; shape; color; habitat; etc. Over 600 drawings. 85 plates. xii + 490pp.

21949-6 Paperbound $4.00

COMMON BIRD SONGS, Donald J. Borror. 33⅓ 12-inch record presents songs of 60 important birds of the eastern United States. A thorough, serious record which provides several examples for each bird, showing different types of song, individual variations, etc. Inestimable identification aid for birdwatcher. 32-page booklet gives text about birds and songs, with illustration for each bird.

21829-5 Record, book, album. Monaural. $3.50

FADS AND FALLACIES IN THE NAME OF SCIENCE, Martin Gardner. Fair, witty appraisal of cranks and quacks of science: Atlantis, Lemuria, hollow earth, flat earth, Velikovsky, orgone energy, Dianetics, flying saucers, Bridey Murphy, food fads, medical fads, perpetual motion, etc. Formerly "In the Name of Science." x + 363pp.

20394-8 Paperbound $3.00

HOAXES, Curtis D. MacDougall. Exhaustive, unbelievably rich account of great hoaxes: Locke's moon hoax, Shakespearean forgeries, sea serpents, Loch Ness monster, Cardiff giant, John Wilkes Booth's mummy, Disumbrationist school of art, dozens more; also journalism, psychology of hoaxing. 54 illustrations. xi + 338pp.

20465-0 Paperbound $3.50

THE PRINCIPLES OF PSYCHOLOGY, William James. The famous long course, complete and unabridged. Stream of thought, time perception, memory, experimental methods—these are only some of the concerns of a work that was years ahead of its time and still valid, interesting, useful. 94 figures. Total of xviii + 1391pp.
20381-6, 20382-4 Two volumes, Paperbound $9.00

THE STRANGE STORY OF THE QUANTUM, Banesh Hoffmann. Non-mathematical but thorough explanation of work of Planck, Einstein, Bohr, Pauli, de Broglie, Schrödinger, Heisenberg, Dirac, Feynman, etc. No technical background needed. "Of books attempting such an account, this is the best," Henry Margenau, Yale. 40-page "Postscript 1959." xii + 285pp. 20518-5 Paperbound $3.00

THE RISE OF THE NEW PHYSICS, A. d'Abro. Most thorough explanation in print of central core of mathematical physics, both classical and modern; from Newton to Dirac and Heisenberg. Both history and exposition; philosophy of science, causality, explanations of higher mathematics, analytical mechanics, electromagnetism, thermodynamics, phase rule, special and general relativity, matrices. No higher mathematics needed to follow exposition, though treatment is elementary to intermediate in level. Recommended to serious student who wishes verbal understanding. 97 illustrations. xvii + 982pp. 20003-5, 20004-3 Two volumes, Paperbound $10.00

GREAT IDEAS OF OPERATIONS RESEARCH, Jagjit Singh. Easily followed non technical explanation of mathematical tools, aims, results: statistics, linear programming, game theory, queueing theory, Monte Carlo simulation, etc. Uses only elementary mathematics. Many case studies, several analyzed in detail. Clarity, breadth make this excellent for specialist in another field who wishes background. 41 figures. x + 228pp. 21886-4 Paperbound $2.50

GREAT IDEAS OF MODERN MATHEMATICS: THEIR NATURE AND USE, Jagjit Singh. Internationally famous expositor, winner of Unesco's Kalinga Award for science popularization explains verbally such topics as differential equations, matrices, groups, sets, transformations, mathematical logic and other important modern mathematics, as well as use in physics, astrophysics, and similar fields. Superb exposition for layman, scientist in other areas. viii + 312pp.
20587-8 Paperbound $2.75

GREAT IDEAS IN INFORMATION THEORY, LANGUAGE AND CYBERNETICS, Jagjit Singh. The analog and digital computers, how they work, how they are like and unlike the human brain, the men who developed them, their future applications, computer terminology. An essential book for today, even for readers with little math. Some mathematical demonstrations included for more advanced readers. 118 figures. Tables. ix + 338pp. 21694-2 Paperbound $2.50

CHANCE, LUCK AND STATISTICS, Horace C. Levinson. Non-mathematical presentation of fundamentals of probability theory and science of statistics and their applications. Games of chance, betting odds, misuse of statistics, normal and skew distributions, birth rates, stock speculation, insurance. Enlarged edition. Formerly "The Science of Chance." xiii + 357pp. 21007-3 Paperbound $2.50

PLANETS, STARS AND GALAXIES: DESCRIPTIVE ASTRONOMY FOR BEGINNERS, A. E. Fanning. Comprehensive introductory survey of astronomy: the sun, solar system, stars, galaxies, universe, cosmology; up-to-date, including quasars, radio stars, etc. Preface by Prof. Donald Menzel. 24pp. of photographs. 189pp. 5¼ x 8¼.
21680-2 Paperbound $2.50

TEACH YOURSELF CALCULUS, P. Abbott. With a good background in algebra and trig, you can teach yourself calculus with this book. Simple, straightforward introduction to functions of all kinds, integration, differentiation, series, etc. "Students who are beginning to study calculus method will derive great help from this book." Faraday House Journal. 308pp. 20683-1 Clothbound $2.50

TEACH YOURSELF TRIGONOMETRY, P. Abbott. Geometrical foundations, indices and logarithms, ratios, angles, circular measure, etc. are presented in this sound, easy-to-use text. Excellent for the beginner or as a brush up, this text carries the student through the solution of triangles. 204pp. 20682-3 Clothbound $2.00

BASIC MACHINES AND HOW THEY WORK, U. S. Bureau of Naval Personnel. Originally used in U.S. Naval training schools, this book clearly explains the operation of a progression of machines, from the simplest—lever, wheel and axle, inclined plane, wedge, screw—to the most complex—typewriter, internal combustion engine, computer mechanism. Utilizing an approach that requires only an elementary understanding of mathematics, these explanations build logically upon each other and are assisted by over 200 drawings and diagrams. Perfect as a technical school manual or as a self-teaching aid to the layman. 204 figures. Preface. Index. vii + 161pp. 6½ x 9¼. 21709-4 Paperbound $2.50

THE FRIENDLY STARS, Martha Evans Martin. Classic has taught naked-eye observation of stars, planets to hundreds of thousands, still not surpassed for charm, lucidity, adequacy. Completely updated by Professor Donald H. Menzel, Harvard Observatory. 25 illustrations. 16 x 30 chart. x + 147pp. 21099-5 Paperbound $2.00

MUSIC OF THE SPHERES: THE MATERIAL UNIVERSE FROM ATOM TO QUASAR, SIMPLY EXPLAINED, Guy Murchie. Extremely broad, brilliantly written popular account begins with the solar system and reaches to dividing line between matter and nonmatter; latest understandings presented with exceptional clarity. Volume One: Planets, stars, galaxies, cosmology, geology, celestial mechanics, latest astronomical discoveries; Volume Two: Matter, atoms, waves, radiation, relativity, chemical action, heat, nuclear energy, quantum theory, music, light, color, probability, antimatter, antigravity, and similar topics. 319 figures. 1967 (second) edition. Total of xx + 644pp. 21809-0, 21810-4 Two volumes, Paperbound $5.75

OLD-TIME SCHOOLS AND SCHOOL BOOKS, Clifton Johnson. Illustrations and rhymes from early primers, abundant quotations from early textbooks, many anecdotes of school life enliven this study of elementary schools from Puritans to middle 19th century. Introduction by Carl Withers. 234 illustrations. xxxiii + 381pp.
21031-6 Paperbound $4.00

THE PHILOSOPHY OF THE UPANISHADS, Paul Deussen. Clear, detailed statement of upanishadic system of thought, generally considered among best available. History of these works, full exposition of system emergent from them, parallel concepts in the West. Translated by A. S. Geden. xiv + 429pp.
21616-0 Paperbound $3.50

LANGUAGE, TRUTH AND LOGIC, Alfred J. Ayer. Famous, remarkably clear introduction to the Vienna and Cambridge schools of Logical Positivism; function of philosophy, elimination of metaphysical thought, nature of analysis, similar topics. "Wish I had written it myself," Bertrand Russell. 2nd, 1946 edition. 160pp.
20010-8 Paperbound $1.50

THE GUIDE FOR THE PERPLEXED, Moses Maimonides. Great classic of medieval Judaism, major attempt to reconcile revealed religion (Pentateuch, commentaries) and Aristotelian philosophy. Enormously important in all Western thought. Unabridged Friedländer translation. 50 page introduction. lix + 414pp.
(USO) 20351-4 Paperbound $4.50

OCCULT AND SUPERNATURAL PHENOMENA, D. H. Rawcliffe. Full, serious study of the most persistent delusions of mankind: crystal gazing, mediumistic trance, stigmata, lycanthropy, fire walking, dowsing, telepathy, ghosts, ESP, etc., and their relation to common forms of abnormal psychology. Formerly *Illusions and Delusions of the Supernatural and the Occult.* iii + 551pp. 20503-7 Paperbound $4.00

THE EGYPTIAN BOOK OF THE DEAD: THE PAPYRUS OF ANI, E. A. Wallis Budge. Full hieroglyphic text, interlinear transliteration of sounds, word for word translation, then smooth, connected translation; Theban recension. Basic work in Ancient Egyptian civilization; now even more significant than ever for historical importance, dilation of consciousness, etc. clvi + 377pp. 6½ x 9¼.
21866-X Paperbound $4.95

PSYCHOLOGY OF MUSIC, Carl E. Seashore. Basic, thorough survey of everything known about psychology of music up to 1940's; essential reading for psychologists, musicologists. Physical acoustics; auditory apparatus; relationship of physical sound to perceived sound; role of the mind in sorting, altering, suppressing, creating sound sensations; musical learning, testing for ability, absolute pitch, other topics. Records of Caruso, Menuhin analyzed. 88 figures. xix + 408pp.
21851-1 Paperbound $3.50

THE I CHING (THE BOOK OF CHANGES), translated by James Legge. Complete translated text plus appendices by Confucius, of perhaps the most penetrating divination book ever compiled. Indispensable to all study of early Oriental civilizations. 3 plates. xxiii + 448pp. 21062-6 Paperbound $3.50

THE UPANISHADS, translated by Max Müller. Twelve classical upanishads: Chandogya, Kena, Aitareya, Kaushitaki, Isa, Katha, Mundaka, Taittiriyaka, Brhadaranyaka, Svetasvatara, Prasna, Maitriyana. 160-page introduction, analysis by Prof Müller. Total of 670pp. 20992-X, 20993-8 Two volumes, Paperbound $7.50

JIM WHITEWOLF: THE LIFE OF A KIOWA APACHE INDIAN, Charles S. Brant, editor. Spans transition between native life and acculturation period, 1880 on. Kiowa culture, personal life pattern, religion and the supernatural, the Ghost Dance, breakdown in the White Man's world, similar material. 1 map. xii + 144pp.
22015-X Paperbound $1.75

THE NATIVE TRIBES OF CENTRAL AUSTRALIA, Baldwin Spencer and F. J. Gillen. Basic book in anthropology, devoted to full coverage of the Arunta and Warramunga tribes; the source for knowledge about kinship systems, material and social culture, religion, etc. Still unsurpassed. 121 photographs, 89 drawings. xviii + 669pp.
21775-2 Paperbound $5.00

MALAY MAGIC, Walter W. Skeat. Classic (1900); still the definitive work on the folklore and popular religion of the Malay peninsula. Describes marriage rites, birth spirits and ceremonies, medicine, dances, games, war and weapons, etc. Extensive quotes from original sources, many magic charms translated into English. 35 illustrations. Preface by Charles Otto Blagden. xxiv + 685pp.
21760-4 Paperbound $4.00

HEAVENS ON EARTH: UTOPIAN COMMUNITIES IN AMERICA, 1680-1880, Mark Holloway. The finest nontechnical account of American utopias, from the early Woman in the Wilderness, Ephrata, Rappites to the enormous mid 19th-century efflorescence; Shakers, New Harmony, Equity Stores, Fourier's Phalanxes, Oneida, Amana, Fruitlands, etc. "Entertaining and very instructive." *Times Literary Supplement*. 15 illustrations. 246pp.
21593-8 Paperbound $2.00

LONDON LABOUR AND THE LONDON POOR, Henry Mayhew. Earliest (c. 1850) sociological study in English, describing myriad subcultures of London poor. Particularly remarkable for the thousands of pages of direct testimony taken from the lips of London prostitutes, thieves, beggars, street sellers, chimney-sweepers, street-musicians, "mudlarks," "pure-finders," rag-gatherers, "running-patterers," dock laborers, cab-men, and hundreds of others, quoted directly in this massive work. An extraordinarily vital picture of London emerges. 110 illustrations. Total of lxxvi + 1951pp. 6⅝ x 10.
21934-8, 21935-6, 21936-4, 21937-2 Four volumes, Paperbound $16.00

HISTORY OF THE LATER ROMAN EMPIRE, J. B. Bury. Eloquent, detailed reconstruction of Western and Byzantine Roman Empire by a major historian, from the death of Theodosius I (395 A.D.) to the death of Justinian (565). Extensive quotations from contemporary sources; full coverage of important Roman and foreign figures of the time. xxxiv + 965pp. 20398-0, 20399-9 Two volumes, Paperbound $7.00

AN INTELLECTUAL AND CULTURAL HISTORY OF THE WESTERN WORLD, Harry Elmer Barnes. Monumental study, tracing the development of the accomplishments that make up human culture. Every aspect of man's achievement surveyed from its origins in the Paleolithic to the present day (1964); social structures, ideas, economic systems, art, literature, technology, mathematics, the sciences, medicine, religion, jurisprudence, etc. Evaluations of the contributions of scores of great men. 1964 edition, revised and edited by scholars in the many fields represented. Total of xxix + 1381pp. 21275-0, 21276-9, 21277-7 Three volumes, Paperbound $10.50

ADVENTURES OF AN AFRICAN SLAVER, Theodore Canot. Edited by Brantz Mayer. A detailed portrayal of slavery and the slave trade, 1820-1840. Canot, an established trader along the African coast, describes the slave economy of the African kingdoms, the treatment of captured negroes, the extensive journeys in the interior to gather slaves, slave revolts and their suppression, harems, bribes, and much more. Full and unabridged republication of 1854 edition. Introduction by Malcom Cowley. 16 illustrations. xvii + 448pp. 22456-2 Paperbound $3.50

MY BONDAGE AND MY FREEDOM, Frederick Douglass. Born and brought up in slavery, Douglass witnessed its horrors and experienced its cruelties, but went on to become one of the most outspoken forces in the American anti-slavery movement. Considered the best of his autobiographies, this book graphically describes the inhuman treatment of slaves, its effects on slave owners and slave families, and how Douglass's determination led him to a new life. Unaltered reprint of 1st (1855) edition. xxxii + 464pp. 22457-0 Paperbound $3.50

THE INDIANS' BOOK, recorded and edited by Natalie Curtis. Lore, music, narratives, dozens of drawings by Indians themselves from an authoritative and important survey of native culture among Plains, Southwestern, Lake and Pueblo Indians. Standard work in popular ethnomusicology. 149 songs in full notation. 23 drawings, 23 photos. xxxi + 584pp. 6⅝ x 9⅜. 21939-9 Paperbound $5.00

DICTIONARY OF AMERICAN PORTRAITS, edited by Hayward and Blanche Cirker. 4024 portraits of 4000 most important Americans, colonial days to 1905 (with a few important categories, like Presidents, to present). Pioneers, explorers, colonial figures, U. S. officials, politicians, writers, military and naval men, scientists, inventors, manufacturers, jurists, actors, historians, educators, notorious figures, Indian chiefs, etc. All authentic contemporary likenesses. The only work of its kind in existence; supplements all biographical sources for libraries. Indispensable to anyone working with American history. 8,000-item classified index, finding lists, other aids. xiv + 756pp. 9¼ x 12¾. 21823-6 Clothbound $30.00

TRITTON'S GUIDE TO BETTER WINE AND BEER MAKING FOR BEGINNERS, S. M. Tritton. All you need to know to make family-sized quantities of over 100 types of grape, fruit, herb and vegetable wines; as well as beers, mead, cider, etc. Complete recipes, advice as to equipment, procedures such as fermenting, bottling, and storing wines. Recipes given in British, U. S., and metric measures. Accompanying booklet lists sources in U. S. A. where ingredients may be bought, and additional information. 11 illustrations. 157pp. 5⅝ x 8⅛. 22090-7 **Paperbound $2.00**

GARDENING WITH HERBS FOR FLAVOR AND FRAGRANCE, Helen M. Fox. How to grow herbs in your own garden, how to use them in your cooking (over 55 recipes included), legends and myths associated with each species, uses in medicine, perfumes, etc.—these are elements of one of the few books written especially for American herb fanciers. Guides you step-by-step from soil preparation to harvesting and storage for each type of herb. 12 drawings by Louise Mansfield. xiv + 334pp. 22540-2 Paperbound $2.50

INCIDENTS OF TRAVEL IN YUCATAN, John L. Stephens. Classic (1843) exploration of jungles of Yucatan, looking for evidences of Maya civilization. Stephens found many ruins; comments on travel adventures, Mexican and Indian culture. 127 striking illustrations by F. Catherwood. Total of 669 pp.

20926-1, 20927-X Two volumes, Paperbound $5.50

INCIDENTS OF TRAVEL IN CENTRAL AMERICA, CHIAPAS, AND YUCATAN, John L. Stephens. An exciting travel journal and an important classic of archeology. Narrative relates his almost single-handed discovery of the Mayan culture, and exploration of the ruined cities of Copan, Palenque, Utatlan and others; the monuments they dug from the earth, the temples buried in the jungle, the customs of poverty-stricken Indians living a stone's throw from the ruined palaces. 115 drawings by F. Catherwood. Portrait of Stephens. xii + 812pp.

22404-X, 22405-8 Two volumes, Paperbound $6.00

A NEW VOYAGE ROUND THE WORLD, William Dampier. Late 17-century naturalist joined the pirates of the Spanish Main to gather information; remarkably vivid account of buccaneers, pirates; detailed, accurate account of botany, zoology, ethnography of lands visited. Probably the most important early English voyage, enormous implications for British exploration, trade, colonial policy. Also most interesting reading. Argonaut edition, introduction by Sir Albert Gray. New introduction by Percy Adams. 6 plates, 7 illustrations. xlvii + 376pp. 6½ x 9¼.

21900-3 Paperbound $3.00

INTERNATIONAL AIRLINE PHRASE BOOK IN SIX LANGUAGES, Joseph W. Bátor. Important phrases and sentences in English paralleled with French, German, Portuguese, Italian, Spanish equivalents, covering all possible airport-travel situations; created for airline personnel as well as tourist by Language Chief, Pan American Airlines. xiv + 204pp.

22017-6 Paperbound $2.25

STAGE COACH AND TAVERN DAYS, Alice Morse Earle. Detailed, lively account of the early days of taverns; their uses and importance in the social, political and military life; furnishings and decorations; locations; food and drink; tavern signs, etc. Second half covers every aspect of early travel; the roads, coaches, drivers, etc. Nostalgic, charming, packed with fascinating material. 157 illustrations, mostly photographs. xiv + 449pp.

22518-6 Paperbound $4.00

NORSE DISCOVERIES AND EXPLORATIONS IN NORTH AMERICA, Hjalmar R. Holand. The perplexing Kensington Stone, found in Minnesota at the end of the 19th century. Is it a record of a Scandinavian expedition to North America in the 14th century? Or is it one of the most successful hoaxes in history. A scientific detective investigation. Formerly *Westward from Vinland*. 31 photographs, 17 figures. x + 354pp.

22014-1 Paperbound $2.75

A BOOK OF OLD MAPS, compiled and edited by Emerson D. Fite and Archibald Freeman. 74 old maps offer an unusual survey of the discovery, settlement and growth of America down to the close of the Revolutionary war: maps showing Norse settlements in Greenland, the explorations of Columbus, Verrazano, Cabot, Champlain, Joliet, Drake, Hudson, etc., campaigns of Revolutionary war battles, and much more. Each map is accompanied by a brief historical essay. xvi + 299pp. 11 x 13¾.

22084-2 Paperbound $7.00

CATALOGUE OF DOVER BOOKS

MATHEMATICAL PUZZLES FOR BEGINNERS AND ENTHUSIASTS, Geoffrey Mott-Smith. 189 puzzles from easy to difficult—involving arithmetic, logic, algebra, properties of digits, probability, etc.—for enjoyment and mental stimulus. Explanation of mathematical principles behind the puzzles. 135 illustrations. viii + 248pp.
20198-8 Paperbound $2.00

PAPER FOLDING FOR BEGINNERS, William D. Murray and Francis J. Rigney. Easiest book on the market, clearest instructions on making interesting, beautiful origami. Sail boats, cups, roosters, frogs that move legs, bonbon boxes, standing birds, etc. 40 projects; more than 275 diagrams and photographs. 94pp.
20713-7 Paperbound $1.00

TRICKS AND GAMES ON THE POOL TABLE, Fred Herrmann. 79 tricks and games— some solitaires, some for two or more players, some competitive games—to entertain you between formal games. Mystifying shots and throws, unusual caroms, tricks involving such props as cork, coins, a hat, etc. Formerly *Fun on the Pool Table*. 77 figures. 95pp.
21814-7 Paperbound $1.25

HAND SHADOWS TO BE THROWN UPON THE WALL: A SERIES OF NOVEL AND AMUSING FIGURES FORMED BY THE HAND, Henry Bursill. Delightful picturebook from great-grandfather's day shows how to make 18 different hand shadows: a bird that flies, duck that quacks, dog that wags his tail, camel, goose, deer, boy, turtle, etc. Only book of its sort. vi + 33pp. 6½ x 9¼.
21779-5 Paperbound $1.00

WHITTLING AND WOODCARVING, E. J. Tangerman. 18th printing of best book on market. "If you can cut a potato you can carve" toys and puzzles, chains, chessmen, caricatures, masks, frames, woodcut blocks, surface patterns, much more. Information on tools, woods, techniques. Also goes into serious wood sculpture from Middle Ages to present, East and West. 464 photos, figures. x + 293pp.
20965-2 Paperbound $2.50

HISTORY OF PHILOSOPHY, Julián Marias. Possibly the clearest, most easily followed, best planned, most useful one-volume history of philosophy on the market; neither skimpy nor overfull. Full details on system of every major philosopher and dozens of less important thinkers from pre-Socratics up to Existentialism and later. Strong on many European figures usually omitted. Has gone through dozens of editions in Europe. 1966 edition, translated by Stanley Appelbaum and Clarence Strowbridge. xviii + 505pp.
21739-6 Paperbound $3.50

YOGA: A SCIENTIFIC EVALUATION, Kovoor T. Behanan. Scientific but non-technical study of physiological results of yoga exercises; done under auspices of Yale U. Relations to Indian thought, to psychoanalysis, etc. 16 photos. xxiii + 270pp.
20505-3 Paperbound $2.50

Prices subject to change without notice.
Available at your book dealer or write for free catalogue to Dept. GI, Dover Publications, Inc., 180 Varick St., N. Y., N. Y. 10014. Dover publishes more than 150 books each year on science, elementary and advanced mathematics, biology, music, art, literary history, social sciences and other areas.